THE BANDITS AMONGST US

A THRILLER

JOSHUA TORENN
SOLOMON ISLANDS

Paperback ISBN: 978-0-646-87280-3

First Published in 2023 by
First Nations Writers Festival International Limited
A Registered Charity (ABN 79 655 932 979)

T/as First Nations Publishers

2/53 Junction St, Nowra NSW 2540, Australia.
Phone: +61 491 851 353

Email: firstnationswritersfestival@gmail.com
Web: www.firstnationswritersfestival.org
FB: www.facebook.com/firstnationswritersfestival

Typeset: Carly Mitchell
Printed and bound in Australia by IngramSpark
Line Edited: Anna Borzi AM 2022
Cover photos: Anna Borzi AM 2022

*Dedicated to my late Father, Mr Martin Tangithia,
who introduced me into the world of books.*

And to my Mum for the folklores and custom stories.

AUTHOR'S NOTE

In the part of the world where I grew up, serial murder cases were committed by people who had ill feelings towards certain individuals or groups. Or, they were only hired to do just that. Kill.

Of all the serial murder cases committed there are two common scenarios. First, the victim is found in a serene state, often negating any suspicious thoughts but conclusive as to the victim's fate. The second scenario, the killer leaves his/her victim with brutal marks, as if to convey a message. This book was inspired by both scenarios.

KEY CHARACTERS

THE BANDITS

Bernard Maneboko: Bernard himself

Alfred Riola: Alo

Nimrod Gimo: Nimo

David Bokito: Deve

Irvin Tumusipu: Osama

Thomas Tumusipu: Toxic

Sikua Ruka: Stonie

VILLAGE LEADERS

Chief Henry Ko'oga: Chief of Ghombua

Elder Moses Ravu: Church Elder of Ghombua

Chief Jonah Pelu: Chief of Aola

Chief Joseph Sukulu: Village Elder of Adeade

THIBO TRIBE CHARACTERS

Jim Pegoa: Pacific Loggers Land Coordinator

Jemes Toki: Thibo Tribe principal Landowner

Merre Toki: Jemes Toki's wife

Edna Toki: Jemes and Merre's daughter

PACIFIC LOGGERS COMPANY

Atkinson Brown: Managing Director and Owner aka *Bossman.*

Mendana Dana: Camp Manager / Logistics Officer

Suiono Lee: Operation Manager/Site supervisor

ISATABU RESISTANCE MOVEMENT

Nicodemus Kebe: Aka Steel Face, leader of the Isatabu Resistance Movement

POLICE

Lieutenant Jackson Kilua: Police Chief of Tetere Police Station

Lieutenant William Wale: Police Chief of Central, Honiara

Officer Peter Pai (Dan Bako): Police Detective of Tetere

Officer Julie Arofa: Police Officer of Tetere

Officer Brian Legu: Police Officer of Tetere

INTERNATIONAL PEACE MONITORING TEAM (IPMT)

Superintendent Addam McColl: IPMT Guadalcanal Commander

PROLOGUE

11:34 AM, Tuesday, June 10, 2003

A figure sneaked through the bushes, panting. In tow are whooshing images of his accomplices squeezing their way forward, leapfrogging for space. The leader slowed down, shifted the weight on his shoulder, tweaked back a compulsory glance, and continued running.

At the foothill, he dropped the duffel bag. He bent over as if in a yoga class, collecting his breath. His followers caught up and took their positions around him.

'One, two, three, four - where's...?' The leader did a headcount between breaths.

No response, only puffs, and blows filled the silence.

He double-checked. 'All fine?'

'What?' a member erupted, lungs bursting. 'We looted the vehicle, is what you mean?' He snapped; irrational fear crushed his conscience. 'I am out. We'll all go to prison for this.'

'No one is going to prison.' The leader assured, ignoring the lurking sensation developing inside him.

The member accused the leader. 'You think you're a rebel?'

'No, I am not. None of us is a rebel.' The leader loosened up his arms in his jacket, gesturing his —*So what?* 'But I am not a coward.' He barked in a brisk voice, demonstrating his adulthood to the other members who watched in silence.

'Who's a coward?!' The members marched spitefully forward; eyeballs protruded. 'I am not a coward. I am not scared of you. Not a bit!"

The leader stood his ground and watched his enraged opponent demonstrate his masculinity. 'None of us is a rebel. No one.'

'You call me coward?!' The member challenged, squeezing his fists into balls.

The leader observed as his colleague evolved into a monster; voice reeked of a devil. His mouth twisted; muscles engaged. The leader tactically stepped sideways to dodge the blow. The punch flew past him like a rocket propelled grenade. Taking advantage of his opponent's spark of energy, he lunged forward and flung him at the lower back. The exerted force is enough to reel his opponent down the slope and fall face-down with a crash.

'So what?' The leader gloated.

'Stop it!' Deve as the eldest member intervened on time. 'What are all these dramas?'

'He's one picking a fight.' The leader justified his side. 'My action is self-defense.'

'Doesn't matter, self-defense, karate, or whatever the crap.' Deve glared at the enraged member, cleaning up the dirt from his face. 'Come on, man up and apologise to Bernard.'

Slowly, he picked himself up. The counter- challenge has vaporised his resentment.

'We are comrades, don't you forget? We have created enough enemies.' Deve added, eyeing the two members who had just joined them.

Deve switched his attention to the disputing parties. 'Come on Bernard,' he talked to the leader, then gazed at the fallen comrade, 'stand up Nimo.' Accepting the call, both members stepped forward.

After repeated pleading, the two reconciled with a handshake.

'Good, we are all grown-up, start acting like one,' Deve retorted.

The sound of approaching footsteps startled them.

'This way.' Bernard hefted the load on his shoulder and tore through the thicket up the steep slope.

I

A transistor radio blaring on the table. A male, raspy voice -whistling backed the song on the radio. The news on the radio prompted the scrawny fingers to fumble for the volume knob. The mid-day news bulletin started with a groundbreaking ceremony of a proposed tuna cannery, followed by the government bilateral agreement to be signed and upcoming overseas trips. It dumbfounded him when the name of his community was aired.

'Hear that?' A metallic voice exploded in his ears followed by a loud blow, and before he realised it, the transistor radio flew in a projectile motion up in the air. The commotion squirmed at him like a hinge, unsure of the incident. His eyes met two owlish eyes staring at him. A muscular profile stands tall like a statue. A scarf on his head, a sloppy army camouflage shirt and is armed with a machete. *Yes, a machete in his hand.* He posed with a rowdy look.

'Nephew?' Chief Henry Ko'oga turned dull; face thawed instantly into a confused lump.

'The news.' A voice snarled.

'News?' Chief Henry Ko'oga froze. He could smell the eerie hatred.

'Are you struck deaf?' Bernard scowled, swinging the machete as if to slash him into two halves.

'Hear, eh-yes.'

'Any word for me?' Bernard's eyes darted outside; the village is clearly empty. All able-bodied men and women have already left for their gardens and plantations. Some to Honiara city.

Chief Ko'oga's wife stood at a distance, shaking feverishly as if infected with malaria. Chief Ko'oga lost the words in his language within a second.

'What's-what's going on?' Chief Ko'oga collected his thoughts, but the right words don't come out.

'Chief, first you are deaf, now you out of your *freaking* mind.' Bernard scowled. 'You heard the news, eh?'

'Please, I know noth-.'

'Old man, I don't have time for your old tricks.'

'P-please…' he faltered.

Bernard signaled for action. They manhandled the old man and placed a cloth bag over his head – a blindfold.

2

A white Toyota Cabin Land cruiser rocks along, maneuvering its way along the bumpy road. The vehicle does not carry the blue and white checkered sign, nor a G-plate, it's an X-plate with the word IPMT printed on its side, *International Peace Monitoring Team.*

The vehicle safely runs at 60km/h. The personnel had been briefed before departure from Tetere Police station. Here, no one bothers to spoil their drive about their mission. That will be discussed when they arrive in the village.

Vivified by the scene, IPMT Officer, Superintendent Addam McColl couldn't deny his admiration. 'Beautiful.' The blue-hued vista of the central mountain ranges was so vivid, 'I wish I could wake up to this scene every morning.'

'Vatupochau.' Officer Peter switched the topic. The iconic mountain slanted thirty kilometers inland. The mountain is iconic and is venerated by the local people, it's the biblical Eden for the Guadalcanal people. The genesis of the island can be traced back to that very mountain.

7

They meditated on the passing scene in silence. Heaven is said to be everywhere, it's true for Guadalcanal and its spectacular mountain ranges. It's comforting to gaze upon.

McColl asked. 'Do people live up there?'

'Not now, but before, yes. It is where the people of Guadalcanal were said to be originated.'

'Ow, must be damned scary up there, so they migrated out.'

'From what I heard, it's the vicious giant that forced people to migrate.'

'Giants? I thought they were folklore.'

'That's the oral history of this island.'

'I see,' Addam McColl said, not convinced.

'Lucky me. We have no mountains, neither giant, only boulders and crabs.' Officer Julie scoffed.

'Which island is that?' Addam enquired, judging that it's a bit late for introduction as they've been in the vehicle together for an hour already.

'Tikopia,' Julie responded, 'Polynesian outliers close to Vanuatu.'

'I see. Small has its own beauty too.' Addam nodded, admiring the young lady, finding her place among men. Julie Arofa comes from a family of Police officers; it's her family legacy, though she wanted to be a nurse during her school days. She has height with a matching physique that could attract a second look. She is endowed with a high cheekbone and full lips, toned with her soft tawny brown skin.

'Oh, thank you, never been proud to my island.' The Polynesian lady beamed.

Traditionally, the larger land masses are usually controlled by one dominant race. In the Solomon archipelago, it's the Melanesians with the dark skin complexions. The Polynesian and Micronesian descendants inhabited the remote outliers that defined the epoch of their arrival. And are more resilient and able to adapt, eking out their living from what is available. It's life, not a choice as off grid living.

'If only guns are all surrendered.' Superintendent Addam removed his round brim cap, tossed his bald head back. 'Solomon would be paradise.'

'Which part of Australia you from?' Officer Julie enquired out of curiosity.

'Townsville, way up north,' Addam McColl said, 'my wife works for a logistic company there.'

'Townsville? Officer Julie caught the word in mid-air. 'That's where they signed the Peace Agreement two years ago.'

'Correct, in the year 2000.' Addam couldn't say more, recalling his days in East Timor.

'How big is Townsville?'

'Same as Honiara I guess.' Addam cut the details.

'And Sydney is the capital city of Australia, right?' Officer Julie assumed from the story.

'No, Canberra. Sydney is more like a commercial hub.'

'How big is Sydney?' More questions poured out like water released from a weir.

'How big?' Addam McColl lost words and tried to make a comparison. He can only presume they get the picture. 'Twice the Island of Guadalcanal.'

'Two times the size of Guadalcanal?' Officer Brian gazed at the distant mountains to make a comparison – astonished still.

'It's a city of three million people.' He pondered to himself- *when is the last time I saw the statistics?* 'Maybe more.'

'I only saw it in pictures.' Julie admitted, 'My elder sister married an Australian.'

'Where about in Australia?'

'Sydney.' Her face beamed, couldn't find any more suitable word for it.

'I see. Maybe one day you can visit your sister.' Addam McColl meant to say it's no point comparing Sydney to Honiara. As in Honiara, one in five people at least knew each other. And Tetere Police station, it's manned by only five Police officers who know each other like the back of their hands.

'I wish.'

Addam McColl looked toward the only female officer, beamed with confidence. 'Do you like your job?'

'My job?' She managed a suppressive smile, 'my education does not qualify me to be a medical doctor.'

'You don't need to,' Addam McColl assured her. 'You look smart in those uniforms; you should be proud of yourself. After all, it's about saving lives.'

'Thank you,' she responded. 'I only reached form five, which is no different from a pre-class nowadays. Everyone needs a job.'

'Lucky you. How long you've been with the Police?'

'A year now. We're the first to be recruited.' She nodded towards Officer Brian in the driver's seat, and Officer Peter, sitting opposite her in the back cabin.

'My advice is, acquaint yourself to these gentlemen.'

'Slowly adjusting,' she said.

'Here we are,' Officer Peter announced as the cruiser turned towards the river.

Officer Julie politely waved at women who crowded under the shade of a tree, hiding from the afternoon sun. Officer Julie can feel the cool breeze of the river whizzing through the tree branches. Her focus briefly switched to the little children who cuddled close to their mothers for safety. She could see fear in their eyes, one reserved for outsiders.

'Hello everyone,' Officer Julie greeted with a placating smile.

'Hello, helloooo...' The bird sang from the branches above, prompting the women to shriek.

Officer Julie startled, looked up, taken aback to see the talking bird sitting on the lower branch right above her. 'Wow, lovely bird.'

'Wow, lovely bird,' the tamed bird imitated her voice, cocking its head about to take an observant look at the Police officer.

'Shoo- commander, shoo.' The kids hurled sticks at the branches, prompting the bird to flutter and flew off.

'You have a nice village.' Officer Julie diverted the conversation. She extended her hand to one of the women, with eyes wide open, ready to lip out her response. *Not too soon, lady*, Julie thought to herself. 'We're from Tetere.' The faces flinched to hear the word *Tetere*, the name itself is a nasty recipe.

'Good you come,' the spokesperson smiled, the best gesture she could muster. Officer Julie darted around, giving a toothy smile, while waiting for her colleagues to arrive.

Officer Julie sensed the gender disparity. *Where are all the men?*

The presence of the White man was a magnetic north, it attracted all eyes toward him. 'Hello everyone?' Addam McColl managed a beefy grin. 'How do you say hello?'

The staring faces reeled Addam McColl. The women mumbled to each other perkily. They gawked at him, unsure if he is talking with his mouth or nose. But after a passing moment, the words find meaning in their conversation.

'Ropo doku.' a woman from the group responded, face radiant-all smile.

'Robo dogu?' Addam McColl faltered. The women laughed in chorus, entertained by the trite pronunciation.

'ROPO DOKU, it means good morning,' Peter corrected him. He reacted to the mismatched translation, knowing the equivalent for *hello* is missing in many languages in the Solomon Islands. *Doku* is ostensibly an accepted word that can mean *hello, welcome* or *situational acceptance* in a broader sense.

'Ropo doku.' Addam McColl said the words, but feebly pronounced them. His presence caught speculating eyes. He is a White man, and seeing one around is sporadic. 'Me and my colleague want to talk to you. We come for peace.' He crosses his hands to show peace. His illustration prompted heads to bob as if floating on water. Addam McColl put on a practiced smile, 'is there any elder around?' Addam McColl looked for clues in the ocean of staring eyes, but nothing. They were absorbed in their discussion.

The mumble subsided, allowing the speaker to respond. 'They go to gardens. Some fella go long town.' She shifted her head automatically to others. 'Bae no back quick time.' Only one woman volunteered as a spokesperson, the others fed her with details as if hinting a student who don't know how to spell.

'Me like talk long village leaders?' Officer Julie deliberated in Pidgin-English, a creole that liberally eases the difficulty of communication, cautious not to say superfluous stuff about *chief*, right time will queue in by logic.

Addam McColl scurried around for no particular reason. Satisfied with his quick observation, 'I guess we'll have to proceed.' By default, he doesn't even bother to ask for young boys too, he had heard enough.

'Julie, you talk with the women and children, we'll have a look around.'

'Look around?' Officer Julie ran her eyes to the group of women, who stared back half-assuredly. Without wasting any more time, she starts sharing the gifts with the children inscribed with the peace mantra, *No more guns*. As said, if they can't smile, bring them a smile.

3

The distance back to the village is short. Chief Ko'oga is ten kilograms lighter and twenty years younger-if you wish to say. The bony ball-headed figure sneaked through the bushes, and before he even realised it, he was at the backyard of the village. A cocoa plantation expands the size of the playing field, does not even bother him. He spied on the vicinity-all clear.

Ghombua villagers are mostly subsistence farmers, mostly cocoa beans and coconut oil as a source of income. Chief Ko'oga adjusted his pace according to his heartbeat. *Slow down, all is fine.* He thought to himself, but his heart beat does not comply. He spied towards the river bank; the white vehicle was still parked where it stopped half an hour ago. His eyes dart towards a group of women forming a crowd around the Police officers.

Chief Ko'oga produced a note from his pocket, and twizzled his head in haste before opening up the letter. He scanned the content; it was only written halfway down the page. His mouth mumbled through the letter word by word, repeated twice while walking. A

13

single line followed by bullet points, nothing much. The writing is very legible and signed off with an initial, not even a name. It's a seven-letter word, all in capital letters. He swallowed in a trace of saliva, accepting the dryness of his mouth. 'BANDITS.' He mumbled the word and marched for the village.

Superintendent Addam McColl walked the length of the village, and cozily looked around. Halfway through the village is a playing field covered with grasses reaching knee-height. A distance further along the river is a church, centrally located, which is no surprise. In a matter of minutes, McColl quickly established the geography of the village in his head. Or what he is telling himself.

Chief Ko'oga's house is next to the playing field. In a typical community setting, a chief or people of elite status conventionally lives at the center of the village, and ordinary citizens' residences sprawl out in circles. The less fortunate will be at the outermost end of the village. Not a village mandate, it's how society works, and everyone fits into it.

Addam McColl and Officer Peter approached an elderly man, who gazed across the river as if in deep meditation.

'Hello, it's such a sunny day.' Addam McColl greeted him with a warm smile, cautious not to scare him with words, though their presence already did.

A pause. 'Hello.' the old man returned a grin he didn't feel.

'My name is Addam McColl.' He extended his hand for a handshake, 'me from Australia.'

The old man smiled in benevolence. 'Pegoa.'

'Peo-. Sorry, come again.'

'Pegoa. George Pegoa.' He succinctly pronounced.

'George Pegoa.' Addam McColl cannot say the word correctly, requires lingual practice. 'Nice to meet you. Me and my colleagues here ...' Addam McColl puckered, not sure if it is necessary to spit out details at that stage.

Pegoa read the details. Age defined his wrinkled face, dropped jaw, and shriveled chest muscle. Despite his frail appearance, his ears can still detect minute decibels long distance away.

'We are from Tetere,' Addam McColl said, 'you have a beautiful place.'

Kind words work miracles. 'Thank you and good you come. This community has lost peace with each passing day.' He munches as if chewing something, glancing towards Chief Ko'oga's house, he read it on their faces.

'Quick question.' Addam McColl seized the cue of the conversation. *There you go.*

'What are your thoughts on the work of the Peace Monitoring team here?' Addam McColl asked before he even think about the words, not a good start as far as the sensitivity of the situation is concerned.

Pegoa shot a confusing look at Addam McColl as if he needs a translator.

'Is it possible-?' Addam McColl meant to make a point but was interrupted.

Pegoa inflated into a question mark. 'You Police?'

The response thwarted Addam McColl.

The old man rubbed the mist off his eyes. Statistics have it, at eighty-three, George Pegoa is the oldest person around. He could tweak the epoch of the community in a minute, faster than what Addam McColl could learn about Ghombua in his remaining life. He witnessed the transition from paganism to Christianity, the era of the British colonisation, the battle of Guadalcanal, gaining independence, and twenty years down the line, living to experience the plight of an ethnic crisis.

'I am wearing this uniform. Partly correct, but without the support of the community, little will be achieved.' *Collective effort* is the word that registered in Addam McColl's head as an afterthought.

The old man gaped, the second guess to the conversation - thinking hard like Addam McColl but in two dialects: Lengo language and lingua franca, broken Pidgin-English.

15

'Is that your house?' Addam McColl derailed the topic for a while, allowing his brain to recharge.

'My son's.'

'Grand.'

'No, not my granny's. It's my son's.'

Addam McColl read the misunderstanding and just swallowed it. The building is a two-story permeant building painted in dark green. It is the biggest house in the community as far as Addam McColl could tell.

'Jim used to work for the government. He looks after the office.'

'I see.'

Pegoa turned to face Addam McColl as if remembering something. 'He was the Manager, boss man like you,' he continued, 'and returned home during the crises.' Truth be told, Jim is the first local to graduate from a college. A success story old man Pegoa still bragged about.

Addam McColl diverted the father-son praises and queued in his questions. 'George, can I ask you a question?'

'Sure.' George nodded. *I know you will.*

'Do you have any idea where they took Chief Ko'oga to?' Addam McColl snapped the name from his memory. He preferred the question about the location of those involved. His experiences proved to him that location is the hardest part of any questioning, as the people responsible can retaliate anytime unexpectedly.

Old man Pegoa's face sparked up, cocking his head sideways. 'Mr-eh, that's a good question. I wish I can tell you.' The response came in a native voice. 'I heard you have the machine to see through thick jungles,' he looked towards the distant hills.

'Machine?' Addam McColl wondered.

Pegoa stared at Addam McColl, eyes squinted and enquired. 'You joined the army?'

'A soldier, yes, used to be.'

'Tough job.' The old man hit his familiar note. 'I spied for the Americans soldiers.'

'You were?'

'Yes. I was twenty-three years old.' He counted with his fingers, added up his age. 'I was young. The Americans supplied us with food and cigarettes. And clothes.' Like many old men on Guadalcanal who lived to experience the plight, the Second World War was deep-rooted and permanent in their memory. Vivid as a glossy page.

'You also carry guns?'

'No.'

'Right.' Addam McColl knew, but just to create a conversation.

'Not allowed. No one of us was allowed.'

'So, what do you do?'

'I am a carrier. I carried bags and rations. It's no easy job.' He squinted again, gripped tight to his walking stick. 'Fighter planes flew across the island like devil birds ready to poop. The noise was frightening.' He paused and swallowed hard as if a dose of adrenalin pumped into his veins, eyes locked on the visitor.

The description of the fighter planes amused Addam McColl to smile. 'Interesting to hear your story. It's the battle of the century, actually.'

'You should receive a medal for that.'

'No. Only a few were awarded.'

'Sir Jacob Vouza. He's famous for his bravery in the battle of Guadalcanal.'

'Right, I saw his statue at the Police headquarter.'

'He helped the Americans.' George continued. 'The Japanese soldiers captured him, lucky for him he escaped.'

'Escaped?' Addam McColl said.

'Yes. The Japanese soldiers thought he was dead-covered in blood.'

'That's war, such things happened,' Addam McColl said.

'Ethnic tension is not a war.' Old man Pegoa witnessed the extreme of the Second World War and its adversities (pardoned me, not mean to be rude, but numeration of wars is the stupidest thing ever). Back to the story, world wars accumulated ammunitions that comprised machine guns, warplanes and massive artillery. Soldiers were defined by regiments with casualties in unspeakable carnage.

'Ethnic tension only ignited more social problems,' Addam McColl admitted, knowing well that peace they wish to restore is not the absence of war, but rather social cohesion. 'Reason for being here today, to help restore law and order - peace.'

The word *peace* sparked a glint of joy in the old man's eyes.

'What's that...?' The conversation was cut short by screaming sounds. Addam McColl looked to Officer Peter for confirmation. The sound came from the women and children. Addam McColl was instantly struck with a thought. 'Officer Julie.'

4

A paunchy figure emerged from a white Toyota Hilux, straightened his blue floral Hawaiian shirt to his khaki shorts, and marched towards the building like an elephant. He glanced at his Rolex wristwatch. 11:45 am. *Forgive me for fifteen minutes.*

The sky-blue concrete building is centrally located, facing the main road. Two other nondescript buildings on both sides. Some distance behind, a vast vacant space, which he correctly guessed as a football field.

'Hello.' He snatched the attention of the front desk officer. 'I am here to meet with Lieutenant Jackson.' He used the first name; this will change in the coming days.

'This way, he'd been expecting you.' The officer led him inside the office. The interior is spacious enough for a boxing ring, sparsely furnished just as he expected. Lieutenant Jackson's office is situated at the back of the building, partitioned by two shelves crammed with reports from an array of incidents, defined the brain of the office bearer.

'Mr. Brown.' The Lieutenant removed his eyeglasses and shot a rather investigative look at his visitor.

19

'G'day Lieutenant.' A firm handshake followed. They both took time to study each other mildly, the beginning of a rapport that will conglomerate in the coming days. Lieutenant is the chief of all staff; Provincial Police Commander is the title labeled against his desk. It was his dream job since entering the force in ninety eighty-three. It took him two decades and tons of patience to climb the hierarchical ladder.

'That empty seat is waiting for you.' He pointed to an empty chair.

'Thank you.' Atkinson stooped tall. He is bulky in the middle and smaller at the top and bottom, like a Japanese paper lantern, covered with disheveled hair, a handlebar mustache and a thick beard. It took him seconds to crumple his bottom on the chair.

Atkinson studied the Lieutenant like a book. At first impression, he could tell he must have been a rough guy in his young days. He still maintained his shape and luster. Flat face, big eyes, and rawboned nose locking the reading glass in place. Imagine an owl wearing a reading glass. My apology. This does not mean disrespecting this office bearer. Respect.

His desk was filled with battered files in piles. A two-way radio on the shelf to his right. Next to it is a tag of keys. The paper pinned up on the wall captured Atkinson's attention: *Be sure your sins will find you out. Numbers 32:23.*

'How can I help you today?' The Lieutenant looked deep into the visitor's eyes causing him to feel awkward for a second.

'Give me a new heart.' Atkinson chuckled. Sensing the staring eyes, Atkinson continued. 'No dramas, pray I will not die from a heart attack,' he said. 'I just got back from Straya yesterday.' He responded with a heavy Australian accent.

'You have a bold heart,' Lieutenant commended.

'Is this compliment or is it my face looks like a dropped pie?' Atkinson grinned and snuggled into the chair.

'No, it's a good compliment.' They both laughed.

'Good to see you again.' The Lieutenant gets on to the formalities without a delay. 'We are getting there, surely.'

'As you said-.' Atkinson nodded his approval.

'The situation in the village had been under our radar lately.' The Lieutenant removed the reading glasses from his eyes.

'It's all in the news,' Atkinson said, not even intimidated by it. He's a hell of a man who runs forward when everyone else escapes the scene. 'So, what can we do about it?' he enquired expectantly, caressing his bushy beard.

The Lieutenant placed his reading glass on the table and fiddled his fingers. 'Our officers are there with IPMT as we speak. We'll ensure those culprits are locked behind the bar as long as time permits.' He digested his own words. 'Local boys were the suspects, called themselves Bandits. I lost my appetite for this melodrama.'

'Heard from Jim Pegoa everything is ...' Atkinson trailed off, allowing the imagination to complete the details.

'That's my fear Mr. Brown,' Lieutenant added. He sized the paunchy figure facing him, wearing a white polo shirt too scarce for his size. 'Stories came out from the village. The media said one thing, the locals said the other.'

'Media is all rotten pig.' Atkinson's face tensed, 'it's more on making money, and very little in providing information.'

'You right, but after all, this is Guadalcanal Mr. Brown.'

'Atkinson. Mr. Brown is my father.'

'Right Atkinson.' Lieutenant eyed him studiously, making a connection. 'I know your father, Mr. Forest Brown.' What a coincidence, he deserved the name that denotes trees and soil. 'He was the Manager for Lever Company here at Foxwood.'

'Right, in the 1980s.' Atkinson reminisced about the past, the passing years deemed him old for a moment. 'I inherited this company after the asshole passed away.'

Mr. Forest Brown was an Irish descendant, which means he's not from Australia. Just like all who entered the country centuries back. This descendant thing means nothing to Atkinson. His grandparents migrated to Australia and settled in Fremantle, Western Australia. This makes Atkinson a second-generation Australian. But unlike his father, Atkinson's young days were equally spent between Australia and Guadalcanal, an asset to his public relations skills.

Atkinson looked with a face-*how do you know my father?*

'I grew up about a kilometer from Foxwood timbers. My tribe is a landowner there.' He revealed his cultural identity. 'Ghaobata tribe.'

The word rings a bell. 'You relate to the *Ghaobata tribe* in Ghombua?' Atkinson enquired with a sluggish movement of eyebrows.

The Lieutenant tilted his head. 'It's complicated. Though we are of the same tribe, we have clans, which categorised us into smaller groups. So, I would say yes and no.' This dual response is the cause of numerous land disputes over the years, because, within a tribe, there are smaller clans, and oftentimes, they fight themselves to death over land ownership. But do they actually own the land? It's yes and no. Complicated the way it is.

'I heard *Ghaobata tribe* is the biggest?' Atkinson remembered his initial conversation with Jim Pegoa.

'It's the big tribe depicted by our totem.'

'"Totem?'

'Eagle is my totem. Tribes on Guadalcanal have birds as an emblem, representing their tribes.'

'So, you are an eagle?' Atkinson visualised a bird gliding with open claws. Tribes in Africa, Australia, and the Native Americans also practice *ornithomancy*, divination of birds as an emblem of power. His mind revolved in thought. 'So what bird is *Thibo tribe*?'

'Dove.'

'A dove? What does dove have to do with tribal totem?' He could be right, a dove as a warrior is ironic. The dove symbolises peace.

'Forget about size. It's not about how big or small the bird is.' The Lieutenant looked around as if searching for answers. 'Different birds have different powers and can show you signs.'

'Signs?'

'If there is an impending threat, your totem can show. Be it in a dream or while awake.' Lieutenant continued. 'Can also reveal to you the past happenings.'

'Wish I have that instinct, I should be a Prime Minister by now, who knows.'

Lieutenant grinned. 'I can go on the whole day on this, but that's another story.'

'A good hook for a *mystery* novel,' Atkinson added.

'Excuse me.' The Lieutenant grabbed the microphone to answer the incoming signal.

For a while, he listens, mouth dropped opened, 'Attack? Who?'

5

'Julie was attacked.' Peter's voice fractured on the radio. 'Repeat, Officer Julie was attacked. Over.'

The Lieutenant nodded towards the microphone. 'Copy. Is it severe, over?' *Silly creeping creatures.*

'Negative. Over.'

'Return now --' he automatically spilled out what his mouth can say, not from his head.

'Copy.'

Lieutenant Jackson shifted his attention back to Atkinson as if he was the cause of the disturbance. Flinched.

'Is everything ok?' Addam McColl's mind throbbed with racing thoughts, at least the situation is relevant to their discussion. And timely too.

'You heard me, right?' Lieutenant snapped, losing his temper from the news. His mood is fluid as always. 'There are people there still acting like blood-sucking, blood-sucking eh- eh-damn it.' The word that slipped off his head is leeches. 'And you insist on proceeding

24

with your operations?' He paused, 'You might not like it, but your operation will not proceed.' He tightened the grip of his hands.

Atkinson mildly considered the Lieutenant's reactions, 'tell you what, the operation of this logging is important for yourself. Important as your job.' He responded in a brisk tone. 'I paid tax to your government, right? The government used the money to pay teachers, doctors, nurses ...and police too.' *Including yourself, Lieutenant.* Little to the Lieutenant's knowledge, Atkinson has been evading government taxes that peaked at several million in local currency, and he has mastered the vice as like riding a bicycle.

'You *are partly* right but don't talk to me about tax and stuff. My point is on security.' Lieutenant's eyeballs popped out; his authority is being manipulated. 'Whilst your operation is in the best interest of the government, we must also consider the safety of our officers. I will not put my men into the mouth of a vicious reptile. No-no way.'

'Look, we are not against each here, right?' Atkinson shot a well-considered thought; a mistake means putting the operation in a crimp. 'What I mean is to support each other. I also employed local boys as security.' Atkinson lied. It's a plan, and like all plans, it's fluid.

'I get your point, but we also have our downside. We are ill-equipped and understaffed.' He eyed across the office space, 'tell you what, a recent survey on Guadalcanal shows that one police officer for every three thousand people. Three thousand.'

'I am not here for the statistics.'

A long pause. 'And what do you expect from us, ballistic missiles?'

Atkinson watched Lieutenant riveted as if no words came out of his mouth. *The ball is in your court.* He stood up, 'this discussion is not over, I will call you-eh-' and walked towards the doorway. He knows it's rude, but under such circumstances, he has to act. 'I hope your men return safely.'

Lieutenant watched the disheveled hair figure storm out the door, but was glad about himself as if winning a speech contest.

Obsessed with money is dangerous, my arrogant friend.

A group of chickens scattered with a cluck, wings flapping to aid their escape. Addam McColl appeared behind the bushes -panting. 'I lost the damned pig. He must have ...' He looked towards the tall trees at a distance, enough for one to hide.

'Idiot,' Addam McColl said, panting.

'That's them,' Officer Peter said.

'Militants, militants....' commander, the talking parrot flew by, flapping its wing, and landed at a nearby tree.

They ignored the bird.

'We must move out now.' Addam McColl looked around one more time, feeling hostile.

6

At 5 feet 9, Bernard stood upright like a mast. He wears a black kiwi windbreaker jacket, the only thing that reminded him of his late father.

'Police, get out of my sight.' Bernard's added in a hushed voice, sweeping the binoculars around. As the only kid in the family, he has no one to compete with or compare himself to. During his childhood days, he fancied the biblical story of young Joash ordained king of Judah at age seven. His dream shifted when he entered high school. Science stood out to be his favourite subject, he memorised the first twenty elements of the Periodic Table within in a day with the aid of a mnemonic. As his dream job, he wants to be a Police officer, specialised in Forensic Science.

As he moved higher in his education, he became passionate about the history of freedom movements, the like as of *South Africa Apartheid, the Indian Independent movement, the Black Panther movement of the United States* plus others. His interest ramified to the secret societies like t*he Illuminati, the Freemasons, the Knights Templar,* and many

27

others, of which he often borrowed textbooks from the library to satisfy his ego. As Theodore Roosevelt rightly stated, he became part of everything he read, which culminated in the creation of the BANDITS.

'Thank you chief.' Toxic added from the back. 'Thank you, uncle and grannies,' he mimicked Chief Ko'oga's voice followed by a snigger.

The boys blurted out in laughter.

After seconds of hilarity, 'It's not funny.' Osama intervened with a solemn voice, 'It's because of him they drove off. If not ....' He jerked his head, leaving the sentence hanging in the air like a bubble –scared if it burst.

'They would have snooped around for us.' Deve gave a twitch at his dreadlocks. 'Chief have power.' He peeped towards the village, a feeble nod to how things work.

'Police are not foolish,' Bernard said, 'they don't buy crap from people like us. It's not over guys, they are like dogs searching for a buried bone. They will continue to sniff around until they gnaw on something.' He weighed the prospects.

He eyed the team nodding their heads.

'We have to stay alert. 'Bernard retorted. 'I will set out rules to guide us.'

Announcing this made heads bob about. They hated rules and are not good in abiding with a single one. The village they escaped is full of rules. It's obligatory and boring.

'What do you think?' Bernard said.

'Not bad.' Deve added little weight to the prospect. At twenty-six, David Bokito *aka Deve* is still single. He is of average build, standing 5 feet 6, masculine and tough as his voice. His head is shaped by his dreadlock hair with bushy eyebrows and stout jaw. Deve once joined the Guadalcanal militants during the ethnic crisis, executing plunder and pillages around the island. Besides Deve, the rest of the team members were teenagers, or late teens looking for some thrills in the gang.

Nimo shrugged and mumbled. 'Sounds stupid, we are no longer in pre-class.' Other members were undecided, they sat as if untouched by the words. Everyone knows Nimo is a scaremonger, good at spreading fear among members. He's the type who escapes the scene when problems arise, he cannot be trusted.

'Stop thinking like a cave dweller?' Bernard added. 'Get some education.'

'I am not educated as you, but I have a brain too, same as you,' Nimo said, 'why come up with rules when we can't keep the law?'

'Because some of us don't know how to shut our mouth.'

The silence queued in eeriness.

'We must set rules to protect us.' Bernard gave an unwavering talk. 'Truth is, logging is coming, this will change everything- the community.'

Heads frozen, still speechless.

Bernard is resolute as a brick wall. 'See this.' He produced a map from his jacket pocket.

The boys looked at each other, grumbling among themselves.

'Is there an agreement?' Nimo jerked his head.

'All papers already signed; nothing for us. So will have to set our rules.' Bernard may overreact, but he read a lot about battles, both won and lost. Sun Tzu came up with the *Art of War* to guide his comrades, knowing the engagement rules are as important as the war itself-*Jus ad bellum* is the term.

The team nodded their feeble agreement. No concrete answers.

Without wasting more time, Bernard announced. 'These are our principles, RULE ONE; landowners must have their say in the signed agreement.' The team nodded their agreement.

'RULE NUMBER TWO; No middle man. If there is one, he is our enemy.'

The second rule was announced followed by low grumbles. The boys all knew this, and as the name implies it causes problems than solving them.

'RULE NUMBER THREE; locals are a priority for job recruitment.' The boys received the third rule with no objection.

'And finally, RULE NUMBER FOUR: don't trust the government.'

The fourth rule raised eyebrows. Silence is permanent.

Nimo raised his hand. 'Talking about the government, you mean the Police too?'

'Of course, Police is the face of the law,' Bernard responded ardently. 'Government is as good as its police.'

~

'They will come up with something. They will.' Bernard continued walking, binoculars in his hands. 'I can only imagine them cramped in a meeting room, discussing how to capture us.'

'Who?' Stonie enquired under gasp.

'The Police. What are you thinking?' Bernard barked at Stonie, who snorted like a pig.

'Ok, I thought you mean -?' Stonie is two steps behind Bernard, gasping for breath, looking at the village below.

Bernard adjusted the binoculars and mumbled to himself. 'That's what police do, locked criminals behind bars, it's their job, regardless -.' The thought of it tingled raw anger down his spine. 'The ex-militants were said to be fighting for freedom, see what happened to them now, locked up for life.'

'Why not take up arms again, we still have guns around,' someone erupted. It's gang member Toxic, responding with his habitual negligence.

'Seven of us against the police? It's suicide.' Nimo smirked at Toxic.

'Can you come up with something reasonable?' Bernard demanded.

'Like what, surrender ourselves?' Nimrod argued. 'Abduction is a big mistake.'

'Mistake? Whose fault?' Bernard argued. 'We planned it together - stop your blaming game'

'It's a *damned* mistake.' Nimrod continued his argument, flinching around.

'Look, if that is how you see it, then leave,' Bernard ordered.

The silence landed like a hailstorm. Unwelcoming and irritating. Nimrod is a mirror reflection of Bernard's character; his reactions are plain contradictions. Raised by a single parent, he goes by the name Nimrod Gimo.

'We should plan our action in the first place. Not abduction.' Deve reasoned out what he thought was a mistake. 'Nimo is right,' he indicated his position. Other team members froze, weighing the pros and cons in their heads.

If we do not abduct Chief Ko'oga?' Nimo paused, allowing others to ponder. 'Things would turn out differently.'

'Seriously?' Bernard contended. 'We looted the vehicle. It's a crime in the first place. Abducting Chief Ko'oga is not the only reason.'

'What Nimo trying to say is—' Deve stopped short with the interruption.

'I know what he meant. I don't need a translator.' Bernard stood his ground, staring blankly down the hills. His mouth puckers in anger.

'Talking about land. I am not a *Thibo* tribe, so I don't care a bit.' Nimo dropped it without a second thought.

'Nonsense. *Thibo* tribe, *Ghaobata* or whatever, we all landowners. Are the gardens own by *Thibo* tribe, is the water we drink owned by *Thibo* tribe?' Bernard hammered back. 'Come on, put a brain to your words.'

'What will you do? Start a military coup?' Nimo challenged the leader.

Fed-up with the argument, Bernard flashed in frustration. 'Fine, those who disagree, go.' He darted around, every inch of his muscles tensed. 'Leave, now!'

7

The Tetere clinic is empty. As this time of the day, most sick patients had already left for their respective homes.

Inside the clinic are two figures, Officer Julie and the nurse. The other nurse clocked out early.

'You can't trust anyone. And I mean no one should,' Officer Julie said, and she meant it. 'No one is around to help us, only women and children.' Julie lies face down, allowing the nurse to do the rest. The blood clot jutted across her back, from the left shoulder down her spine, a diagonal cut. Julie offered a silent prayer, *thank you Lord for saving my life...* The pain is overpowering, especially on her back where her hand is unreachable. She bites her lower lip, accommodating the pain.

'You lucky, the cut is not deep,' The nurse said. 'It'll be over soon.'

'I want to squeeze the neck of that prick.' Julie's face crumpled in pain. 'He's wearing a mask, like some joker. I wish I saw him coming.' She hissed at the nurse who is not paying attention to her brooding tone.

32

'Sorry,' the nurse added with a comforting voice, 'I felt sorry for the women and children.' She continued with her work, acknowledging the routinisation of her job. Second, by second, minute by minute, she stitches the wound. She had the face of the carver who was about to achieve the job.

Officer Julie recalled. 'The idiot said something about Bandits. Right, he's a stupid Bandit.'

Chief Ko'oga's house is next to the playing field. Three houses up the river is the Church. Moses Ravu's house is the one next to the Church. Moses Ravu is the Church Elder, but he preferred to be called Elder Moses, more relevant to the Biblical Moses. Elder Moses visited Chief Ko'oga as part of his duty, counseling and praying for the church members.

Elder Moses sat on a white plastic chair, facing Chief Ko'oga. 'I felt sorry for our community, we are losing our normal way of life.' Elder Moses spoke with a benevolent voice. 'What they've done was unacceptable, it's a total disgrace.' He knuckled his hands together, adjusting his back onto the chair that fits perfectly for a short man like him. He stood only 5 feet 1, but one cannot misjudge his prominence through his height. He's going towards his 70th birthday. Elder Moses lost track of it, his mum passed away when he was still a kid. From memories, he's somewhere between sixty-eight and sixty-nine years old. Whatever the number that ticks, he cares a little.

Unlike elder Moses, Chief Ko'oga has lost weight over the years because of his age, leaving him just enough flesh to hold his skin intact. His lips pursed, forehead pales with crinkles, and wearing a small pointy beard. 'Thank you for your assuring words and prayers.' He paused. 'Their point is valid. They strongly opposed logging; I mean Bernard.' He recalled their discussion. 'They do not mean to hurt me; they are desperate for help. They want the community's attention, that's all'

'You believed them?' Elder Moses intervened.

'A little. Hard to believe Bernard succumbs to that life. A quiet kid, well-educated, you know.' The thought revolved in his head.

Elder Moses continued, 'poor Bernard, that boy grew a violent bone after he lost his parents.' He frowned, unsure if it was worth continuing with the discussion.

Chief Ko'oga continued, 'Deve is also with them, and also the two brothers. Thomas and Irvin.' He paused. 'They used names which I do not understand. One is called Osama. The other is… I, I can't remember all the names. All make-up ones.'

'Youths, it's no surprise. They can do something crazy on a whim.' Elder Moses caressed his beard.

Chief rubbed his back against the chair. 'Their camp is at the vantage point, looking down at the entire village. They have a thing they look into -.'

'You mean a spyglass?' Elder Moses asked.

'Yes, spyglass, a map, and other items.' He nodded indicatively.

'Those are stolen items, right?'

'Where else can they get it from?' He swallowed and darted around. 'They denied burning the Police vehicle, but who else can do that.'

Elder Moses remains silent, consuming the details.

Chief Ko'oga continued. 'I don't know. Maybe they lied to me.' He cocked his head as a matter-of-fact look.

Elder Moses face turned dull. 'But why they attacked the Police officer, that's another criminal case, a felony.'

'I don't think they involved, Elder. All the seven members were up in the camp when they released me. I can vouch for their innocence.'

'Innocent?' The thought riddled involuntarily in Elder Moses' mind. 'It's possible they can still make it to the village before you.'

Assuming enough talk has been done, Chief Ko'oga passed the note. 'This is their request.'

8

Atkinson is good at keeping his words. He returned to Tetere Police Station as he promised. He has to learn a bit about Guadalcanal and its people. The culture.

As the largest island on the archipelago, Guadalcanal is undisputedly complex with its tribal system. For a foreigner, it will take unnamable years to understand and appreciate the cobwebbed composition of the society. Atkinson is no exception; he has to understand the culture by all means possible.

'Thanks for lecturing me on the tribal system of Guadalcanal. That's very helpful.' Atkinson commended Lieutenant.

'That's the foundation of Guadalcanal. It's a long –long story.'

Atkinson's face appeared vacant. 'I have a question. Assume I am a *Thibo tribe* who got married to a woman from a *Ghaobata* tribe. What tribe will my child be?'

'Guadalcanal is practicing matrilineal, so the child will be rightfully *Ghaobata*.'

'I can't understand why the child has to be *Ghaobata*, since I am the man who will fight for land, not woman?'

'I understand your point. It's even trickier when a *Guale* man married a woman from another island. The child will be -.'

'Landless?' Atkinson interposed, digesting what has been said.

'Not necessarily landless, but will not entitle or inherit to any of the tribes.'.

'This is ridiculous. That's the problem with such land inheritance.'

'That's partly the reason for the ethnic tension too.' Lieutenant frowned. 'Some children are born as such.'

'So why inherit land through women?'

The Lieutenant accepted the question leveled at him, of which he grinned. 'Let me tell you the story of my Guadalcanal.' He cleared his throat. 'In the very beginning of the beginning, we have only *Ironggali*- the creator of this island called *Isatabu*. *Ironggali* created the tribes and designated leaders to different parts of the island. However, as history goes, only two tribes survived the ages. We called them *Garavu* and *Manukiki*- *or simply big and small tribes*.' He straightened his back, getting himself to a comfortable posture. 'This represented the two brothers who killed the vicious giant that once ruled the island. It's another story.' He fiddled his fingers on the table, creating a considerable background nuisance to his subordinates in the office.

Atkinson was absorbed by the indiscernible account, begging him to continue.

Lieutenant continued. 'All people vacated the island and fled to nearby islands- *Ngella, Savo, Malaita, Isabel* and *Makira*. All except a pregnant woman, left behind because she was an abomination to her people and the community. To cut the story short, the two sons of the abandoned woman killed the giant, allowing the people to return to the motherland. As a token of recognition to the mother, a matrilineal system of land ownership was adopted ever since.'

Atkinson pondered with unblinking eyes. 'That makes complete sense, she was the one who nurtured and trained those brothers.'

'Twins actually,' Lieutenant corrected him, 'they were *baso malaghai--twin* warriors.'

'Everyone has their story.' This was all Atkinson could say, weighing out the difference between truth and folklore. He has his own story, but again as Lieutenant Jackson rightly put it, it's another story.

9

T he glass door carries the notice, 'We're Open. Always close the door.' Sounds generously reasonable for the Office that dealt with different classes of people. Pompous businessmen, oil smeared mechanics, shabby drivers and desperate landowners. The interior is comparatively empty. Facing the main door is the reception desk, manned by a worn-out looking woman in her late fifties who hardly does any work besides answering the incoming calls.

Opposite the reception desk is a man, gawking at the posters on the wall. The silence is numbing, and the only sound heard is the buzzing noise of the air conditioning system.

'Can I help you?' the receptionist's face beamed up, professional and eloquent.

'I have an appointment with bossman.' He glanced at his wristwatch. 'At ten o'clock.' He's twenty minutes late.

'Name please?' His official attire struck her eyes, which emanates halo of authority and power.

'Jim. Jim Pegoa. He knows about this.'

'Jim Begoa?'

'P for Pencil,' he emphasised his second name, assuming it as the cause of the follow-up question. 'I have an important meeting.' He pronounced with a showy nod.

The receptionist lifted the phone automatically, punched the numbers, and dials. After seconds of head nodding, she dropped the phone. 'He's coming.' She responded immediately, acknowledging the importance of the meeting. She proceeded to scribble something down in the visitors' record book.

'Thank you.' He reverted his attention to the map hanging on the wall. It is the map of the Solomon Islands dotted with 992 islands cobbled together into nine provinces, from Shortlands in the west to Tikopia in the east. His eye settled at the center of the map where Guadalcanal is located. He pictured his village on the map. As the village name implies, it's ostensibly dotted at the center of the island. *Ghombua* means center.

The creaking sound of an interior door got his attention. 'G'day mate!'

'Good morning,' Pegoa replied.

'Come in, take a seat,' Atkinson said, all smiling. 'You look younger every time I see you.'

Pegoa walked in and took a seat.

Atkinson continued. 'Great seeing you again, when is the last time we talk?'

'A month ago.' Pegoa responded instantly, contemplating the passing days and weeks.

'It's just like yesterday, time moves so swiftly that we forget to keep track of our age.' Atkinson beamed, allowing the numbers to add up in his head.

'True, days are flying.' Pegoa said.

'What have you been doing all the past weeks, busy with community stuff, I guess?'

'Right, you know in the community it's always a busy time. The Church annual programs, school board meetings, family matters and such,' Pegoa uttered with an air of authority.

'I see. That must put a hell of a lot of pressure on you.' Atkinson scrutinised the lean figure in front of him. From a quick guess, he is in his early fifties, robust with an average height, 5 feet 6 is the number that is stamped. He had a bony nose that is too large for his chiseled face with thick eyebrows. His hair cut shaped his head like a mushroom, neatly trimmed to give a gaudy hairline. A white striped shirt buttoned halfway up to his neck, tucked into drab khaki shorts, a stunt for his professional gesture.

'True, as a village leader, I accepted the work for the betterment of our community.'

'Got it right. So, what is new?' Atkinson diverted the discussion.

'I guess you must have heard the news, 'Pegoa said.

'Of course,' Atkinson agreed. 'But media as we knew, sometimes exaggerated their stories to make it newsy – too much bullshit.' He curled his lips, to make his point relevant.

Without a word, Pegoa only nodded.

'I am thinking, Pegoa.' He paused composing his words. 'Let me put it another way, who else owns the land?' Atkinson queried to the best of his interest. As much as he knew, land on Guadalcanal, like other neighboring islands is own by tribes, which genuinely means more than one signatory is expected. He knew from experience, that other tribes will also claim access fees if somehow, the operation passed through their land.

Pegoa caught the question by the head. 'We are. The other landowners are quite busy, so I represent our tribe.'

Atkinson quizzed himself with a response, 'What's the tribe again?'

'*Thibo. Thibo tribe,*' Pegoa answered, stroking his bony forehead.

'It's just one tribe, right?'

'Yes,' Pegoa responded, '*Thibo* tribe-my tribe.'

'Pegoa.' He paused, knowing he just pronounced his name close to fluency. Whatever the name holds, 'I want this operation to proceed. But, unless the safety of my machines and employees are guaranteed, I cannot ...' He stared at the figure in front of him, weighing his thoughts.

'Safety, right. Police will be stationed in the community.'

'Is that confirmed?' Atkinson flushed. *Where did you hear that?*

'That's the plan.' He sounds ambitious, tapping his knees and looking relaxed.

'What's the closest Police station?'

'Tetere.'

'Right, but it's still fifty or sixty kilometers away.' Atkinson stared at the map.

'Yes, right, closer to Honiara than Ghombua.'

Atkinson thinks to himself, 'I am not sure if Tetere Police Station has the manpower,' he said. 'By the way, do you know Lieutenant Kilua?'

'Lieutenant Kilua?' Pegoa stared vacantly at the wall, searching his brain database.

'He's the PC for Tetere,' Atkinson explained, 'Police Chief.'

'He's from north Guadalcanal, right?' Pegoa's eyes widened, a weak surprise.

'I guess so.' *Damn it. He picked the man by the name.*

'Not at a personal level, but he is a *wantok*.'

'I see, Wantok.' Atkinson understands the buzzword -- speaking the same language.

Atkinson tossed his head backward. 'Great, I am thinking if we could meet anytime. He is the man of the game. Very charismatic.'

'What made you say that?' Pegoa dug for more. *Damned, what does it mean?*

'Restoring law and order when guns still in abundance like bush knives requires a brave heart.'

Pegoa vacantly nodded. 'True, big job.'

A thought struck Atkinson. 'Pegoa, the incident. What is that all about?'

'It's those boys. They need something to occupy their time. You know youths.'

'Such a shame. What do community leaders do about this?' Atkinson queried with an engaging look.

'Well, as said, it took a village to raise a child. We are working with the elders to address the problem. Not only Ghombua, but the surrounding communities as well.'

'Very encouraging. I am willing to help in any way possible.'

Pegoa massaged his chin. 'Good, I will talk to them.'

'Talking about tribes, can you bring someone with you next time? The tribal leaders.' Atkinson has to play it safe. It's like walking on waterlogged ground. Slippery.

IO

The sky is clear, cirrus clouds formed weaving patterns, scattering across the sky. Under the shades of the trees, figures move about, discussing. Planning.

'We are not statues,' Bernard imposed, 'we have brains, arms, and legs to defend ourselves.' He beamed around with an iota of confidence.

Not all members agreed, the silence says it all.

Bernard continued. 'We have few good elders we can talk to.'

'Again?' As expected, Nimo interposed on a whim, 'you mean we see the elders?'

'You heard me, right?'

'I had enough with those *brain-dead* elders,' Nimo said.

'I thought you already left the team?' Bernard said. 'Your presence gives me a headache,'

'Nimo, listen,' Deve interrupted, not wanting to see another bout. 'Listen for a second. What's the matter with you?'

43

'I don't have a matter with me. The matter is what we are now in,' Nimo snapped back, angling his head at Deve.

'I know, can we put our heads together for at least one more time?' Deve said.

'We have been doing that all along. Look at us now, we're trapped, can't you see?' Nimo shot an outrageous look.

'That's why we have to stand together and plan our way out,' Bernard said.

'Yes, we are BANDITS. And the elders are framing us up,' Nimo smirked.

No more words to say, Bernard lifted the duffel bag onto his shoulder. 'Who is with me?'

'IPMT do not use guns. You can criticise, but the protocol is protocol.' Lieutenant Kilua marched across the tattered tiled floor.

'I am curious about the end outcome, especially dealing with ex-militants. These are rebels, they have guns,' Atkinson said.

'It's ridiculous to even think of it. When dealing with guns, one has to be armed.' Lieutenant snapped, debating the thoughts in his mind. 'At first, that is my thinking, but I was wrong, weapons free approach works well in the communities. Weapons were surrendered, hundreds of them.'

'How can you be sure all weapons are surrendered, what if they surrender the homemade ones, and keep the high powered?' Atkinson asked.

'That's the question I cannot answer,' Lieutenant said. 'But I can assure you, everyone wants peace in their communities. Crystal clear.'

Lieutenant paged through the files. 'I believe in the theory of instilling fear in the locals. It works. Some kind of high-tech lie, like saying using special equipment to locate guns through walls and roofs.' He allowed the words to run through his mind. 'Many ex-militants swallowed that high-grade bullshit. It's safe to say that

IPMT weapons-free campaign is a milestone, but maybe two years is not enough. They are pulling out in a month time.' He paused to catch his words. 'This is the copy of their exit report.' He flagged the report as if telling is not enough. Sensing he had dominated the talking; Lieutenant rubbed his mouth as if to zip it shut.

Atkinson glanced at the report with disparagement. 'After their exit, what?'

'Yes, they are leaving.' The Lieutenant misread the question.

'I mean the International Peace Monitoring Team,' he partially responded, followed by a sigh. 'After they left, what is their exit plan or whatever crap you called it?' Though he was familiar with the situation, Atkinson selected his cards well. As his dad always says, *always grip your nails, the ground could be slippery.* This has become his mantra.

'Oh, sorry, the local counterparts will take over. Mostly ex-Police officers and former government officers.' *Damned gutless bureaucrats.*

'So, the plan is to continue with the *unarmed* approach?'

'What I know.'

'At the top of your head, how long do you think it will take? Criminal activities still rampant in the communities.' He locked his eyes on Lieutenant Jackson wondering if the person he is talking to is even sane. Or worst, if the approach selected is the only one that existed, otherwise what are the synonyms for stupid?

My question all along too.' He mistakenly raised three fingers. 'IPMT has both advantages and disadvantages.' The discussion put the Lieutenant in an awkward position, seeing Atkinson is impatiently eager to get assurance for the success of his operation.

Atkinson's face is ashen in a second, probably need a cigarette.

Lieutenant continued. 'Counting on their advantages, combatants from both sides now surrendered their guns, and many, I'd say most communities are now weapons-free. The fruit of the *No more guns* campaign.' He tilted his head, 'disadvantages as you know, not all guns are surrendered. I'd say ten percent is still out there, and wherever these guns are, I can vouch that, they are high-powered ones. Ninety percent of weapons surrendered are mostly homemade.'

Atkinson grimaced with a snub, 'My whole point. You can't fight rebels empty-handed; you know that. Even David armed with a sling and stones to kill Goliath.' He nodded, at least his Sunday school classes meant something after those years.

Like other ordinary citizens, the Lieutenant questioned the capacity of IPMT in restoring law and order. While placing a premium on the restoration of law and order in a broader sense, one will have to consider Police officers and civilians alike that will be at stake. To larger degree, IPMT is a transitional buffer to address the failed Townsville Peace agreement. TPA as they abbreviated, looks appealing on paper, but had little impact on the ground, and the signing was a bit rushed, riddled with loopholes. 'The government will intervene with fully equipped overseas soldiers,' he paused, 'this is the plan.'

'Sorry, what is the timeline we are talking about?'

'One month.'

'Let's be realistic on the timing, I don't have time to waste.' Atkinson sighed, reading the figure who responded, not the brain he expected. He knew well nothing will happen within the said timeframe. He switched his attention to the page on his table, a signed logging indenture. He glanced at his wristwatch; two things clicked in his mind. One, it's time for a cigarette.

Two, from the discussion, he will have to execute Plan B.

II

'Town life is expensive.' Pegoa munched his dinner. 'Water, food, transport, electricity, everything is money.'

His wife is busy roasting plantains on the fire, sufficed a hollow nod.

'Today, one street kid asked me for a dollar,' Pegoa continued. 'One dollar.'

'Everyone needs money to survive.' His wife added with a breath of compassion.

'I know, but they should work, not sit and ask. I hate lazy people.' What came to Pegoa's mind is the proverb that became his mantra- *give a dollar to a struggling kid, and he will prosper, give a dollar to a beggar, and he will be a beggar still.*

He munched like a cow. His wife cooked it to his preference. She placed the plantains in a stone oven, allowing the banana to cook slowly, enhancing the aroma and the taste.

'Everyone needs money. Even here in the community, we need money too. People can say bad things about money, but money is

47

now part of our daily lives. We need salt, sugar, soaps, kerosene -,' the wife pithily stated. Pegoa's wife is from Isabel province, the longest island in the Solomon Islands archipelago. She has a neutral view of town life and meant what she's talking about. Twenty years has been lenient enough to embrace her with the local traditions of the *Guale*.

'Correct, money is now part of our everyday living, but one will have to sweat for it, not begging the streets.'

'But some don't have the resources to make ends meet, not all the town people are employed.' The wife added, with tongs in hand cooking the banana.

'I want the Prime Minister to put a law allowing only ones with genuine job and business to live in the city,' Pegoa said. 'Those without job will have to go back to their respective islands and plant gardens.'

'True, but sorry, you are not the Prime Minister.' The wife chuckled.

Pegoa continued munching. 'Where're my beautiful kids.' He resorted to ask an exit question, appreciating he has a son and daughter in their teens.

'They joined the Church choir.'

'How's Elizabeth? Does she find someone?' Pegoa asked, knowing his eldest daughter turned seventeen.

Pegoa looked outside, darkness greeted him. The village is quiet and the sky is starless.

'There's a boy,' His wife added.

'Who is the future in-law?'

'Oa-.'

A voice in the background interrupted their conversation.

'Oa, it's me,' a voice repeated.

'Who is it?' Pegoa squinted his eyes into the pitch darkness, knowing the word *Oa* in the local dialect equivalents to *hello* in English. Loosely fitting, more of a synonym.

'It's me, Jemes.' The response is gruff.

'Oh Jemes, good evening, I cannot see you.' He mumbled to his wife, probably to see if they have enough food left. 'I am having my dinner, come join me.'

'Thank you, I had enough.' Jemes gave a terse response.

'How's Merre and Edna?' Pegoa jumped in with a question.

'At the river,' he responds sparingly. Jemes gave no prior notice about his sudden visit which prompted Pegoa to abandon his sitting position and head for the door.

'The night is selfish and refuses to provide us stars,' Pegoa said.

Without wasting more time, Jemes said. 'Sorry for show up without notice. I have something to discuss.'

'Ok? Not a crime.' Pegoa stared at the silhouette of Jemes against the distant light. 'It's a shame we hardly visit each other these days as if we are on a different side of the island. Come in.' Pegoa scanned the distance behind Jemes to confirm he was alone. 'You alone?' he enquired to confirm his eyes.

'Yes.' Jemes darted around in the dark.

'What's the worry, come inside and have some cooked plantain.'

'I don't mean to be disrespectful, but I already had enough.' Jemes said.

'Fine, just come inside,' Pegoa said.

'I heard you went to town?' Jemes finally hit the lurking topic, something for Pegoa to fiddle on for a start.

Pegoa sensed an incoming storm. 'Yes, eh-right.'

'You visit Pacific Loggers office?' Jemes queued in a leading question.

'Yeah-right. I did,' Pegoa affirmed.

'Any news?' Jemes queried in a concerned tone.

'Not much, I went there, but bossman is busy, no time to story.' He lied, channeling the thoughts in his head. 'We will sit down and talk first before we meet with bossman.' He used the word *we*, literally involving himself. Pegoa is also a *Thibo* tribe, but another clan, different from Jemes' *Luvu Malaghai* tribe.

'What I've been thinking.' Jemes has to depend on someone for such advice. His two elder brothers married to the other side of the

Island and settled permanently there with their families. The last time they paid a visit was when their father passed away, some ten years back. In their absence, Jemes took on the crown. But like a king, he is even bored with the power invested in him. 'Better we know what is in the paper before sign,' Jemes stated.

The fire flickered and cracked, slowly extinguished, leaving only an ember to glow on the wood.

'We have to agree first Jemes, that's how it works.' Another pronoun was used. He threw back the bag of responsibility, knowing Jemes does not have many family members alive, besides bloody relatives.

Jemes stood silent for a moment. Not a word. He needs time to compose himself together before saying anything gross.

'We need to confirm the land boundaries too,' Pegoa said. Another *we*.

'Boundaries?' The land bordered with *Ghaobata tribe* to the south and *Thogo tribe* to the east. A discrete noise suppressed the discussion. It's familiar, the sound of approaching feet.

Silhouetted in the dark was a wall of mute figures, standing like Moai of the Rapa Nui. For seconds, no sounds came out from them, prompting Pegoa to mistaken them as ghosts. He believed in ghosts but not at dusk when people still move about. From memory, ghosts love white, less black, and always a single lady in a white long dress. Ask the devil.

'Oa, who is it?' Pegoa enquired with a controlled voice, audible enough for them to hear.

'The boys.' Followed by a long pause. 'You forget us?' The voice growled.

'Who?' Pegoa eyed Jemes who was mesmerised by the group and the awkward silence it yields.

Nobody speaks. A slight movement showed they had planned their move. To stand still and remain silent, except for the one who does the talking.

'Me and Jemes here if you need to talk.' *Why me?* Pegoa questioned himself, his guts knotted like cotton, he smells the intention.

'We want to talk with you, in private.' The voice interrupted with a flat tone, loud enough for Pegoa to hear.

Pegoa's heart missed a beat. *Lord help me.*

Without a second thought, Jemes slowly sneaked out in the opposite direction. *I had enough problems, let this be someone's.*

12

T he island of Guadalcanal is distinctive, one will not mistake it on a country map, both its shape and size. It looks like a plump giant footprint embedded in the mud. On the 1:25,000 scale, the 5,302 square kilometers island is large enough to show all the sixteen major rivers traversing across the plain on the northern side of the island.

'This is the place that stole the show.' The Lieutenant pointed to the northern side of the map. 'We are here, and Ghombua is somewhere there.' He indicated it on the map as if they were tourists visiting for the first time. 'It's approximately thirty kilometers. This is the distance we'll cover.' He searched around for collective responses. 'I argued on the ground of our safety, but the company boss stands his ground. Such an arrogance t,' Lieutenant said, 'we'll only provide support in escorting the machines on land.'

'Excuse me, Lieutenant?' A rusty voice interrupted.

'Yes, Officer Peter.'

'What's the number you are thinking?' Peter looked around anxiously, knowing their number is scant. The others rumbled too, fiddling through the plan - to accept or discard.

'That's a good question. Will come to that later.' Lieutenant Jackson cleared his throat. 'We have protocols. Our job is to escort only. And follow-up investigations to the previous cases. We have *all* valid reasons to be part of this mission.'

'Excuse me, Lieutenant,' Officer Brain asked, 'do you consider Central police in this mission?' The question floated around in the room for a while.

'Unfortunately, Central Police put the responsibility on us,' He announced. The response is not what the team expected, it's open for debate. The whole plan is questionable somehow.

Officer Brian bobbed his head, 'we all know what the bandits are capable of, so it's better to have a plan, and do we need support for that plan, and if yes, how?' He spoke out his intention, eyes leveled at his colleagues.

The Lieutenant listened with half-opened mouth. 'Listen, we can always seek support from Central Police if need be. Specifically on circumstances beyond our capacity.' The Lieutenant looked around the faces, unsure if their capacity matched the task. 'Will think through that. And yes, the company has its own securities too - we are not alone. They are the ones who will take the leading role.'

Lieutenant Jackson continued. 'Camp there for a few days, three weeks maximum.' This sentence goads the faces to twist, weighing the intensity of the job.

'Lieutenant, what I assume from the discussion are two missions.' Officer Peter enquired with profound thought. 'One to escort machines and second, to hunt down the culprits.'

'Yes, correct,' Lieutenant said.

Officer Peter continued. 'I have a five-cent thought. For task one, I think we are comfortable with that. One or two of our officers can help escort the machines. But for the second task, we need a team. And to be frank, we need to prepare for task two.'

'You read my mind, officer.' The Lieutenant summarised his thoughts. 'And that leads to your question. How many officers to be deployed.'

'Police can't devise a plan quicker?' Atkinson said. 'Are they building a rocket?' He leaned back on his cushion chair, puffed a lungful from his cigarette and blows out onto the newspaper. The thoughts raced through his mind, or at least thinking about something.

'It's all excuses,' Suiono supported. Suiono Lee is a seasoned logging Operations Manager. Averagely built and stood 5 feet 6, broad face with a quivery lip and a peanut dry skin. He has been with Pacific Loggers for over a decade now. He left Malaysia, crossing three international borders with no legal documents. Like those who illegally crossed borders, he landed on any available menial job, from a punctilious tool boy to unflagging bulldozer crew, before being promoted to bulldozer operator, and later to austere supervisor. At forty-nine years old, he managed the Pacific Loggers operations.

'These iron ladies are ready to roll.' Suiono combed his hair with his fingers, staring at the machines.

'Good, it gives my brain comfort.' Atkinson nodded with a satisfied look 'Tetere Police are ready.' Atkinson stroked his bushy beard, watching his cigarette butt creating flame in the ashtray.

'What about our security?' Suiono stared with an asian gleam, mouth opened for two seconds without a word.

'Pegoa is handling that.' Atkinson said.

Suiono looked at his watched 2:49 p.m. 'We have two gentlemen here this morning, looking for a job.'

'What job?'

'Operators, they both had some logging experiences.'

'Well, get them on board? We'll also hire locals as part of the agreement.'

'As you said, boss.' Suiono agreed.

'Good, ready to roll.' Atkinson stared at the map on the wall for a few seconds, gathering words for the call. Fifty kilometers north of Guadalcanal lies Malaita Island. On sunny days, one can easily see the tip of the island come to view. It's sad to see fellow men of these two islands fighting each other. 'One last thing, *Guales* are the priority, as in the agreement.'

Bernard snatched his bag. 'For once or twice I don't believe in ghosts. Now I am convinced.' He darted towards the direction of the village and start walking. 'They framed us for all the nuisance in the community.'

'I need a gun and five bullets,' Toxic cracked, sensing the awkwardness of the situation and stop walking.

'Someone is hiding behind white teeth,' Bernard said.

'Maybe he also against logging,' Stonie commented with an undecided look.

The silence fell on the boys, except the sound of evening creepers announcing the approaching darkness.

'You think Chief Ko'oga betrayed us?' Osama queried out of shaky curiosity, reverting the discussion to point zero again.

'He's a coward,' Toxic snarled, 'too righteous for such thing.'

'The note is not delivered,' Alo admitted.

Bernard shrugged. 'I hope Pegoa keeps his words to speak on our behalf.'

'Pegoa is cow dung.' Toxic added convincingly, slowly picking his paces.

'What is he discussing with Jemes?' Osama queried.

'Logging, what else can they talk about.' Deve intervened. 'Papers already signed.'

'That's my guess...' Osama tried to reason out the meeting they interrupted.

Nimo felt the need to speak as he always did. 'Papers may be signed, but without the consent of the landowners, it's never going to happen. See what happened to the police officer, speaks loud about people's view on logging. Even Chief Ko'oga spoke against logging.'

Silence landed expectedly as they reached the plateau of the hill. New night, new camp. For the past few days, they have been living like vagrants. They sensed an unusual feeling the community is planning a plot to capture them. Under any circumstances, they will have to fight.

'Talking about the masked man.' Deve swerved the discussion, 'they suspected us.'

'Bullshit,' Toxic spat blindly. Circumstances forced him to speak blindly, that's what humans do in a flustered state.

'Hey, did you hear Chief Ko'oga? Something about people from Aola?' Osama queried at length.

'Right.' Stonie reinforced the discussion. 'He said that.'

'But what is it to do with the Police?' Toxic enquired loudly.

'The attacker has a motive. Tell you what? Police are interested in this community, not because they want to bring law and order. No. They are interested in our land. Our trees.' Bernard got a joule of energy radiated on his face. 'Whoever is involved in this nuisance, whatever they have in mind, we will stand on our principles. We will fight.'

'Only if we have guns,' Toxic said.

'I know where we can get guns, high-powered,' Bernard said, looking towards the mountains.

13

Pegoa mutely meditates on the dull wall in front of him. In his hand is a piece of paper handed to him by the *boys*. He scratched his steel wool hair, frowned, and scanned the note again. He shifted his thought to what Jemes queried about. He put on his shirt, got the Bible, and headed for the church.

The church is sparsely filled-usual for morning devotions. Only the regular ones attended, mostly the elderly ones. Pegoa is one of them. 'I love stories.' Elder Moses started his sermon in a low-pitched voice.

Pegoa scanned the faces vacuously, Chief Ko'oga also among them. Chief Ko'oga was all in white, polo shirt and khaki shorts, make a conspicuous contrast with his lean and bald head structure.

'Stories can make you laugh, cry, or even angry.' Elder Moses continued, moving out from the podium in a halting limp as his left leg is shorter than the right. He is short and only stands five feet high. And for a man, that height is not attractive.

Pegoa's mind is set on fire, like a volcano that's about to erupt. He scanned the walls; it was all grey, like his thought. The interior can accommodate a congregation of a hundred heads, including children. It takes years and years for the locals to construct up to this stage. Despite its current state, it's already a landmark. They sacrificed their time, money, and energy. But it is for the good cause. How many more years will they invest to complete the work? Two or three years is unrealistic. Probably ten or more is reasonable. Pegoa recalled the biblical stories where the slaves built huge temples. Such a hard life.

Nowadays, the machine replaces all the manual labor, and speed up the rate of construction work. Though in the age of the machine, this building is still intensively labor-based menial work. No machines, the foundation was all manual; shovels and picks used, gravel and timber on bare shoulders. Pegoa recalled, that he was a teenager when the church foundation was laid, construction is still progressing, and no sign of stopping. The story of Noah building an ark kindled in his head.

The river slithered a couple of meters away. Its bank is lined with trees. A rendezvous for the women to share stories, often gossiping under those trees, where a glint of invidious thoughts can turn to words, and words into action.

'The moral of the story is ...,' elder Moses concluded his sermon. 'In our individual lives, our families, and our community.' The sermon ended, with heads nodded as if electrically controlled. 'Thank you. Please, all stand for a benediction,' he announced.

'Great sermon, uh?' Jim Pegoa commented as they exited the church building.

'Yes. Definitely,' Chief Ko'oga growled.

'We all have a part to play in the story,' Chief Ko'oga continued, 'I always like Elder Moses' sermons. Short and sweet.'

'I prefer short sermons.' Pegoa agreed without even looking at the figure he's talking to.

Chief Ko'oga cleared his throat to queue in a diversion. 'What is the issue last night?'

Pegoa coughed. 'You know young boys.' He shrugged his shoulders. 'They enquired about the attack of the officer.' Pegoa has to tell the truth since the argument content is loud and clear like a pre-school song.

'Sorry?' Chief enquired; eyes fixed on the road sensing the scarcity of the details. 'What is it they enquired about?'

He paused and tilted his head. 'They said they know nothing about the attack. But who else can we blame?'

'The women witnessed the attack.' Chief Ko'oga looked around, 'so what did you say?'

'Yes, the attacker is wearing a mask, we cannot tell,' Pegoa said. 'We'll allow the Police to do their investigation.'

'Right, but just be careful when dealing with media and police,' Chief Ko'oga said, speaking from his experience.

'As community leaders, we can always try to help where we can, that's all.' Pegoa elaborated in a civil tone. His house is at the far end of the playing field down the river, so will walk past Chief Ko'oga's house and past the playing field. Next to his house is Jemes family's house.

'You right.' Chief's face furrowed. 'Good talking to you Pegoa. See you around.' The Chief turned to his house. No-one is eager to talk about the note each received from the boys.

14

Atkinson cupped a phone in his ear and punched five digits by heart

'Tetere Police station?' A male voice responded in a robotic voice.

'Can I talk to Lieutenant Kilua please?'

'Just a second.'

The phone went silent for a moment before gaining life. 'Lieutenant Kilua speaking.'

'G'day Lieutenant.'

'Hi mate, how are we doing?' The Lieutenant responded in borrowed words and tone.

'Defo! We are ready to move.'

'It's your call, what do you expect me to say?' Lieutenant responded.

'We are departing at 9 a.m. tomorrow.'

'Fine, and one thing, we have protocols. We just cannot carry our bags and go. We need to ensure the safety of our officers is guaranteed.'

'I know. Can we talk over this?' The line went silent again for a second. 'What about we meet at Mendana Hotel this afternoon? Say 3:30 p.m.' Atkinson clings tightly to the phone, gauging the plans in his head.

'Sure,' Lieutenant responded. 'See you then.'

'Excuse bossman,' a voice startled Atkinson who still hold on to the phone. He must have been waiting for the whole phone conversation, which gives Atkinson a creepy feeling.

'Who's it, come in.'

From the look, Atkinson can tell. It's Pegoa. And he is with another man. One at the back seized Atkinson's attention, he is so black that Atkinson has to squint to see.

'Good morning, bossman,' Pegoa said.

Atkinson welcomed them in. 'Good morning, come inside, take a seat.' He does not want to bother them with too many words, for a start.

'Thank you for coming, I've been expecting you two.' Atkinson shared glances between the two, nodded.

'This is Jemes.' Pegoa announced. 'Mr Jemes Toki is a principal landowner.'

Jemes was unmoved and remained standing. He looked around for familiarity in the room, a used rice sac converted to a tote bag hung across his shoulder. He took a few steps and stopped as if hitting a wall. He stood right up, wearing a white singlet and a battered jean cut above the knee, obviously well-worn and dated. His hair is trimmed to a box shape matching his flat forehead and a strong jawline. A trait that is dominant on his father's side.

'Take a seat.' Atkinson offered the cushion chairs with a hospitable smile.

'He is the leader of the tribe and a big man in our community,' Pegoa added.

'Oh, heavy is the head that wears a crown.' Atkinson grinned to expose his tobacco-stained teeth, 'That's a saying, meaning leaders have a lot to do.' He simplified it though not literally hitting the meaning.

Jemes remained standing and still had not reacted to the reception. Considering the unreceptive silence, Atkinson wasted no time. 'Anyway, let's give it a crack.' He ran his fingers through the files on his table. 'I guess you are here about the agreements.'

'Excuse me, I got to go to the washroom.' Pegoa walked out in haste.

Agreement? What agreement? Jemes thought aloud. He landed his eyes on the files lying open on the table, watching Atkinson's fingers flip through the pages. *It's a tiresome job, how does he know which is which?* Jemes has never seen such stacks of files in his life, and his wonder heightened even more. *What's in them? Logging, cutting trees... on my land?*

After seconds of searching, he produced a page. 'I got it.' Atkinson looked through the page one more time before handing it over.

Jemes accepted the page as if he had no other option. His mind juggling with a dozen thoughts, cramming his head like wedge.

'So, Jemes. You are the head of the *Thibo* tribe, right?' Atkinson asked, trying to connect with the figure he is facing

Jemes nodded with a vague look, prompting Atkinson to wonder if he understands the English language at all. Or worse, if deaf.

'Please look through and let me know if you have any questions.' Atkinson pulled out the drawer of his table. 'Here's the pen.'

Jemes ran his eyes on the page. The logo above the page provides the detail of the company. The logo is comprised of a tree and a thin curved line under it. The curvilinear probably represents a road or the ocean surface? The document outlined a brief profile of the company, followed by details and empty spaces. Jemes is lost in the words. It's all words, all typed in black. The whole page is bunch of words, not attractive to his eyes.

Fifteen minutes passed unnoticed. The entire office is hushed. Only the air –conditioning system creaked a background noise. Jemes was preoccupied. *Where is Pegoa?* He wondered.

Atkinson focused on other things. Or at least he pretends to, by opening one draw after another as if searching for a lost diamond.

In such a situation, keeping one's mind occupied is healthy for negotiation. It allows the blood to circulate easily which boosted the brain's performance in responding to misunderstandings or confusion. Often, argument can brew if the signatories are not happy with the contract. Atkinson has mastered his art.

Jemes scanned the content of the page from top to bottom and bottom to top. And repeated as if it will make any difference. *What is this? Am I going to do this? What's the point of all these papers?* He fidgeted, staring at the page as if he saw his own shattered reflection in it.

Atkinson studied the character in front of him. He has a broad shoulders and lengthy feet. He has big round eyes with eyelashes as whiskers. He had an immaculate haircut with beard well-groomed. Probably maintain the style from his younger days. He can tell from his furrowed face, he's in his early forties. As one goes beyond the thirties, the smile line created a permanent mark.

Atkinson went over to the fridge and produced a bottle of orange juice. He poured it into two disposal cups. Pegoa is nowhere to be seen.

'Here you are.' Atkinson tried to create a casual environment for them, sensing the eerie delay, longer than what is reasonable.

'Thank you. Thank you.' The first words Jemes said since he entered the office. He continued staring at the page as if looking at an ancient knotted code that was yet to be deciphered. The paper in his hand is an undisputable enemy for the past fifteen minutes, he hated every square inch of it.

'Is everything in the paper understandable?' Atkinson voluntarily intervenes for support.

'What?' *Understandable?*

'I mean the agreement, do you -?'

'Oh yes, the agreement.' He trivialised his response.

'You ok with it?'

'Yes, eh...I would like to talk with Pegoa first.' Jemes wobbled for the door, smeared with sweat. Swamped.

15

The reception area of Mendana Hotel is sparsely occupied as expected. The lobby is spacious to use as a school assembly hall. The reception desk is a varnished wooden bench imprinted with glamorous designs and patterns; the creative work speaks for itself. Less reasonable to say, but it stood out to be one of the top choices for diners. Lieutenant Kilua glanced at his wrist watch and glances around a couple of times.

He took a seat in the lobby, grabbed the daily newspaper, and riffled through the pages. No news is good news. The national column of the newspaper grabbed his attention. The government is sealing a deal for regional interventions for security support. The situation is beyond the capacity of the local Police to address. He wondered; *Illegal weapons were still in the rural communities. Most of those in rural areas still possess illegal weapons. Especially, the troubled islands of Guadalcanal and Malaita. The peace talk signed by these two rivals did little towards curbing criminal activities that rampant in rural areas. But what have*

64

we got from this Townsville Peace Agreement? Ex- militants still hold on to their guns.

'Hi mate. Sorry for keeping you waiting.' Atkinson extended his right arm for a handshake. 'Let's grab a table.'

They walked past the reception area towards the waterfront. They located an empty table at the beachfront. From their table, they have a vibrant view of the harbor, vivid to one's imagination. The coastline is sprawled with hotels and resorts. To the east is a bay where sailing boats are moored. Further out in the deep sea are passenger vessels traveling to the islands, it's another day in paradise. Their view is being disrupted by a moving figure in a dark suit.

'Can I get you something?' A waitress gently asked, switching her glance between the two.

'Can we have drinks, please?' Atkinson ordered.

'Sure. What drinks do you want?'

'Eh, get me something smooth. Red wine will do.' Atkinson had a penchant for red wine, especially for business talks.

'And you?' the server turned to Lieutenant.

'Same.' Lieutenant Kilua nodded his response, watching the waitress jotting on the order pad. 'Anything else?' she asked amicably.

'Fine for now,' Atkinson advised.

Lieutenant Jackson watched as the waitress padded away. 'How often do you come to this place?'

'How often? When I need to wind up a crook day with a few beers.' Atkinson looked in the direction of the bar. 'My Camp Manager hates to come here. His name is also Mendana.'

'Seriously? That's a good reason to be a regular.' Lieutenant scoffed. In his mind, he recalled how the Spanish name became naturalised in this town. It traced four centuries back when a Spanish explorer *Alvaro de Mendana* discovered these islands in 1567. *Discover?* Maybe that's gross, probably *landed* is more appropriate terminology as the ancestors discovered these islands thousands of years back before the Spanish even conceived the idea of exploring the world. What our friend Alvaro de Mendana did was *only* document the Islands and the people. And he deserved a goodwill medal for his daring journeys into the uncharted waters.

'Mendana sees it differently. He does not like to introduce himself with the name. *Hello, my name is Mendana, nice talking to you Mendana.* That sounds ridiculous when you are in a hotel that also bears the same name. Anyway, he has his own judgement.' Atkinson said.

'Now Lieutenant, if I may ask you. How many languages do you speak?' Atkinson struck a least related question to the meeting. Like Lieutenant, Atkinson is unpredictable, he can switch his thought on a whim like a wind.

'An average Solomon Islander can speak at least three languages. Mother tongue language, Pidgin-English, and English.'

'That's trilingual.' Atkinson looked at Lieutenant and continued, 'What a shame, I only speak one. But I could count Pidgin-English as my second. I would comfortably be bilingual.'

'Some can speak up to four or five languages. Depending on where their parents came from. Solomon has about eighty native languages and dialects.' Lieutenant Jackson continued mumbling out the facts.

Atkinson stared at Lieutenant Jackson trying to register the statement in his brain. 'Do anyone you come across someone who could speak all those eighty languages?' he subtly enquired.

'No, never in my life. That's almost impossible.'

Atkinson paused. 'A hell of a challenge for the British back in the days. A hard nut to crack.'

'That was the birth of pidgin - English.' Lieutenant Jackson added. 'It united the islanders through a single language they could use to communicate with each other.'

Atkinson continued. 'I read it somewhere that Pope John Paul II spoke ten languages.'

'Seriously?'

'Yes, there are few who have that feat.'

'The pope must be a genius.'

'He's a polyglot.'

Lieutenant wondered. 'Poly-what?'

'Here you are.' The waitress elegantly placed the glasses on the table. They both appreciated the service with an aura of admiration. It's an art the waitress has to master, by all means, especially handling glasses on tiled floors.

'Thank you.' Lieutenant can't hide his fondness for the wine glass, sparkling with tiny bubbles.

'Great view huh?' Atkinson put a little twist on the conversation.

'Dollars deserved to be spent here,' Lieutenant agreed.

Atkinson took a swig. 'See that Landing Craft? That's the one we're going to use.'

'That's big enough to transport a house.' Lieutenant imagined. 'How many machines can it transport?'

'It depends. In our case, we'll only transport big machines,' Atkinson snuggled into his chair and sipped his second mouthful of wine.

'What's the plan?' The wine gave a comforting feeling to Lieutenant, putting some weight on the discussion.

'9 O'clock tomorrow,' Atkinson said, 'three Police officers in uniform is sufficient.'

Lieutenant Kilua stared at Atkinson as if he needs a translator. But the language is conceivable. Unlike Atkinson, he can speak three languages fluently. The one they are using in the discussion is one of the three.

Silence crept in for a while before Atkinson broke it. 'You know, most times we exhausted our resources to find a golden solution, and misuse our resources, bad decisions. But simple answers are there, we need to think, think out-of-the-box.' Atkinson tried to convince the Lieutenant of the proposed approach.

'You think three officers is practical?' Lieutenant enquired as if he has an option.

'Exactly. Let's keep a low profile, go for a simple plan.' Atkinson took another sip from his glass. 'I already negotiated with the landowners. So, fingers crossed.' He pulled out a cigarette and lit it automatically.

'You need one?'

'I quit smoking a long time ago.'

'Good for you.' He puffed his smoke and scanned the vicinity to refresh his mind. Like a human being, the brain needs a break. But it is up to each individual to find an activity that suits the mood. Some go for a cup of tea; others take a short walk or some take a deep breath. And smokers do as Atkinson did.

'Waiter!' Atkinson flagged the server who stared blankly at the customers. He turned towards the Lieutenant and said, 'Plan B activated.'

The sun had already dropped behind the western clouds when the pickup truck arrived at the village. Sitting in front with the driver is Jemes, lost in his thoughts. When the vehicle came to a stop, he handed over his fare and said thank you to the driver. He slowly picks his weight up from the passenger seat and squeezed his way out the door.

Standing outside, he tapped his side tote bag, to ensure the envelope is there. Happy with the content of his bag, he strode across the river to his house. He knew Pegoa is still in town and will arrive later in other public transport. It has been a long day; he thought to himself.

16

T he July sun shot whizzy beams on the wall of a two-story building. The paint had been plucked off from recurring exposure to heat, giving the walls a mundane look. From a distance, it appears matte white like a passenger boat washed ashore by Tsunami.

The machines of various make assembled in a distorted row, Caterpillar, Komatsu, Mercedes-Benz, Hino- apparently purchased from second-hand dealers. Mendana checked through the list; two bulldozers, a Loader, a Road Grader, two forklifts, three logging trucks, two dump trucks, and one Toyota Land cruiser.

'LC Pacific Logger, do you copy?' No response. 'Pacific Logger, do you copy?' The Camp Manager repeated, voice amplified after each call.

A voice gasped a response. 'Rajah, copy,'

'We'll start loading at 9. Over.'

'No problem, will dock by then.' The radio mumbled with an almost inaudible tone.

'Come again?'

'Happy Independence Day.'

'Oh, sure.' Mendana dropped the icom two-way radio and stole a glance at the digital clock, registered July 7. *What have we achieved as a country to be proud about? Ethnic crisis? Greedy politicians?*

He brought the map onto the table, spread it out, and studied the proposed landing site. From the signed indenture received, the landing site is owned by *Thogo Tribe*. To coincide with the agreement, the fee had been paid for landing rights. Mendana traced his index finger over a blue line that slithered like a string, connecting *Tuvu* and *Ghombua*. The distance from landing area to the proposed logging site is roughly ten kilometers inland. *Not bad.* It would take at least twenty minutes on average for muddy roads.

The incoming call seized his attention. He strode over and snatched the phone.

'Atkinson's office, hello.' Mendana responded casually.

'Hi, this is Lieutenant Kilua from Tetere Police Station. I would like to talk with Atkinson.' The Lieutenant was lenient in his introduction.

'Sorry, Atkinson is still not in the office.' Mendana felt accomplished, at least not alone in hitting the office at 6 am. 'Should I get a message for him?'

The phone hung up.

An hour later, Atkinson walked in. The thick folders on his table addled his brain. He impetuously shuffled through the pages trying to locate something that keeps popping into his head for the past few days. A knock on the door distracted his concentration.

'I am moving the machines now.'

'Great. One thing -.' Atkinson lost his focus. 'Crap, the name of the Chief slipped off my head.' In such a situation, millions of thoughts can run through one's mind at synaptic speed. Atkinson knows that. 'Anyway, proceed with loading.'

'Lieutenant Kilua try to call you this morning,' Mendana reminded him.

'I get it. Now go.'

17

A white cabin cruiser signaled its indicator as it turned to the spacious parking lot. The driver admired the building that was once his office. A low concrete structure, painted off-white, and lined with a strip of navy blue and white checkered at the bottom. The vehicle came to an abrupt stop at the front of the building, facing the reception desk.

'Good morning, Sir,' a voice echoed from the reception desk.

'Good morning comrades.' The Lieutenant waved to the front desk officers. 'How's the Police job treating you?'

'As always, hated by many.' The officer simpered.

'Forgive and forget. Is Captain William in?'

'Yes. You are on time' The desk officer nodded.

Lieutenant spied at his watch. 'Right, my appointment is at 9.'

'Wait a minute.' The front desk officer dialed the phone. Lieutenant Jackson scanned the interior of the office. A lengthy front desk partitioned the area, with a shelf behind the desk officer occupied with radio-controlled units. Reminding him of his young days when

71

he started his career as a junior officer. Most of the officers seen around are new. He could tell from their faces. His age groups were now promoted to senior officers and even to captains. Or became Provincial Police Commanders like him in other provincial stations.

'He still not answered his phone.' The female desk officer dropped the phone and redialed it. She did it as if it was her only option.

Lieutenant Kilua watched the officer who still held on to the phone. She must be one of those newly recruited officers. Probably out of high school and right into this office. She has an average height that matched her feminine structure. Enough to convince the person interviewing her for the job.

'Hello. Lieutenant...Eh.'

'PC from Tetere?' He completed the sentence for her.

Captain Lieutenant William Wale's office is at the back. As a protocol, a prior appointment was made for this meeting – it's the formalities. Lieutenant William is heading towards his retirement age of fifty. Despite his age, he still maintained the masculine shape of a thirty-year-old, it being incumbent on the job to stay fit and maintain some good shape.

For the first couple of minutes, they exchanged pleasantries, good old days, and a bit of politics, slowly the topic switched to work.

'How's everything at Tetere?'

'Improving slowly, but surely. My new officers are determined.'

'Good to hear that. I wish they maintained the freshman enthusiasm.'

'Right.' He agreed, couldn't find the right word. 'Unfortunately, only one female officer.'

'It's time to balance the workforce, Kilua.' He used the name they acquainted each with. It's more informal when they talk among themselves, even during working hours. Oftentimes, they gossiped like old women. But they are human too, like everybody else.

'I heard a lot about Ghombua in the news lately.'

'It's all *garbage*.'

'If it's so, why you are here then? Do you need additional support?'

'Yes and No.'

'Yes, we need experienced officers. Probably Special forces. However, that will only escalate things for the villagers. What we try to avoid at all cost.'

Captain scrutinised his colleague's face as if he's a lost kid looking for his mum. 'So, what's the plan?'

'We do not need additional force,' Lieutenant Kilua assured. 'We will only send one police officer. This is important to regain the trust of the community.'

'Are you sure about that? Guns still out there, you know that, and you will run into the risk of losing your officers.'

'Right, that is the point. I will only send one officer to work more like a community negotiator than police.' Lieutenant Kilua said.

'You know the place and people more than me Jack, I trust your judgment on this,' Lieutenant William said. 'Brief me on the modus operandi.'

Lieutenant Kilua cleared his throat. 'He will assist the locals. It's a community thing, and have to be solved at a community level. I was wrong in the first place to send in patrol troops.'

'I see, like a community policing?'

'Yes, Sir. Correct. He's at the village now as we speak.' Lieutenant Kilua dropped it.

A twig snapped behind the cascading trees, seizing their attention. They turned towards the noise, expecting to see someone approaching.

'Who's that?' Nimo cocked his head to listen.

'It's me.' The voice emanated behind the bushes, yielding nothing but more questions.

'Itsme, do you have a name?!' Toxic shouted.

Contradicting their anticipation, a kid appeared behind the bushes. The team stood up, allowing him to proceed, entering their territory.

'What do you want Mr...?' Bernard craned his neck and saw a kid, panting as he staggered forward. 'I don't expect you here little Pegoa?' *How the hell did you locate us?*

'They sent me... to give you this.' He stuttered words between gasps.

'Who?' Bernard wedged his thought for words.

'My dad.' He flagged the note in the air. 'He wrote this.'

'Your dad?' Bernard waved the kid to walk closer. The members watched attentively, uncertain of what the next big thing will be. With a dramatic pose, Bernard grabbed the note.

The boys wonder in sundry guesses. *Is it a call to surrender to the Police? Do they know we are here?*

Bernard glanced at the note. His eyebrows furrowed, for a moment he scrutinised the details. 'As I expected ...,' he announced with no glint of surprise in his tone.

'What did it say?' Toxic stepped forward from his sitting position.

'Bad news.' Without wasting any more time, Bernard announced it throatily. 'Logging machines are coming... today.'

'Today? You mean now?' Toxic marveled.

The messenger boy only stared back, unsure himself.

'That's what it says here.' Bernard tilted his gaze at the note.

'I knew it,' Deve agreed, tossing his dreadlocks about. 'What is the good news?'

Bernard weighed his words. 'Good news is, our names are automatically included in the payroll,' he announced. 'Stupid amnesty, we are not ex-militants.'

'Amnesty? You mean,' Deve queried out of his subtle curiosity, knowing that it's relevant to him more than any of the members. And the word *amnesty* flickered hope.

'Yes, remember? The police charged us. They are looking for us.' Nimo intervened. He is always concerned about the fate of the team. Unlike Bernard, Nimo dreamed to live a good life, and by that, he finds it disquieting to accept the crimes they committed.

'I do not understand, looting vehicles was all we did,' Deve admitted.

'Be it one or a million, a crime is a crime, and we break the law,' Nimo rebuffed.

'This is the note.' Bernard passed it to Deve.

Just as it looks, the letter resonated mixed reactions. Some accepted it on a whim, some not. One or two don't even feel a thing about it, come what may. Stonie is in that category. Fatherless and raised by a single mother, he learned his promiscuous values from his peers. Not even completed standard four in his school days, but at least he knows how to spell his name in clumsy handwriting. And of course, do basic math and read warning signs.

'My name is in the payroll,' Toxic admitted in a rowdy manner.

'Good for us.' Nimo twitched. Of which, others agreed, Bernard is not. Besides Bernard and Stonie, Alo also undecided. Thinking that logging is not for them, not now. That is as far as Bernard's point is concerned.

Alo eyed around with his single eye. 'I don't support logging, whatever you guys think, I will not involve myself. At least I have some cells in my brain functioning.'

'Think carefully,' Bernard said.

Osama like Deve accepted the news. 'Machines arriving today? That's fast.'

'Means, the police will be here too.' Nimo added, leaving others to sink their thoughts in defeat.

Without further talking, Bernard advised the young boy, 'Tell your daddy, we'll join. But first, remind him, I am the landowner, not him.'

'RULE NUMBER TWO, no middleman,' Stonie bragged.

The messenger boy nodded his head apprehensively, turned, and trod downhill.

'Tell your sister, I love her,' Toxic said. The words are irrelevant, but they metamorphosed the grim-looking faces into laughter.

'Shut up Toxic!' Deve commanded. 'It's already taken.'

18

The motorcade slowly approached the village, creating an impulsive excitement among the locals. It's been the talk for the past few days, 'the logging machines will arrive'. Much to their excitement, the locals crowded the opposite river bank, frozen in complimentary gestures, not wanting to miss each passing view. One by one, giant machines rolled onto the riverbank. The noise is disturbing but was accepted as part of the fun, hearing how the engines coughed and sneezed, and blowing their noses as they arrived in queue.

In a well-mannered reaction, they stood and watched at a safe distance, allowing the village elders to put things in order. Which they did.

'Good day everyone. 'Atkinson jumped off his seat, and looked around conscientiously, posing as a most revered candidate campaigning for a national election.

'Welcome to Ghombua.' Pegoa walked over to meet him. 'We've been expecting you. I told the people after returning from town. We do not go to the garden. See.' A grotesque nod melted to a grin.

'Thank you,' Atkinson humbled by the greetings. 'We come with Tetere Police and IPMT.' He looked towards the officers who stood close to their vehicle, watching and cautious. 'We are a bit behind schedule. Anyway.' He tapped his pockets and tucked his shirt loosely into his khaki shorts.

Pegoa was engrossed with the machines, hardly realising the police officers standing at a distance. 'This is the area for you to camp for the night.' He surveyed the sky and the hills behind the village. 'No rain.'

'Right, no rain.' Atkinson stood upright, hands akimbo and turning around like a turnstile.

'Tell me, what is the general rule around here?' Atkinson wants the operation to run smoothly. And he prepared to spend the money if necessary.

'I will seek permission from the elders for you to pass through the village. You know, village protocols.'

'Fine, am ok with that. So can we meet with the elders?' His face melted to grin when Jemes walked over. 'Hi Jemes, how are you doing?'

'Good.' He nodded conservatively, eyes settled at the machines, sensing the dreadful stink emanating. 'Big machines-eh.' Seeing the threat the machines pose; he shooed the children not to move too close to the exhausted monsters. The children obeyed and stood afar, maintaining their distance, changing their staring eyes between the visitors and the machines.

'These are light machines. Heavy ones will land at *Tuvu*.' Atkinson oriented his clients.

Pegoa gave a ghost of smile, not too obvious. 'You will be sleeping here tonight?'

'I wish. Only my operators and securities.' A thought came to his mind. 'Talking about security, are the boys here already?'

Pegoa responded after a second of eyeball rolling. 'Yes. They will be here soon. The message already passed.'

'Great.' He removed his round brim cap. 'The police will not be stationed here. I trust your boys can handle it. This is your company, so respect the properties.' Atkinson put some decency to his words.

'No problem.' Pegoa all smiles.

'I wish to talk to the boys, if it's ok before I leave.'

Pegoa turned to Jemes and discuss for a couple of seconds. 'They will be here later. I do not inform them of the arrival time. Sorry.' Pegoa lied, which Atkinson naturally accepted. Pegoa looked around as if trying to locate the boys. No one stepped forward.

'Are they happy to join?' Atkinson scavenged for details.

'Of course. Who would refuse the note with the head of the Queen of England stamped on it?' He turned to the village, crowd intact as if watching a football game. 'Some of them can help unload the machines at *Tuvu*.' Pegoa generously assured.

Atkinson looked up at the sky searching for the sun, which already beaming 2:30 pm shadows over the machines. 'How many of them?'

'Four.' Another lie.

'I thought you said seven?'

'Yes, right seven. I forget to count the other three.' He mumbled doubtfully.

~

'LC Pacific Logger, do you copy?'

'Copy,' cracked a recognisable voice.

'Position, over?'

'Approaching Adeade bay. Expect to land 4:00 pm. Over.' Mendana responded.

'You know the rules of the game boy.' From the time registered on his wristwatch, it's a bit late to offload the machines. 'The name of the village chief to talk to is Sukulu. Cannot remember exactly his other name, Joseph? Whatever, he's the Landowner too.'

'Copy bossman,' Mendana asserted. Mendana is more like a smaller brother to Atkinson. They adopted him when he was fifteen years old. His mum couldn't afford to support him, and with a good heart Atkinson employed him from scratch. He later gave him the second name of *Dana*, with no significance besides rhymes with the first name. He started as a tool boy, later ventured his stride as a bulldozer crew before joining the survey team. The passing years have been very kind to him; he is now a Camp Manager.

'Local boys will provide security around the landing area. Already sorted this over with Chief Sukulu and Pegoa.'

'Copy loud and clear. We'll offload tomorrow morning.' Mendana walked out to the front of the Landing Craft, surveying the coastline. If one thing could assure him, it's the captain of the Landing Craft. He has been doing his job for decades, so fingers crossed.

Night settled in the village like an uninvited guest. Villagers crowded at the river for evening washing and bathing, the last chore of the day. For the little children, still playing their never-ending games that started late in the afternoon, prompting elders to bark orders for them to stop.

The makeshift tents and machines silhouetted at the opposite bank against the starry sky. The police had already returned to Tetere, so had Atkinson. One officer remained. He's different from others, yes, his attire. He wore a round brim black hat and a time-worn pair of jeans which presented him with a jaded profile, more like the Scarecrow character in 1939 The Wonderful Wizard of Oz (for Millennials out there who are not familiar with the Scarecrow, imagine an erected frog wearing a round brim hat). Atkinson provided him with the hat as a gift. He tried to be comfortable around his new colleagues, though anxious. He got the feeling one gets at the airport when an immigration officer studied you, trying to verify the person in your passport.

'We have food here.' The asian sounded casual, yet to stamp names.

'Thank you, sir, I will come over.' He stood to face the man, eager to strike up a conversation, but words don't form. After a long pause, he managed. 'Where's everyone?'

'Long day, you know.' Suiono dusted his face.

'Right.' He darted around.

'You will be in charge of the local boys.' The asian dragged out a cigarette. 'You smoke?'

'No.' ignoring the offer, he continued. 'How many boys?'

'Seven is what I heard.'

The man did some thinking. 'Seven?' The number of the BANDITS, it's an emblematic figure, a perfect number; seven days in a week, seven wonders of the world, seven colors of the rainbow, seven rivers that separate Ghombua and Honiara. He can't wait to meet them in person, more like colleagues than the wanted thugs.

'Two already here.' The asian showed the direction towards the machines. 'Ok Dan, when you're ready, collect your food.'

'Thanks, Suiono.' *Damn, did he just call me Dan?* That's his new moniker he will have to assume for the coming days and months. Daniel Bako-a security incognito.

19

The scene struck with familiarity. Line of trees, flowing river, doves cooing at a distance. After a minute or two, his thought blacked-out like a computer screen. The cooing sound of the doves subdued into a brittle female voice, which he recognised at the instant like his own breath.

'I am here to protect you. Don't believe what you hear from them.' A voice *from a distance and slowly moving closer.*

'Protect me? I am fine.'

'Listen, when I am talking.' A female figure glided forward with lips moving, saying something inaudible. *'I have been there and know what was going on. They tried to set you up.'* The dress she wore protracted out like an umbrella, hands bidding him to pay attention.

'I will not. I am a grown-up man now; you cannot decide for me.'

'You always like that since you were a little boy. Aggressive and always like to do things on your own. You are very much like your father, violent and stubborn. The reason your grandfather hated him. My father passed away without forgiving

81

your dad for all his nuisances. Same to my deceased mother, the grave knows if she forgave him.' She moved closer and continued. *'Everyone hates your father. Everyone...'* her voice flattened out.

Bernard locked his eyes, unruffled. *'I don't care about what people think.'*

'You should see those men, they use you.'

'Who-what men?'

'They killed us.'

'Who killed- I thought you...?'

'Wake up Bernard.'

Her body soaked sluggishly and sunk after each word. She fumbled around, struggling to stay afloat.

'Wake up! Wake up, Bernard.'

Alo's voice startled Bernard. He was drenched with sweat and his breathing rhythm was triple.

'What is it?' He stared straight into Alo's face.

'You were moving and uttering indistinct sounds.'

Bernard breathes heavily, 'bad dream.' He slowly twisted his head sideways, an attempt to clear his mind. Outside the tent, nothing but darkness, freezing. Alo stared at Bernard's face in the dark expecting him to spill out the dream. Instead, Bernard stood up and tramped to the corner of the tent, groping around for a water bottle. He filled his mouth and walked out to greet the chilly night.

The sky is quiet, exposing dots of stars displaying a dazzling Milky Way sprawling across the heavens. The screechy sounds of bats intermittently disturbed the hushed night sky. Bernard dares not think of the dream, no time to reminisce about the past. He has to focus on the future. But considering that prospect; it's not guaranteed considering his present life. No brother, nor sister. The doctors diagnosed his mother with an ovary cancer after he was born, he knows what it's like to be without siblings. He felt like planet Pluto in the universe of people. *Why does everyone hate my father? Because of his truculent manner?* His thought swerved to his father. As a kid, he loved swimming in the river. The fun part was climbing onto his father's shoulders to get height and dived into the river. Mum would watch happily at a distance. *Why my life end in this mess? Why me? His dream job is to be a police officer.* The warm pool of tears trickled down his cheeks.

'Who is the man in a cowboy hat?' Bernard flickered with curiosity.

'He is the chief security,' Stonie snorted.

'Security?' Bernard raised both eyebrows. 'I thought... anyway he's a security cowboy.'

'Cowboy with no horse.' Alo burst into a suppressible laugh.

'He supervises all security officers, including Osama.'

'What about Nimo?' Bernard sounded more cynical than curious.

'Nimo work with the operators.' Stonie coughed out the cigarette from his lips. 'And Toxic is with the asian.'

'Because the asian man has stocks of cigarettes,' Alo smirked. 'What else can we expect from that friendship?'

'They also want to recruit Scalars for tallying logs.' Stonie continued his report. 'Deve is joining them.' It's no surprise, Deve completed his primary school. He is an easy pick for the job, considering his age and muscles.

'Suits Deve, Scalar needs someone who can withstand the scorching heat of the sun,' Bernard said.

'Not an easy job.' Stonie frowned.

Bernard thinks it over. 'Uncle Jemes will be fooled. It's like leading a blind person to water, thinking it's shallow, whereas it's not.' He paused for emphasis. 'Do you know what it means? He will drown before he even realised it.' Bernard was right on this, as the famous saying goes, *real eyes realise real lies.*

'Smoke?' Suiono asked.

'Yes, boss.'

No better way to start a conversation than sharing cigarettes.

'Eh-good, no rain today.' Suiono introduced as a weather reporter. Weather is the topic everyone has a fair idea about. Striking a conversation with someone who is new to you can be dreary, but a little weather chat can do the trick.

'No more rain.' Deve looked at the machines, imagining the horrible damage they can cause. 'Big trucks.'

To spice up the conversation, Suiono changed the topic. 'Are there houses up the hill?'

'The village has two layers. One line of houses along the river. The second line houses at top of the hill.'

'Big village.' Suiono puffed his cigarette. 'What is the population?'

'Seven hundred, I guess.'

'You guess?'

'Yes, no one count people like chickens. The government did that prior to election.'

'But you should know the rough figure.'

'That's what I am guessing.'

Suiono surveyed the community and puffed his cigarette. He expected the number to reach a thousand plus. Later he realised that this is not China after all. 'So where do you live?'

'Up the hills.'

'Ok, so you-?' he furrowed his eyebrows as if to ask, *you married?*

'I have a small house.'

Suiono can tell he's not married, he's reluctant to talk about it. Even the size of the house speaks a lot about himself. 'Is it far?'

'Five minutes' walk.'

'I see.' Suiono nodded understandably. He took another lungful, and slowly exhale. 'Do you know someone who owns chicken?'

'Chicken? Yes. We have a lot. I can get you one.'

'For free?' Suiono grinned out of his curiosity.

'No free, you have plenty money-yah?' He tried to mimic an asian accent.

'No money.' Suiono not bothered by the pleasantry. 'How much for one?' He enquired.

'Depend. Fifty dollars, Sixty dollars?'

'I want one tomorrow.'

'Ok, I will look for one. Sixty dollars?'

'One hundred dollars.' Came a sharp response behind them. Toxic's face expanded to a grin. 'I am kidding you.' He smiled at Suiono as if already knew him at length.

'Hello boss. My name is Thomas.'

'Thomas.' Suiono nodded, smoke rushed out from his nostril.

'My friend called me Toxic.'

'Toxic? That's a dangerous name,' Suiono smirked.

'No, it's a good name. And you boss?'

'Suiono,' his response linked to a question, 'you are the security?'

'Yes'

Damned. What part of security does he know? Suiono studied Toxic for a while. Stout and masculine with a flat face that matches his big nose.

'Good. You will also join -.' Suiono looked towards his colleague who is yet to have a name. 'I gave him a new name, Rasta.'

'Rasta?' Toxic glimpsed at Deve.

'Yes, Rasta because he has dreadlocks.' Suiono beamed.

'Rasta,' Toxic uttered, 'that is a good name. Right Deve?'

Deve tweaked his nose. 'No problem, anything can be a name. Except for feces.'

They all shared a peal of laughter.

'There are names that mean feces in some languages,' Suiono said.

'Like what?' Toxic enquired with a glint of interest.

'*Paska* is a name of an Easter bread in some countries, but it can mean *feces* in some places too.' Suiono smile.

'Paska! Paska! that is a good name.' Toxic face melted with a chuckle.

'We'll call you Paska,' Deve intervened.

'No, I already have a name and am happy with it.'

The pun was disturbed by a crackling noise of an incoming call, of which Suiono robotically obliged.

'Base one. Do you copy? Over.' Came the voice.

'Go ahead Mendana?' Suiono responded.

The conversation went on for a minute, and the subject is not welcomed as portrayed by Suiono's face. 'What demand?'

'It's about the landing fee, they are here right now -ten of them.' He talked like a sports commentator, except no cheering in the background.

'Ten? Who the crap are they?'

'Landowners, what they said.' He knew, asking a lot of questions can be misinterpreted for a threat.

'Landowners. Where the hell is Chief Sukulu?' Suiono queried aloud.

'That's what I am asking too,'

'Tell them to see Sukulu.'

'Already told them. No one seems to buy my explanation.' He sighed with a tone of defeat. The radio cracking sound is nerve-jangling without a conversation.

Suiono swore, but no words came out. '…. all payment already been done.'

'You will have to come and explain it to them. These are landowners, and they can be big-headed like animals.' Mendana slammed as if reminding a kid of a danger.

'I know, but we cannot do much now.' Suiono put his hand on his head, sensing the mounting pressure. He dropped the microphone that landed with a thud. *Idiot. Some people see money as a gift - always.*

20

'Somebody told me about it...! When I was still a little boy...!' Bernard lost in a song. For a moment, he forgot his fears and worries. 'I am a prisoner, -ahh priiisoner...' Bernard stuttered with a lilting voice, dancing with both legs hardly planted on the ground. 'Lucky Dube is a prophet.' He reeled forward, a bottle of homemade brew dangling in his hand. He freed the binoculars from his shoulder and threw it over, 'Alo, update me.'

Alo delightedly took the honour to do the work. He prostrated himself with his eyebrows puckered towards the center of his forehead. In past days, they have been monitoring the village for any happenings. Even more fun is the use of the spyglass.

'Ghombua, what's new?' Alo protruded his only functional eye to the lens. He mumbled, 'three logging trucks, two dump trucks...'

'And a white land cruiser?' Bernard queried, enthralled by the movement of the vehicle. Of all the vehicles, the land cruiser has been accumulating mileages lately.

Alo winkled the scene out in the binoculars. 'No - I did not see it. Nothing.'

'Check close to the tents, behind the trucks. Check everywhere,' Bernard demanded.

Prolonged silence. 'Nothing, it's gone.'

After thinking it through, Bernard's face relaxed. 'Must have gone to the landing craft.'

'Hello you two, Nimo and Osama.' Alo buzzing with curiosity, as if discovering a new species.

'Working very hard-yeah?' Bernard shrugged his shoulder, *waste of time*.

'That's what they are going to do, right? Monitor everything and everyone,' Alo simpered.

'Yeah, check on who is in, and who is out,' Bernard said.

'And who is going to the toilet.' Alo chuckled.

'These guys will shit in the river.' Bernard murmured.

'Where else can they go?' Alo imagined the impact as far as his knowledge allows. Truth be told, no one cares about the environment, as it always finds its own way to heal itself. Its nature. But with big development like this, it raises a question.

'Do you see the asian man?' Bernard queried.

Alo was engrossed in his menial duty as if counting bacteria in a microscope. 'No asian man, I hope this thing is not racist.' The hustling sound on the dead twigs is obvious. Alo locked his gaze at Bernard. 'Hear that, is it my ears ...?' He placed his index finger to his right ear and twirled it.

'Hi, it's me.' A fat figure appeared behind the trees, panting.

'Stonie, what brings you back?'

Stonie stopped, and raised his hand, bidding them to stop bombarding him with questions. He came to a halt, puffing, and slowly taking in the air like an inflatable bag.

'Are you going to talk?' Bernard asked.

'Damn hill,' Stonie rebuked.

'What happened? Any news for us.' Alo said.

'They are waiting for you two,' Stonie announced.

'Waiting for us?' Bernard smirked. 'We were born only once and what we say is final.'

'They want you to join, your space is there.'

'And you?' Bernard asked.

'Me?' Stonie was taken aback by the question unexpectedly. 'I am your man - you know.' He shrugged his plump shoulder.

'Seriously?' Bernard sneered.

Stonie flinched, tried to explain, but no words favored the circumstance.

'I know why they don't hire you.' Alo chuckled. 'They don't need a babysitter.'

Stonie ignored the nagging and continued. 'I hated the operation Manager. He wanted people with damned skills. What is skill without people?'

'Stonie, we do not need jobs to survive. Air we breathe does not have a price tag.' Bernard assured him. 'Water is free. We have food, what do you need money for? To buy noodles?'

Stonie yanked a cigarette packet from his pocket. 'What about this, do we need to pay for it.'

'That's my boy.' Bernard grabbed the packet in a single snatch. 'Let's kill ourself with these.' Carefully, he unsealed the plastic cover and opened the packet. 'Birds do not have a house, no gardens, nothing. They feed on the abundance of the earth, which humans are too busy to see.' He threw one cigarette to Alo.

'Breaking news.' Stonie puffed his cigarette. 'Machines will cross the river today.'

'They have to pay first, or I will dispute, RULE NUMBER ONE,' Bernard demanded.

'What if your uncle already received the money?' Stonie gawked, with the face - *what you hear is genuine.*

'RULE NUMBER TWO means dispute. I know where my support will come from.' Bernard said.

21

The locals convened in groups like mud crabs, they shifted around the newly cleared camp. Stirring feelings along the process. No one wants to be left out.

Mendana rushed out from his makeshift tent with a perturbed face. 'The operation Manager will be here soon.'

'Do you tell him we do not have the whole day?' One member barked, summoned with air of authority.

'He's on his way as we speak,' Mendana said.

'Good and better be quick.'

Mendana shifted his weight to his right leg, eyeing the newly bulldozed road. The operators did a splendid job that should have taken a hundred men to accomplish in weeks and months.

'Will the company build houses for offices?' The conversations switched, one boy asked in a crispy tone.

'No, only these.' He pointed to a 20 feet container placed next to the coastline. 'It's a complete house. Canteen. Office. Everything.'

Mendana knew the logging life well, it's not a luxury. It's basic, with no proper accommodations, no dining table, nothing. Shipping containers were used, but Mendana prefered tents for some reasons. 'That is my house.' He pointed to the tent.

The locals mumbled among themselves, pointing at the container. Probably suggesting where to position the container in their preference.

'Do you own land in Ghombua?' Mendana queried before realising, maybe not a good diversion topic. But at least it will give him time to think

They all looked at each other, unsure if they meet the criteria.

'No, Ghombua land is owned by *thibo* tribe,' Willie added. Willie is Sukulu's smaller brother. He is the one who act as spokesperson for the group.

'Sorry, what's your tribe again?' Mendana asked.

'Thogo tribe. We are the landowner here.' They pointed sweepingly along the coast as if no boundaries to consider.

'How many tribes on Guadalcanal?'

Willie counted with his fingers and responded. 'Five.'

'Is that for the whole of Guadalcanal?'

Willie cocked his head, 'Two main tribes-- big and small tribe.'

'Did you say five?'

'Yes, three tribes branched - off from the two main tribes,' Willie said.

Mendana related the story to his own. For him, they have a band of warriors travelled between islands in their war canoes killing people as an exhibition of power and expansion of territory. But history has its glamorous days. It's in the past.

'We have *Ghaobata* as the big tribe and *Thogo* the small tribe. *Thibo* and *Nekama* are part of *Thogo* tribe and *Ghamotha* evolved from Ghaobata.'

'That's a lot to remember.'

'I know, we have to recite it from memory. You can't read these from textbooks.'

Mendana understood Guadalcanal practices matrilineal system, like other islands of the Solomon Islands archipelago. Men usually dominated the discussions and to larger degree always influence the decision making. He stood back, watching the locals discussing among themselves. The approaching vehicle interrupted their conversation.

'That's him.'

'Imagine if someone enters your land.' Willie flicked his forehead. 'It's common sense.' He winced with a - *you are not from here look*. 'You have to seek permission and accept what the owner demanded.'

'I know, that's why we paid the landing fee.' Suiono cut to the chase.

'Who - what money?'

'Your elder brother, Chief Sukulu.'

'He's not our chief. Not to anyone.'

'Whatever you say Mr-.' The Malaysian stood his ground. 'See him and discuss.'

The news dropped a bomb. No one bothers to face it.

'How much?' Willie's face swollen within a second.

'Five thousand something. Can't remember the exact figure.' The Suiono bluntly added.

The boys exchanged glances and clustered into groups.

'I am surprised he did not consult you,' Suiono said, scrutinising the faces. 'It's not good. You have to - just talk to your leader.'

Mendana felt the need to intervene. 'We are happy to assist the community as we've done in other provinces. We provided water tanks to schools and clinics.' He looked toward Suiono for support. 'We must work together, not accusing each other.'

'No one is accusing anybody here.' Willie unconvinced. 'The case here is different, these boys are yet to receive a dollar on the landing consent.'

The other members mumbled in the background.

'If we don't receive money today, we will dispute the operation. Is that clear?' Willie demanded.

Suiono intervened. 'Bossman will come and talk with you, but first, go and see your brother.' Suiono has been in this business for decades and dealing with disgruntled members of such nature is not new. They had beaten him a couple times, which he accepted as part of his job. It's like a fish in flooded water, one has to accept and adapt.

The group dispersed and walk away, muttering about their next move.

'We have to move the machines inland now.' Suiono has been observing their discussion the whole time. And from the tone, he sensed the lurking danger, and if not managed well, it can give vent to trouble. 'Two security officers to be stationed here.'

'Dan will man this camp,' Mendana said

22

A white Mitsubishi Pajero parked at the Kitano Mendana Hotel parking lot. The time on the dashboard of the car read 10:22 AM. He's minutes earlier. *Perfect.* Atkinson leafed through the local newspaper, looking for nothing in particular.

His mobile phone vibrates in his pocket.

'Atkinson speaking.' He opened the door and slowly stepped off in a leap. He tilted his head, eyes leveled at the phone and hand into his shirt pocket, digging for a cigarette.

'Pig ass - what?' He sighed. 'I already signed a cheque.' He stamped his boot on the concrete pavement. He dropped back his unlit cigarette into its pack. The conversation continued, torturing his thoughts. 'I am coming over tomorrow.' He looked around blankly, mobile glued to his ear.

'Listen Suiono, I don't care - how many tribes -,' Atkinson said. 'Are they breeding tribes overnight?' He moved in a circle absent-mindedly. A subliminal state of anger and frustration.

94

'Five thousand?' He transferred his mobile device to his left hand. Freeing his right hand to action his anger. More stuttering and swearing.

'That's what they want,' Suiono said.

Atkinson hunched against his car, accommodating his anger. 'I will come tomorrow. Tell them.' He hangs up. He wanted to squeeze the mobile phone; he had little patience for his plan. He dropped the mobile into his pocket and strutted towards the lobby.

'I am going tomorrow.' Atkinson skipped the greetings, he looked like he was going to punch someone in the face.

'What? You mean...' Lieutenant Kilua abreast with his pace towards the foyer.

'Landowners' demand – I don't understand.' He waved to someone he recognised, not a word. 'It's always about money – nothing else.'

Lieutenant stroked his eyebrows, not surprised at all. He doesn't bother to ask, and doesn't want to fuel the fire.

They entered the restaurant, prompting the automatic sliding glass door to open. Thanks to technology that can cater to their swift pace.

Atkinson looked around the semi-crowded restaurant. 'They are still claiming money.'

Lieutenant Kilua nodded his head, no word.

Atkinson led them to the corner table. 'I'd rather go on my own. I'll try to be neutral as much I can muster.' He pulled his chair out and signaled his colleague for a seat. He stared at the Lieutenant for a few seconds, acknowledging his role. In communities, Police officers are often treated as public enemies by a few. They see the police as the government, corrupt, and cannot be trusted.

'You are not wrong on that; you have to work closely with the locals.' Lieutenant Kilua takes his seat.

Atkinson lowered his voice and frowned at the scenario that kindled in his mind. 'Land coordinator is mishandling this situation.'

'Remove him, pick someone who can do the job...' His mind is searching for words but only brought in silence.

A meaningful silence, par for the course.

23

Bernard jumped with a calculated step and bent down to scoop a handful, savoring every molecule in his mouth. *What is life without water?* He splashed surplus water on his face like an elephant.

'This is Guadalcanal many don't see.' Alo found comfort in the serene surrounding. 'Will be there at noon.' The thundering waterfalls drowned their talk. The walk became arduous and taxing, specifically demanding to place one's foot on the right spot, missing it means sliding down the boulders. It's a risky walk, and worth the cost.

Bernard did some thinking. 'If they ask us, say we fight for the Island.' Bernard vouched for their safety. 'They will suspect us for spying or worst government recruits.' He jumped onto a boulder, gripping his toes, 'you say no. No and no.' He allowed the eerie thought to engrain in his head.

Alo said nothing, digesting the plan in his head.

Bernard stopped, and darts his eyes around suspiciously. Everyone knows the mountain rebels. No one in his sober mind has the gutz to talk about them, even worse - facing them. It's a straight disaster.

They are the faction who refused to sign the Townsville Peace Agreement and deliberately retained their ammunition. The base harbors the stronghold of Isatabu Resistance Movement coined by acronym-fancy media as IRM. Their leader is known for his cruelty; burning homes, exterminating people he suspected as a spy, looting community shops, painful to imagine his barbarism.

'I'll do the talking,' Bernard said.

The air is thin, causing them to pant with every step. Tiring enough, they lost calories as they ascended the steep terrain, fumbling around for support from the nearby bushes.

Alo took the lead, Bernard tottered behind him. The climb is a suicide itself, probably what comes to mind when they chose their base. Any intruder who reached the peak is a dead man.

Bernard darted his eyes around, wondering under his breath. 'Wait,' he looked around and gave a hollow nod.

'What - anything? 'Alo dropped the navy green duffel bag. It's the only bag they took a turn to carry, and sad enough, Alo's turn is when they crawled up the steep slope.

'Nothing, keep moving,' Bernard hushed. *This place, why camp up here?* The thought flickered in his mind. *What enemy they'd expect to fight? Is this indeed a rebel camp or a hideout?*

The rushing waters created a dulcet melody of the surrounding scenario. The river is hundreds of meters below, like a silver thread, creating a line that slithered back and forth at the toes of the mountains. The famous Guadalcanal folklore has it, the mighty giants, who once ruled the island occupied these mountains. Even today, few locals still inherited the traits to converse with the giants; for power and good luck. But to the millennials and generation Zs of *Guales*, it's like the dinosaurs, it has its own story.

Bernard's heart throbbed. The place fits all descriptions of a rebel base, remote and foreboding. He has no room for doubt– this is a rebel base. His breath becomes concrete, solidified in his chest as if he will never breathe again. Bernard is tensed and sweating, though the mountain temperature plummeted below twenty-degree Celsius. They are between the devil and the deep blue sea.

'Eagle.' Alo pointed to a soaring bird, providing comfort to the unnerving feeling. Each step forward was trod with eeriness, engrossed in the feeling of being watched by vicious eyes. Or the thought of a hidden net trap, about to be thrown on them.

Click!

The sound is unequivocal. It's a metallic sound.

Click! Second one.

'Hands up!' A brusque voice blasted in their ears. Two figures appeared from the nearby bushes, armed.

Bernard was convinced; this is it.

Alo had no option but to comply. They both did.

'Hands up!' The voice ordered.

The brigands mastered their skills. No more talking, no more explanation.

Bernard twizzled and saw a metallic barrel jabbed towards the back of his forehead. Automatically, both hands raised.

'Down!' Came the follow-up order.

Before he even musters his response, Alo already on his knees, manhandled by one of the brigands.

Both on their knees, no theatrical melodramas.

24

'I never dream to be rich, logging did it for me.' Jemes dropped the tote bag on the floor. Eyes popped at the bulging white bag as if it falls from the sky.

'This is the access fee.' Jemes announced, family members nodded their heads, mumbled among themselves. What everyone has been expecting when the machines arrived.

'Not for trees yet. That will be paid later,' he said.

The members were flabbergasted, as receiving something free is unusual. Especially money, like a bird, it's not an easy catch.

Jemes looked around happily. He grabbed the money bag and anxiously opened it. Eyes still glued to the bag, mouth agape. He pushed his hand inside the bag and produced files of crispy smooth notes, knotted together with rubber bands. He held up the thick bundles and swayed them around. It's a miracle in their eyes, especially women and children, who never had the chance to see such big money. It had its own surprise.

'Money, money, my money – money - money...wwsooonnncchh,' the screechy sound of a bird made all heads turn around.

Unhappy with the interference, Jemes turned towards his daughter, with constricted eyebrows. 'Edna, take Commander outside.'

The members admiringly glanced, mumbling their admiration.

'Take me where?' The bird whistled and flapped its wings, exhibiting the bright colors of its feather, red, yellow and green.

'What's your name?' The little girl stood up; the bird fiddled with Edna's blonde hair.

'Commander.' Responded the bird in a high pitch tone, twirling its neck cheerily.

'Your date of birth?' Edna repeated the routine lines.

'25th December 1998.'

Edna cavalierly walked out the door with the bird whistling a bird's tune.

Jemes satisfied when they disappeared behind the door. 'Sorry for the disturbance. I gave her as a fourth birthday present.' Eyes following Edna, 'She was born on the Christmas day, same as myself.' he grinned. 'Except that I am forty years difference and with no memory of a birthday present.' His lips lop - sided to a grin.

The women admired the close tie between the bird and the girl, exchanging words adoringly.

Jemes cleared his voice and continued. 'It's five thousand dollars.' He singly counted five bundles of rubber notes. 'We will equally share these among ourselves.'

An elderly member in the room stood up. 'Thank you, nephew, how do you plan to share it? What about the kids?'

'Got you uncle, will include kids too.' Jemes replied understandably. 'Everyone in our family will receive something.' He looked outside, checking no one is eavesdropping.

Members agreed by nodding their heads. The children ran around the interior of the kitchen. In such a situation, children usually take advantage of the gathering to play any game that suits the circumstance. That's the special instinct of kids; they are very creative in developing time-killing activities. Usually, those instincts matured into something else when they grew older. The secret joy of the kids' game will end when one is started to cry, that's when the parents intervene and dissolve the game. It's their little world, an open world with no standard rules, it's where the children learn their values.

Jemes scanned the faces one more time, trying to be nice. 'We have two options. First, we determined the total number and shared it equally among us.' Heads nodded but no constructive feedback from the group.

'What do the others - everyone think?' Jemes sounds receptive to ideas, but still no response. As said, money without a brain is dangerous, so Jemes needs a collective decent brain.

'Second option is to share according to family.' This second option struck faint conversation among the women.

'Not many of us, share with each family.' One member agreed, and look around for support.

'What if we use it for our children's school fees?' A mother at the back added on. Despite the matrilineal system in land ownership, women were usually sidelined during communal meetings.

'Excuse me.' A voice coming from the back of the building. All eyes revolved towards the door where a gentleman stood. His profile created a vertical opaque at the doorway. He is wearing outfits like a cowboy.

'Can I talk with Jemes, please?' A man wearing cowboy outfit stood at the door.

Jemes shattered as if hit by tons of bricks staggered towards the doorway. A group of men standing - bleak eyes of mad dogs.

25

J emes squinted his eyes, watching the band of men approaching like cockroaches. Judging from their exhibited flurry, he can tell something was not right of which he is answerable.

'Stay back.' Jemes is one step out, with very little thought given to the likely outcome. Whatever it is, he prepared to face it head-on.

The group reached a 5-meter boundary and stood rigid as if hitting a glass wall.

A pang of discomfort burned in Jemes stomach. He flickered around for an explanation, obviously no time for weather talks.

'We are here to see you.' Came the terse response, hoarse and dry like gravel.

'Me?' Jemes asked in an impartial voice, sensing a glint of threat.

'Stop pretending, let's settled this in a good manner.' The same voice responded. He is the leader, a stout figure armed with a machete. All of them were armed, with a knife or something else.

'I know, tell me what's all this about?' Jemes dropped it hard, unruffled.

'We are here for our money!' The voice roared a week's worth of hoarded grievance. The women in the house watched in silence, even the children stop crying as well.

'Money?' Jemes face ashen. 'What money you're talking about?' His eyebrows dropped, settling his gaze on the leader. He recognised as the landowner of Tuvu landing area. 'I have nothing to do with your land. This logging is on my land.' He blurts out, controlling his patience.

'Really, what about the wharf?' The leader queried with probing eyes. 'The machines cannot land without one.'

Ignoring the glary faces, Jemes glanced to the kitchen where an envelope still lying flat on the floor. 'You have to see bossman,' he said. 'I signed-.'

'Now you confessed, you signed.' The voice interjected.

'I signed for my land. I am not stupid to sign other people's land.' Jemes knew they misunderstood the payment.

'You signed for landing fee too.'

'What? Who fed you with that nonsense?' Jemes mumbled for the right words, maybe a swearing word will suffice. But not appropriate for this conversation.

Among talks came the response. 'We get our information from a secured source; we are not stupid.'

Jemes twitched, rage incubating inside him. 'I am confused. I got my share for the access fee. Not the landing fee. Two different payments. Landing and entry fee.' Jemes grabbed their attention. They are barking up the wrong tree.

'How much do you receive?' Their speaker maintained his stand and no sign of retreat.

Jemes swallowed hard; body tensed with fury. He put on an understandable face, but not last. 'Hey, go and see the bossman. Go see the boss!' He pointed to the newly constructed road crossing the village into the bush. 'He will explain.' Jemes voice inflamed.

'Will go,' the speaker responded. 'We are not finished with you yet.'

'Go.' Jemes swung his hands in the air, anger now boiling inside him. His size is enough to scare his opponent away. Tall with broad shoulder, long jaw with an unshaven beard. His dark skin was smeared with sweat, causing it to soot-black as that of Dan's.

Jemes moved back with hands akimbo, posing his chiseled features. He looked towards the one with the cowboy hat, whose face struck defensive.

'I am sorry to put you in this situation. We mean to see eh- Pegoa,' Dan apologised. Or at least he tried to fake one.

'Then see Pegoa.' Jemes lost his grip. 'I don't want to see you here, again.'

'I am sorry-he's out so-.' Dan looked like a fool for a split of a second.

'If he's out, then he's out.' Jemes stared at the security, sizing his structure against himself. 'Leave while I still hold my brain's temper, if I have to remind you.' He looked into the kitchen where his people are watching with popping eyes. 'What kind of security are you, go-go. Now!' Jemes exhibited his anger by clapping his hands in the air, taking a step forward to show his masculinity.

Dan rushed forward to disperse the crowd that encroached Pegoa's house. Commotion fermented, hands raised, fingers pointing aided by undue name-callings as if about to crucify someone. Pegoa was bathed with accusation, swallowing the words that has been hurled at him. He knew well, that they need money like everyone else. He stared in silence-*going against the grain will only worsen the situation. Accept what they have to say, prepare your response and deliver it simply and understandably - a leeway.*

'Where is our money?' The leader asked the profound question, amplified with the threat. Members nodded their heads, those armed with machetes shifted the weight to the other hand. 'Week passed and we yet to receive any payment.' The leader continued.

Dan walked forward to Pegoa, who had been seized with a shocked uneasiness. The other security officers also moved closer, like Jemes and Pegoa, lost in the deadlock.

'Excuse - excuse me.' Dan intervened in a throaty voice. 'Pegoa is only an employee. He can report your demand to bossman, but not give the money.' Dan looked around the group in the best of his neutral pose. Toxic, Osama, Deve, and Nimo mingled with the crowd that expands in seconds. As a ball, Stonie rolled his way towards the crowd. Cautious not to get so close.

'Please, allow him time to explain himself. Please listen.' Dan bid the angry voices to calm down.

Pegoa sensed the weight of eyes on him, he darted around briefly, searching for a face he can penetrate with his explanation. You cannot convince the whole group; doesn't work that way. One needs to convince one member at a time, this is the art. And Pegoa mustered his pose well. Unlike Jemes, Pegoa had experience dealing with people of different backgrounds as an ex- government public service officer. And that is his entry point in the conversation.

'Nephew, allow me to explain.' He faced the leader; recognised as William, Sukulu's younger brother. That's his bait to lure him to the hook.

'Your boss lied to us, no need to explain. Give us the money.'

'I understand your point,' he said. 'I can help, that's part of my job.' The moment the fish swallowed the bait, it hooked by the throat. Bingo. 'Let me explain.'

'I say the money.' The leader rebuffed; eyes fixed; arms akimbo.

Pegoa run out of words, silence cued in.

'We don't have time for talk. Enough of your lies, you think you can get away with it? Never.'

'Please, listen.' Pegoa's eyes narrowed, focused on the leader. 'I got approval from Joseph Sukulu, well ahead before the machines landed.' The name smells of puke to them.

Pegoa spewed out the words like magic. 'Sukulu signed the papers.'

'Paper- what paper?' The leader gives vent to a line of questions.

Pegoa continued. 'There's nothing to hide. All the papers are in the office.'

The boys cobbled together, bogged down in grumbles, trying to locate the missing piece of the puzzle. 'We know, it's in the office, do you have a copy to prove?'

'Can I ask, do you see Sukulu before coming here?'

'Sukulu is in Honiara.' Came the blunt response.

'If so, I am sorry, you have to wait for him to answer your questions, not me.' Pegoa advised with a relieved tone.

'You are the Land Coordinator, right?' The elder riddled him with one more question.

'Right. I only do what is within my power,' Pegoa said, arms folded over the chest.

'Good, we'll erect a roadblock.'

No response from Pegoa.

'Mid-day tomorrow is our deadline.'

26

'We don't expect visitors, do we?' He shot them a gruesome look as if they have no valid passports. For seconds, eyes locked on Bernard, head to toe, and end his stare at Alo. He staggered away, still scrutinising for details as if he venerated the statues he just carved. Probably thinking, *is this all?* 'But we do expect enemies, right?' They lead them towards a tent, spread out like a mushroom up the slope. The interior is gloomy, one will have to squint to look inside.

Bernard cleared his throat, robbed of words.

'No talking, you hear me?' the order is explicit.

Bernard's hands locked behind his head, his eyes darted around to locate his friend. He flicked his nose when he saw him a few meters away, beyond whispering decibel. Behind them are two armed members wearing well-worn t-shirts, both competed against the height of Alo. Facing them is a broad-shouldered, barrel-chested man, with eyes unblinking like a lion. He wore an army camouflaged shirt, battered jeans and chinese made flip flops, not a cool military type. This ridiculed Bernard and almost burst out in laughter, but no time for such, his fate is at stake.

They gawked foolishly at anything that is not a human face. A minute is gone, no sign of moving. Two minutes gone, still no one is talking. *What the -, they are probably fooling us?* Bernard stifled a hiss, what he is scared of the most is not total silence, it was what was coming up next. Thinking of the unknown is the hardest part, the odds that flickered at the back of his head. Three minutes gone, he can feel the beat of his heart pounding, equivalent to the ticking of a clock.

Bernard allowed his thought to wonder in vain. Five minutes of silence is eerie.

Sounds of boots are approaching. Bernard turned his head briefly, reluctant to know the details. A man appeared from the tent. He must have studied them the whole time. He took his time to scrutinise them, composing his thought.

'Mongga is derived from *Monggavata*, meaning *divide into two.*' The man echoed in the loudest voice he heard in the past months, besides the usual boring announcements usually made by Chief Ko'oga during village gatherings.

Bernard raised his head slowly to take a glance. A stout figure, eyes of an eagle daunting and also defiant with thick lips and weak jawline. A rough, pockmarked face warped like steel plate, not meant for a smile. Reason for his nickname, *Steel Face. An* obnoxious fat and round face with a scar that looks as if imprinted by a minting machine. Bernard could sense the hatred -a streak of misanthropy in his eyes.

The leader continued in a hoarse voice. 'It divides the island into two equal parts. The east from the west. Sunrise from sunset.' He paused without blinking his eyes. 'This camp is situated in the middle of the island, the heart of this land.' He adjusted the gun on his shoulder. 'Solomon Islands is located in the Central Pacific. On a map, it's located on the equator, an imaginary line dividing the earth in two halves. That imaginary line runs through?'

'*Isatabu.*' The team chorused.

Damned, he brainwashed his followers with his tardy thoughts.

He talked like a geography teacher quizzing his students. 'That means we are at the center of the world.' He stamped his feet on the ground. Third time.

Bernard is perspiring with confusion. He lost his cognitive ability to think. *What are all these? Is this ritual before they kill them?*

The brigand leader continued his raucous speech. 'See these mountains, like us, they have breath too. They feel what we are going through. To fight for this land, protect it from the government.' He paused, adjusted the gun on his shoulder and continued. 'We said no-no to government.'

Bernard is speechless, eyed Alo. *Will they offer us for sacrifice to the mountain god?* He collected his composure, brushing away the floating thoughts in his head. He believed fear is like a child within us that keep bombarding us with ghost stories. That's not going to happen now.

'*Ironggali* is god of Isatabu, the first and the last. The creator of all things.' Brigand leader croaky voice roared the inspirational words like a preacher.

Bernard sweated with lurking fear. *Please Ironggali or whatever god of the mountains, we are just passing by. We knew nothing.* He looked at Alo's feverish face, ashen.

Steel Face lowered to a squatting position. He scooped fresh soil in his hand. 'This is life, our lifeblood. It's not like dust on the road blown here and there by – a passing vehicle. This land is precious.' He looked deep into Bernard's eyes, allowing the words to settle. After a pause, he continued his bleak monologue. 'The government is hungry for this land. They are eager to seize from us, and will continue to do. This is the motherland.' He glanced around briefly, veins pulsing on his forehead as if he hit the climax of his speech. 'But we are Isatabu Resistance Movement, our solemn duty is to protect this island from foreign *greedy* hands.' He stood up and stamped his feet on the ground. 'Isatabu!'. Fourth time. Everyone faced him, digesting his perverse speech- not a sound, like a moment of silence, to pay respect to his words.

He concluded his speech, grabbed his gun, corked it and pointed to the foliage, and pulled the trigger. 'Boom!' He fired one shot. Breaking the silence of the mountains with vibrating echoes 'This crisis, we are not alone. These mountains are with us.'

Did he say this crisis? Someone needs to remind this smelly brigand, it's over.

The leader is getting stronger after each word, revealing his nefarious trait. If Steel Face is a natural disaster, he would be an earthquake. He took his time to exhibit his anger, whilst the outcome is delayed but sure-fire disastrous.

Bernard pleaded in his mind to whatever supernatural power he could ever land a thought of. In his befuddled mind, an idea clicked. *There is one stronger than these brigands.* He made a silent prayer.

'Tie these boys up!' Came the belated order as they both expected. 'Will talk tomorrow,' he ordered.

Like a caterpillar with an undulating body, the bulldozer slowly eats the soil away. It is no surprise the manufacturer stamped the name *Caterpillar* on it. Inch by inch it eats its way into feet and into yards, leaving a trail behind. The ugly machines scavenge the earth's surface - followed by falling trees toppled like dominoes. Two bulldozers tore the bushes on each side of the road, wild as *monsters*.
With controlled breath, a man stood afar and spied on the machines - bulldozing the new access road. The bush is buzzed up with noise. Chainsaws hummed like bees, chopping down trees as if in the Olympics. He glanced at his watch and knew it was time to go. He adjusted the mask on his face, and ducked behind trees to take a last look. He smiled, knowing the blame is on poor Bernard and the boys. A perfect trick.

His face soaked with sweat, and beamed like a vanished statue. He slid the mask from his head and wiped his forehead before placing the mask back in place. He grabbed his knife and was about to walk away when a white vehicle approaches. Puckering up his face, he hunkered while the vehicle passed him. He stooped down and walked off in haste.

The white Toyota cruiser sped up the muddy track, moving with a drag, and shook vigorously in the mud. The organic scent of the excavated soils infused Suiono's nostrils as he stepped on the accelerator and rode up the hill. He peeped outside the window, whistling as he drove along, hitting the horn to capture the attention of the operators.

'That's why we hired you gentlemen, great job.' He showed a thumb up to one of the bulldozer operators. Happy the road was now taking shape. He looked around, fallen trees piled up in heaps. A little distance further, a familiar sound of a chainsaw rang in his ears. He jumped off the vehicle and walked over to meet one bulldozer operator.

'We reached the stream.' The operator swept his arm down the valley. 'Quite steep down there.'

'I trust you can do it,' Suiono agreed, indicating the orientation of the stream. He tilted his head orienting himself with the hill. 'Angle the road on the slope.' As an operator himself, he knew well how to glide the huge machines down the steep terrains. He fancied working on slopes than on flat areas to catch the thrill of the work.

The operator nodded his agreement, mind already processing the task that lay ahead.

'Trees, lots of trees.' Suiono shouted above the noise of the machines.

'This is Guadalcanal,' the operator said. 'See that tree.' He pointed to *Pometia pinnata* species, with its trunk the size of a water tank.

'Possible for shipment in a week's time.' He jerked his head around. The cracking sound of the radio cut short the conversation.

'Suiono, over.' He frowned; face petrified within seconds. 'Is Sukulu returned already?' A few seconds of silence erupted to a 'tell them to be patient for at least a day. They won't die.' Suiono dropped the radio.

27

The branches swayed under the grey sky. The skein of birds dropped and dispersed like dropping leaves, twirling and vanishing behind the distant hills. *What happened? They disappeared as wind.* He watched the empty space, mesmerised by its vastness. It's a space of infinity, so vast and so lifeless. A voice echoed into his ears, conjured up a face - blurry. He stood back in distaste, darted around, disoriented. After a moment, which he could not properly envision, the images zoomed towards him, only to see his own face. It's a mirror, and his face is on it - distorted, skin peeled off as if been weathered to form yet another face. Surreal.

But the face is familiar.

A female figure immaculately dressed as if ready for church. The figure managed a blithe smile, but only a brief one. The smile transduced to a shocking face. She gripped tightly to an object, raising it only to be disintegrated into pieces.

'What is it?'

'Don't tell me you bought their lie.'

113

'What are you talking about?'

'You will see. Events will unfold in your very eyes.'

Silence.

'What events?'

'Our story. The story of our family.'

'Our family? What happened?'

'You will see events unfolding in your eyes.'

'What?'

The unravel. 'Our land, our tribe, our family.'

'Family?'

'You have no family, Bernard. No one left, all gone.'

'Gone?'

'All are dead'

'What - but I am alive.'

'Right, you are not dead, that is why I am warning you.' Her deep grey eyes sunk further into her face, slit just enough to denote life in her.

He watched the female figure twirling into a black hole. He felt the surrounding coldness engulfing, shivering, darkness all around. He was cramped in a cage, the size of his body sitting up.

'Wake up, sleeping dogs!' a voice barked in Bernard's ears. He flinched and fluttered his eyelids, light streaming in and incapacitating his sight - dizzy. 'Do they lock me up...?' He sensed the cage, nothing more than a captured animal. Rubbing his face, he squinted. Exactly what he initially thought a rebel camp looks like.

'Out!' The armed brigand ordered. He is the one that seized them at gunpoint. He recognised his slanting thick eyelids. He opened the cage fastened with vines. 'Move, quick.' His breath reeks of home tobacco. The two grim-looking eyes popped a few inches from Bernard's face. Bony cheek with a steel wool shock of hairs, thick lips, and an oversized nose. 'Move!' He ordered. 'Quick you animal.' He booted Bernard hard at the back. Without a word, Bernard complied, with no point in resisting a gun. Talking now is not a good idea either.

Bernard spied around. Few more cages lined like portable toilets. Another armed member guarded the cages. *Which of those contained Alo?*

The cold air rushed through Bernard's nostrils, shrinking his half-naked body. He walked slowly as far as his energy allowed. Gripped with fear, he stopped. A few steps away is an edge of a cliff. His petrified face locked at the precipice, only a leap away. *I should ask what is going on.* 'Where's my friend?' he managed a question. Eyes locked at the rocky edge.

'Shut up!' Came the ferocious response.

Bernard submissively moves forward, the barrel of a gun poking his back like forever which caused him nausea.

From his position, he could see treetops a hundred meters beyond the cliff, displaying vast swathes of greeny-hued canopies. He felt his head dizzy, stomach twisted enough to puke. A little also to do with *acrophobia* - fear of heights.

'Keep walking!' The order came as if they are running late for a flight.

I am walking, can't you see? Bernard noticed only one brigand in tow. He sized up the lad; he is short, brawny, and armed. *I could have jumped and pushed him off the cliff, watching him pumping his legs as he drops.* And with both hands tied, that would be a suicide. He continued dragging his feet along, marveling at how thick the forest was at the top. One can hide, and no one will spot you for ages.

'This way!' He directed Bernard to where a group of men were standing, probably waiting. It's the brigand leader at another location. Bernard was disoriented, and nauseous. *Damn it, this is a rat tunnel.* He cast his eyes to the level of theirs, can't get his composure together.

'Good morning, Bernard.' The croaky voice growled, calling out his name as if a teacher introduces him to his class. Steel Face is still on yesterday's uniform. One thing caught his attention, all wore masks except their leader. *If this is a sacrificial ritual, then this is my last day on earth. Watchers of the mountains, help me.*

A moment of silence. 'You are here at the courthouse, as you can see.' He pompously glanced at the masked men, 'these are my judges.'

The masks resemble a human skull, white scalp, and intimidating black eye sockets.

Where's my friend? Bernard sensed the grimness. *You horrible creatures.*

'Let's get down to details, shall we?' Came the response. Hiding real intentions is dangerous, and that's what they are doing.

These people are demons. Bernard strengthened his hefty shoulders that play little help among these barbaric creatures. He adjusted the vines they tied his hands with, careful not to alarm their attention. He recalled the incident at Ghombua. The culprit disguised himself with a similar mask. He felt a tense knot in his stomach, pulled from both ends a little tighter.

'We want the truth. Plain truth.' The words were meant to be comforting, but the voice itself is diabolical. No one can read his or her fate from those words.

Bernard wriggled his shoulders, irritating.

'I admire your courage young man, but I don't need any more rules besides the Isatabu laws.' He snapped. Like Bernard, the brigand leader is plumb patriotic. A patriotic man could be on Guadalcanal to fight for his land. Land ownership is everything, it connects and bonds you to your distant relatives, it links centuries of generations to the unseen future, and it's intrinsic. As a man, you have to be courageous and able to raise your manly voice and flex your muscles in representing your tribe. To remain silent on land issues is a sure *coward*, which Bernard understands, but not the Isatabu tut-tutting.

What is he talking about? What Isatabu laws?

'Now prove to me,' the leader said, 'that you are not a spy.' He paused. 'We know, one police officer is stationed at Ghombua, disguised as a Security officer.'

Damn it? Bernard felt his stomach knotted tighter still. *The freaking cowboy-looking guy?*

'There is a group called Bandits.' He hit the catchword.

Please don't say anymore. Anticipation of danger is worse than reality.

'We know you are the leader. Some of your boys now joined the logging company.' Two members stood next to the leader exchanged glances, unmoved like Swiss guards protecting the Pope. 'They now happily employed.' The voice came naturally in an optimum decibel. 'And you are not. No offence, but why?'

None of your business. Bernard cleared his throat, cannot summon up a word. He cleared his throat again. 'We are not ... like you, I am not happy with the government.'

Say no more.

'You should be happy to receive the royalty money.'

Bernard thought over the response. He pursed his lips. It's more than logging. Logging is only a part of the whole thing.

'You are the gifted son, born at the right time.' He scoffed; his words lathered with sarcasm. 'What's your name again?'

'Bernard.' *You psycho.*

He corked his ears towards Bernard, unconvinced, his eyes formed a slit.

'Bernard Maneboko.'

'Never heard of it.' He enquired the most horrific question. 'And your parents?'

Damnit. This is the question. Don't say a word, don't say a word.

'Both at Ghombua.' He compromised with a plump lie he could muster.

More nodding heads. The carious masked faces listened to every word with a material look, weighing the tone, studying the eyes and body languages. They whispered among themselves, tomb silence that follows is intimidating still.

At a distance, Bernard caught sight of something, giving him fear to his bone. Its wooden crucifixes, more than ten, protruding from the heap of soil, covered with crawling vines. The brigand leader signaled the member next to him.

Not me, please, not me.

28

A potbellied figure staggered towards the wrought-iron gate. His sloppy black trousers look like a skirt topped with a blue polo shirt, with unshod feet. He darted around thoughtfully and proceed to march towards the office. The compound is empty except for idle machines squatting like giant cane toads.

He leaped up the stairs, and approached the entrance door with the hanging notice 'CLOSE'. He peeped through the glass door as if the notice is not enough. 'Looking for someone?' The voice startled him. 'Still not open.'

'Oh-yeah. I have an appointment with bossman.' He gawked at his wrist as if to check his time. 'Meeting at 8.'

'You can wait around.' The security officer examined the visitor head to toe, plump with no trace of a neck, only a wide head and a lumpy nose, the size of a noni fruit. His height is average but bulky. The security shot him a *-who-are -you* look.

'I am the landowner.'

'Oh, landowner...I see.' The security acknowledged his status. 'You are the big man,' his dubious look metamorphosed to a face-

118

saving grin, slacking his feet. Landownership on Guadalcanal is more than owning a hectare of land covered with trees and ugly toads and stinking bats, it is deep-rooted in one's life and represents one's hierarchy in society, and imposes great respect.

'I am here for a meeting. Very important meeting.' Returning the grin, the visitor studied the security officer and turned towards the security house. Empty.

'How's the operation going?' the security tried to be casual.

'I guess you will already know what I am here for.' The visitor jerked his head around one more time. The office complex is situated next to a workshop. The cabin blocks occupied the remaining spaces, obviously residence for employees.

The security headed towards the gate, 'come and wait at the security house.'

'By the way, my name is Chief Joseph Sukulu. Call me Sukulu.' He produced a cigarette packet. 'Smoke?'

'Thanks Chief.' The security accepted a cigarette.

Outside the gate, a vehicle stopped. Sukulu took a step back and watched in silence.

'That's him,' the security announced.

Bernard turned to the sounds of dragging footsteps. They escorted his colleague forward. For almost forever, the rebels talked among themselves. For sure, it's not about a fishing trip, nor about their families. *These guys are perverts.*

The leader cracked a cough. 'The mass graves of those who against Isatabu. We have hearts too, so we buried them, we know they loved it that way.' He announced with a peacock look. From the size of the grave, Bernard could imagine how the bodies were piled. Buried dead or alive, who knows, there is no law in these mountains. He vividly recalled the night his father was taken away. Tears pooled in his eyes. *BANDITS don't cry.*

'Now that you know me, tell me about yourself.' The leader leveled his eyes at Bernard. 'Let's start with why you are here instead, I like to do things differently.' He smirked. A feeling that crawled through Bernard's spine was worse than fear.

Seconds yield a minute, staring eyes have their peculiar terror. The tattoo on Bernard's right shoulder caught the attention of the leader.

'What's that tattoo?'

Is this necessary? 'Eagle.' Bernard responded in a guileless voice.

'Eagle?' the follow-up question is a deathtrap; a single mistake and you are a dead man.

'Eagle over Vatupochau.' Bernard asserted.

'Good. You are the true son of Isatabu.' He trudged around them as if inspecting slaves for their manliness. He saw a second tattoo on Bernard's left shoulder. 84. 'What's that number stands for?'

'Date of birth.'

A suppressive laugh followed. 'You tattooed your date of birth? I like you boy.' He grinned, revealing his uneven size teeth. 'We'll engrave that on your tombstone if you're lucky to have one.' He laughed even more, before turning to face Alo.

'One eye boy. What is your number, 42?' he grimaced.

Alo was untouched by the jeering, better silent than saying something that may pull strings of questions.

'Your request for guns, we don't throw pearl to pigs.' The leader switched the gun over to his right arm.

Bernard recognised from a picture somewhere it was an AK47, wooden stock with a SKS 30 detachable magazine.

'No, no. We --' a lump gained root in Bernard's throat.

The leader bade Bernard to shut up. 'I will allow the jury to decide.' He turned to the masked men, who already talked among themselves, allowing one of them to step forward.

One of the skeleton mask men stepped forward. Bernard's heart missed a beat.

'Government is corrupt,' the masked man announced.

Bernard's mind clicked. *My bag?*

29

'I am not a fool. I have a brain that directs me on how to do things correctly. You are jeopardising my operation.' Atkinson stood tall behind his table, throwing his hands in the air.

'No one puts your life at risk. I-I-'

'Look Sukulu, whatever your intention, I care so much about my employees.' He marched inside his office, giving him no chance. 'Your people have threatened my operation.' He came walking back, and continued lecturing. 'As a village leader, you should....' He allows the sentences to complete themselves in Sukulu's mind.

With a nodding head, Sukulu responded. 'I will talk to them. They are my people, they trust me.'

'Trust. Now I hear the word I've been expecting from you all along. If that word exists, then this conversation will not happen.' He banged his hand on the table. 'I expected you to come with me and explain to your own people. Will you?'

'I will. I will, that's what I always do.' He asserted emphatically. 'I have come here to create a bank account.'

121

'What bank account?'

'Savings account.' He produced a deposit slip for the unsolicited deposit he'd done.

'So why not explain it. Isn't it that simple?' He sighed. 'Tell you what Sukulu.' He mentioned his name for the first time. 'You are the chief and landowner and I expect a lot from you. Likewise, Pegoa.'

Sensing the lurking distrust, Sukulu intervened. 'Of course, I am the Chief. For *Tuvu* land, it's me, no one else. Ok?'

'Correct, that's why I involved you since day one.' With mouth agape, Atkinson realised he had just spewed more words in a minute. 'Look Sukulu. I respected you as a Chief, and you know what it means to me and my operation.' He spread out his two arms on the table. 'And I have to talk for the safety of my employees and the machines.'

'In case you don't know, I am a retired schoolteacher. I know how to deal with people.'

'Great. Better do something like a teacher, at least for this operation.' He glanced outside the window; the eastern sky is clear.

'Of course, I will and always be,' Sukulu responded.

'Now, prepare to face your people,' Atkinson said.

The morning rays perforated through the clouds in the western sky, illuminating the small shivering waves. The community is still cold and calm. Chief Jonah Pelu sat at his verandah, staring out to the sea. Three buildings away is the clinic. Aola clinic serves the surrounding communities, including Ghombua. A lot of things raced through his mind. As a village chief himself, he shoulders a huge responsibility. Unlike the police who only deal with the law and order of the country, his role is far more than the law and order. He is also responsible for the cultural and social norms of the community. This morning is different, he is not thinking about the community but instead, pondering over the conversation he had with a fellow tribesman. It's about logging operation.

As a landowner himself, Chief Pelu knows what being a tribal leader means. Whatever the decision he made is not for himself, but for the tribe he represents. He recalled from the discussions that one of his fellow tribesmen in Ghombua already signed for the logging. In return, he received a lot of money. Big money.

The bush logging camp was splattered with mud and scattered puddles. For safety reasons, the operators vacated their machines and run for shelter under the makeshift tents. They watched the rainfall patter on the red soil and drain away. Soil erosion took its natural course. No one under the tent give a damn thought what it means to the living things in the streams and rivers. Or at least heed the government environmental regulations.

It took four days for the pile of logs to tower over the tents. Three chainsaw operators discussed while scoffing about their cigarettes, and sharing jokes. Their discussion swerved to their work unconsciously, how many trees they cut, targets for the coming days, and so on. They cut trees of any size, as the forestry division is too bureaucratic that forget to action their words. No culling of trees, no cutting limits, and whatever fabulous mandate there are, as the logs demand overseas is at a premium, and they have a target to meet.

One of the chainsaw operators added. 'I heard we are recruiting?'

Suiono took time to think through the question like a quiz. 'We have some local boys yet to join.' He stood tall under the tent, staring at the raindrops pooling at the edge of the tent. 'Bossman is meeting with *Adeade* boys today.'

'So, we are hiring them?'

'It's their demand.' He lied. It is one way to stop them from causing disturbance.

'The jungles are thick as grandpa's pubic hair,' the chainsaw said.

'You right.' Suiono smirked and lit a cigarette, not a habitual urge, but stress. So much to think about, dealing with disputes and demands, keeping the operation going, and meeting the target for the first shipment. His brain is searching his entire cerebrum for ideas to comfort himself.

'Hey, you guys saw the masked man?' one chain saw operator changed the topic.

'What masked man?' Suiono insinuated his thought, a cigarette in one hand and a lighter in the other.

'Village people hunting for wild pigs.' the other operator shrugged, 'this is their bush.'

'With a mask on, that's strange,' the reporter said.

'I also saw that bum.' The third operator cemented the rumor. 'He wore a black coat and was armed with a knife. He is into something.' He looked around at the staring eyes. 'Doesn't look like hunting for pigs.'

'When is that?' Suiono became engrossed.

'This morning.' Came the first response.

'Yesterday evening.' Came another.

'Someone is watching us,' the third operator said. 'Maybe he is a bush security provided by the villagers.' A wry laugh.

'Not with someone waving a knife at you.' The first operator interjected.

Suiono looked sideways. 'Is Mendana back yet?'

'I don't see stringy hair.' Came the blunt response, followed by mumbling.

'I got to talk to him about this,' Suiono said.

'The police officer was attacked by a masked man.' The revelation landed like a bomb, numbing with an awkward hush.

'And where are the local boys?' Suiono enquired aloud.

'Follow Mendana.'

'I will talk to the securities. They must spread out into two camps.' He looked at the sky, the downpour subsided to drizzle. Suiono leaped out of the tent and marched to his cruiser.

30

The time on the dashboard registered, 1:19 PM. The grey Nissan Navara decelerated to 20 km/hr as it approached the village. The village is unusually empty, no one seemed to be moving about. Atkinson pulled the vehicle closer for a clear view of the roadblock- a coconut trunk lying across the road.

'Stop, close to the road junction,' Sukulu said, gushing heavily.

Atkinson squinted. From the nearby bushes, he saw one or two figures moving about like shadows. 'This it, mate. We expect some debate.' Atkinson wound the glass down, watching expectantly. The trunk blocked the access road linking Ghombua and Tuvu camp.'

'Good afternoon boys.' Atkinson spewed out his trite greeting.

No response, his presence is a gravity, he could feel the glary eyes land on him.

A man in a camouflaged coat stepped forward from the group, armed with a machete. He is wearing eyeglasses covering most of his face. One thing Atkinson learned from those youths; they are fond of army clothes.

All eyes glared at Atkinson. 'Good to see you boys waiting.' The introduction is inquisitive, causing eyes to glare. 'My apologies, I cannot make it yesterday because of other urgent matters.' From the look, no one cares about the delays, or whatsoever. What matters is now. The leader of the group approached him in a practiced stunt. A couple more members in the nearby bushes.

'We were told, that's why we are waiting for you.' The front man approached, seeing Sukulu emerge from the vehicle. 'You too.' His glare was implacable. 'Where's our money?' The first words hurled at them like a flaming spear.

Atkinson is unruffled, negotiating his entry point. 'That's what we're here to talk about.'

With courage, Sukulu stepped forward, insinuating himself in a sloppy voice. 'Listen - listen. Allow me -.' Sukulu was attacked before the rest of the words came out. He is reeling backward with force. The leader landed a punch to his face, a heavy blow.

'We don't need you here.' The other members marched forward with a squabble, clamored with anger. 'You're conman!'

'Stop it- stop it, we can settle this.' Atkinson pleaded hopelessly as the two figures exchanged punches. The leader moved forward and threw a second punch, well targeted and with more exerted effort than the first.

Sukulu limped sideways, helplessly hurling his arms everywhere, fending punches off, defending himself erratically.

'Casino bastard.' The leader stealthily moved over again, now aiming for his neck, to strangle him. Fortunate for Sukulu, his body size accommodated the jabs and managed to fend off the incoming punches. He took his valiant stand, collecting his energy and pushed. The leader staggered backward and landed on his back with a thud. This called the attention of members.

'Punch him, selfish conman!' Three boys accosted Sukulu like rabid German shepherds, causing the potbellied man to wriggle, as if swept by a tornado.

Atkinson lost it. 'Stop-stop!' he shouted repeatedly. 'You are killing him.' It's too late, Sukulu is already on the ground.

The leader of the team picked himself up and released his retaliation with multiple kicks at Sukulu, who lay prostrate on the ground.

The boys slowly swaggered away from the mucky figure. Sukulu fumbled around for support, trying to lift his weight. Traces of blood at the side of his mouth, evidence of when he coughed out blood.

'See - see what happened?' The leader now turned to Atkinson. 'This is the result of telling lies.'

Atkinson pleaded his stand with half-raised arms. 'I am not here to fight. No, no.'

The group stood back in formation and scowled at Atkinson defiantly. If one thing Atkinson trusts, it's his surefire attestation that they will not touch him. It's the money they are after. They confronted Sukulu because they perceived him as embezzling their money; reasonable to cause a discord.

'And the money?' The question leveled at Atkinson, slack and loose like an inchoate agreement signed by Jemes and Sukulu. Glances exchanged, followed by shouts, mostly squabbling as if ready to eat him alive.

'Silence.' The leader put an order to his gung-ho members.

Atkinson collected his wits. 'I know you are angry; you have all the right to. I guess it's misunderstanding--'

'Misunderstanding?' came the response, raw as rat meat. 'This is our land!' One member barked.

'You trespassed!' Another voice bawled from the back.

'Shh-.' The leader signaled his boys to calm down.

Atkinson removed his cowboy hat, allowing heat to massage his scalp. *Be smart. You have the money; you make the rules.*

Sukulu limped back towards the vehicle, his approach was fraught with failure. He lost his dignity to five thousand dollars.

'You trespass.' The words repeated, now from the leader. 'You have to compensate us for entering our land.'

Atkinson fanned himself with his hat, the sullen sun is not showing its face. He was thawed by the glary faces, wishing he had bionic power to turn into a hulk or something. Out of all weighed options, he opted. 'I have the money.' Atkinson looked into the eyes of their leader. That is the secret he learned from his father. To tweak out their weak point, find a common ground and strike. That is what he is doing, 'Follow me.' He led him away from the members. *Play cool, the ground could be slippery.*

Steel Face scraped his thoughts together. He learned the Government had a big plan for him. They pledged a fifteen million reward for his capture. *But who will do that? No one in his right mind will take the risk. It's like promising one a reward to catch a gorilla alive. Catching a dead one is acceptable, but to catch the monster alive, you need to have the instinct of an animal itself. Reckless.*

He assembled the team for a prayer session. This has been the practice for the past months. They conducted devotions three times a day, for their own reassurance, not for forgiveness.

'Let's hold each other's hands.' The team of twenty plus formed a perfect circle, the size of their camping tent. The leader says a prayer, a lengthy one, followed by a song-*We are one big happy family.* The routine was programmed, after the closing prayer, he gave some announcements followed by solemn encouragements - to keep fighting the common enemy. The government.

'That tax eater Prime Minister is putting our heads in a ransom noose.' He raised his gun to his arms. 'We'll expect visitors flooding in under different tags, Church leaders, Provincial leaders, Peace negotiators, whatever the crap title they come under.' He took a deep breath. 'Comrades, from now on, no more visitors. Visitors must be killed. No more negotiations, no. All clear!?'

'Yes Commander!' They all chorused.

He turned towards the cages, where his capturers are locked.

Bernard unsettled in the cage, flinched from side to side. The cage is designed for one person in a constricted and twisted position, restricting movement. He folded his hands around himself for warmth. In these mountains, the temperature can drop as low as twenty degrees celsius. This is unbearable for Bernard and his friend who are accustomed to the warmer coastal temperatures. A single ray of sunlight landed on his face, animating a disc-shaped mark. 'Alo, where are they going?' He looked in the direction of the departing troop. Only one-armed member manned the camp, locking his eyes on the cages.

'I don't know,' Alo whispered. 'Training?'

'Training?' Bernard cried, the bleak thought of being festered out here in this far-flung mountain prison is unbearable.

'What else can they do?' Alo revolved in the little cage.

Bernard looked around, at least seven cages he saw, a couple of meters apart. Including the ones they are locked in. Maybe, there are a few more somewhere. Bernard moved his legs under his buttocks, adjusting his position.

'Hey, don't move.' A raspy voice echoed at a distance. Someone is watching them. Bernard turned to see the source of the voice.

'Brother, what's going on?' Bernard enquired out of curiosity.

The watchman was unmoved like the surrounding trees. 'Shut up, I am not your brother,' he said.

Bernard dropped his gaze - don't want to meet the eyes of the watchman. He was mean. Probably it's the rule not to talk to the prisoners, or maybe he's an uncivilised pig after all.

'Where's everyone?' Bernard is not gagged so he has the liberty to talk - ask questions.

'Messenger is here.' Came the blunt response.

'Messenger, what?'

'You want me to shut that mouth for you?' The watchman said.

Bernard accepted the unreceptive response and utilised his freedom to spy the camp; three tents pitched alongside each other. All empty, no one is around besides the one he is talking to.

Bernard studied the watchman. Tall and emaciated like a refugee. Probably his age, but hardly grow any muscles since teenage, only height. Bernard imagined if he punched him right in the face, he would reel like a propeller a hundred times over.

'Brother, do you have any food?' Bernard got the nerve to ask some more. 'I am starving.'

The watchman shot Bernard a dubious look, then glanced to the tents. No response, making Bernard feel edgy.

'Please, I know you can help.' After a second thought he realised, these are rebels, not soldiers. And if there is food somewhere, it must be rationed on a strict order.

'No, we don't feed pigs.' He glared with a slantwise glance. This is disparaging for Bernard, gross. No one ever called him animal names as far as he could remember, he repulsed the thought of it.

'Water. Just water, I am thirsty,' Bernard asked again.

The watchmen walked towards the cage, unzipped his trousers with his left hand, and started to pee. He aimed his stream towards the cage, inches from Bernard's arms.

'Hey! aim your damned thing somewhere.' Bernard glared at the watchman.

The watchman continues his thing, without a word. When he finished, he shook it, some of the trickles landed on Bernard's foot. This is annoying, but worth no breath to challenge. Can't fight, no point in asking for one when you are in a cage.

'Your time will come.' This is all Bernard can afford to say. His engagement with the security meant they both forget about Alo.

Like a snake, Alo uncoiled the vines, one by one. Before Bernard even realised, Alo exited the cage and tip-toed towards the nearby bushes.

'Joining the rebels doesn't mean you have to treat everyone as an enemy,' Bernard said, trying as much as possible to sound casual.

No response from the security, lips pursed, maintaining his relentless pose.

Bernard subconsciously eager to lure the human out of him to talk, knowing he has a benevolent soul like everyone else.

'My name is Bernard.' He announced as if he did not know. Worth saying something than troubling oneself with depressing thoughts.

'I am Alo!' Without a warning, Alo thumped a dead branch on the head of the watchman, causing him to writhe like a headless chicken down the slope.

Alo untied Bernard like magic.

'Chew that, you skinny rat!' Bernard said in a vengeful tone. 'This way!' They race down the opposite edge of the mountain, along the cliff.

31

The raindrops caressed Jemes bare shoulders, tingling, a numb sensation down his back. He groped for freshwater *gudgeons* and *gobies* along the drains of the newly constructed road. These freshwater fish species colonised the nearby streams and ponds, inhabiting the once pristine ecosystem. It's an unlucky day for the fish, uncalled for, the sediment - laden water flooded their habitat, forcing them to migrate out, only to be caught along the way.

'See, a big one.' He showed it off to his wife. 'How many have you caught?'

'No time to count, ten, maybe,' Mere answered.

'You beat me.'

'I always.' the wife replied jubilantly, not even turning her head. Jemes admired his wife, ten years younger, average looking but endowed with the essential qualities every man needs in a woman; loving, caring, hardworking and of course, child-bearing. Jemes late father knew it, so he picked the right girl for his son.

Jemes surveyed the sky for the sun. He picked up his knife, placed the bag on his shoulder. 'Enough, we are not hosting a feast.'

'I got one.' Mere still groping the muddy waters for more. 'One more. Another one.' She continued, leaving Jemes to stand watching in total silence.

'We have to go. Sun is shifting north.' He darted his eyes around, examining the landscape created by the ugly machines as if dreaming of a foreign land. But that is not all, in his mind, he is thinking about something else. In a few weeks' time, he will receive his first batch of royalty. *What will I do with the money? Give some to my relatives, and keep the rest for myself. I am the leader, so I decide how I will share it. What will I do with the money? Build a big house with three big rooms. One for Merre and me. One for Edna, one for visitors? And I will purchase a brand-new Isuzu pick-up truck. Blue or white? White is better, representing dove as my totem. Also represents white stones of Mongga river. I will decide what should be transported in the truck. Passengers going to town must pay the fare. No hitch-hiking allowed.*

'Let's go.' Merre's voice startled him.

'Access road to the gardens.' His eyes were still locked on the road. 'Now we will not lug mosquitoes on our shoulders.' He gave a smug look.

They picked up their pace and marched home. The sound of the engine humming at a distance seized their attention. The new sound they will have to adapt to.

Jemes turned to see the source of the noise. He stopped to improve his eyes. A figure is walking behind them, a hundred meters away, covered in a yellow raincoat.

'Who's that?'

'Security maybe.' Merre continued walking, not even looking.

'Security, right.'

The figure stopped as if sensing them. The rain continues to pour heavily causing Jemes to shiver.

'Hurry, let's take the shorter route. I am soaking in these clothes.' He glanced in the opposite direction, trying not to stare at the figure directly.

Merre continued walking. 'We should tell the camp manager to warn the employees from roaming around the bushes. It's not safe, especially for us women and girls.'

Jemes said nothing.

'This logging brings in people and problems to our community.' She continued to whine. 'The *Adeade* people now became our enemies,' she growled. 'It's not even a month.'

Jemes utters no response.

'We'll now have feelings against them. Just because-.' Merre continued.

'Stop it!' Jemes retorted, avoiding meeting her eyes. 'I know what you mean, and-.'

'And what!?' Merre snorted. 'Don't respond like you don't know.'

'I understand, you don't have to remind me a hundred times. That's the thing I hate about women. Always whine over petty things over and over again.'

'And if we don't then who will?' Came the sharp response. 'Look, it's no longer safe for us women to go alone in the bush.'

'The bush is always unsafe Merre. Even if the logging is not here, you still cannot go alone. Don't you?' He twitched the raindrop from his eyebrows. 'We have *Vele, ghosts* and whatnot. It's a jungle of everything - anything terrible can happen.' The incoming sound prompted Jemes to dart sideways at an instant. 'Watch out!' He jumped and grabbed his wife as the wild boar tore through the bushes like a whirlwind, disturbing the surroundings with its rush.

They both landed on the wet ground.

'Stupid animal.' Jemes face is only an inch from his wife's face, still holding her firmly. They lay for a couple of seconds, breathing heavily.

'Thanks, and get that weight off me.' Merre interrupted the silence with a command.

'You never said that when we're in bed.' Jemes chuckled, admiring his wife, standing next to him, eight inches shorter but endowed with strong arms and legs, with little features of her girlhood still resonating. The natural blonde of her spongy hair is a unique trait for the *Melanesian* people.

'Shut up.' Merre retorted, adjusting her blouse over her shoulder. 'Help me up.' She raised her hands.

'Lucky, I shoved you quickly.' Jemes sinisterly recalled, pulling her up.

'See this.' Merre's face flushed, the surrounding twigs tore her skirt. She nodded to her husband. 'You look great.'

Jemes nodded *you- are-my- wife* look. Twelve years of their marriage has cemented their love more. 'It's a huge boar.' He described the length of its front teeth, showing three fingers.

'Right, it gave you a present.' She pointed to his forehead, all smiling.

'What?' Jemes rubbed his face and removed a lump of sticky mud. 'Crap.'

'Wash your face.' She pointed to the nearby run-off. Without a further word, Merre re-packed the contents of her bag. The whooshing sound prompted them to turn abruptly, only to see the man in the yellow raincoat, watching them from afar.

32

A new day brings gloom for Jemes. It's like events switched in the snap of a finger. His wife vomited the whole night. As bad news, it has already reached every corner of the village.

A group of women doing their washing at the river and by no surprise are engrossed with the news.

'A masked man was following them.' A woman shared her story. Like everyone else, the group of women indulged in the rumour.

'He threw a stone ....' She tapped her left shoulder and continued.

'No, it's her right shoulder.' One lady corrected her, as if it's going to make any difference.

'Left, right, left-' Commander, the bird talking chirped behind them.

'Shoo, go away.' They chased the bird.

'It will report us to the owner.' One lady cautioned. 'Shoo-.'

The bird flew off, whistling.

'He meant to shoot Jemes.' The woman continued, frequently glancing towards Jemes house. 'Unfortunately, his wife was hit. I felt sorry for her.'

Merre's deteriorating condition engulfed the entire community by surprise. People assumed different version of the story that suits their curiosity. Many alleged it's a sorcery, because of its suddenness. Unnatural as many claimed.

'It's the same man who attacked the police woman.' Another woman added ingredients to the recipe. Rumors are sweet when shared.

'Did any of you recognise him?' She looked around expectantly.

Faces turned with doe—eyed expressions, darted around as their curiosity mounted inside them.

'Bernard.' One woman dropped it. 'That's the only one I think of.'

'But Bernard is tall.' More questions than answers.

'He can impersonate Zacchaeus.' The rumour hung in the air, reluctant to touch it, as it may burst like bubble.

'Could be a member of the ex-militant groups.'

'But why attack a female officer? Such a coward act.'

'Pegoa is working...' The woman looked towards the village, not answering the question. 'Working with Tetere Police.'

One lady looked sideways and added. '*Kaumolo.*'

'Someone must pick her food scraps and gave it to the sick dogs.' They all looked at each other for agreement. Sorcery is still widely practiced and is incarnated through animals and birds, incanted with spells.

'It's *Kaumolo*- a sick dog sorcery, sunken eyes and weak limbs.'

'But who possessed *Kaumolo?*

Bernard tore through the bushes downhill, supporting himself with the tree trunks cascading down the steep hill.

'Wait. Where are we?' Alo enquired, oriented their position with the surrounding mountains.

'To the river.' Bernard dashed forward. From their position, they could hear the rushing sound of water dropping to the channels a hundred meters below, somewhere.

Alo insisted. 'Wait.'

'What?' Bernard dropped his head, hands on his thighs, panting.

'We can't go to the river. They will soon catch up to us.' Alo took five seconds to ponder, despite the urgency to hurry.

'But that is the only way back.' Bernard disagreed. 'We can't hide here; they know these mountains.' He looked at the mountain ranges that rolled out like giant waves.

'They will follow us. We must divert somehow,' Alo said.

'How?' Bernard queried loudly.

'We'll follow the stream, up.'

'Upstream?'

'What I am saying. They will pursue the river.' Alo is smart when it comes to jungle navigation. As a kid, he used to follow his dad hunting for wild pigs. The experiences Bernard lacks, as he spent most of his childhood in classrooms.

'As you said,' Bernard finally agreed.

'Wait.' Alo twitched; eyes looked sideways as if checking his ears.

'They are coming.' Bernard jinked down the adjacent hill.

***

'You fall asleep!?' Steel Face is rigid as a hammer. 'They beat you like a kid.' He walked over to the security, slowly recovering, face pale as a fish. He was in a coma for fifteen minutes. The blow on his head caused him to become unconscious. Luckily for him, he survived the attack. Smears of blood pooled down his gaunt face, with splinters of the dead branch sticking out of his hair.

'No one disowned my command. No chief, no police, no whatsoever, but you.' Steel Face levelled more questions at him, causing the scar to become vivid, disfiguring his gritty face. 'You skinny pig!'

No response, the security felt small and awkward in front of the probing eyes, leaving only silence. He has nothing to say, and besides no one argues with the brigand leader. No, never in a million years, it's like trying to justify your case to a tiger. He will tear you to pieces before you even utter a word.

'You gave away one of my guns. You little devil.' He spat on his face, glared around, members watched in silence. Reverence is part of the protocol; no one talks when the leader is talking, unless he requires a response from you. Which is not always.

The leader walked over, tapped the jaw of the trembling security, and tilted it upwards. 'You will bring back the two alive. Understand!'

33

'Shipment confirmed for next week.' Suiono was tempted to hold out for a cigarette, but the urgency of the meeting forbids him. 'We have next week to transport all the logs.' He glanced at the pile that transformed the landscape.

Mendana slouched against a post, watching the smoke venting from his mouth. Dan and Pegoa sat across him on a log lying across the tent.

'The logging trucks will have to work day and night,' Suiono said, tweaked a glance at Dan. 'Shift for the securities?'

'Sure, my priority task.' Came the response.

Suiono continued. 'We have to put pressure on the securities, no more hitchhiking in the company vehicles.'

Pegoa got Suiono's attention by raising his hand.

'Yes, Pegoa?'

'For the securities, do we need additional ones?'

'I forget, for loading, we will hire *Adeade* boys. Thanks for reminding me.' He made eye contact with each of them, debating the thoughts in his head.

'I'm fine with that,' Pegoa said, 'if you still need security, let me know.' Looking around, he continued, 'just to let you know, Jemes wife is sick. So be considerate when driving through the village,' he said.

'How is she?' Suiono enquired more out of wonder than compassion.

'I can't say a word. She is bedridden for two days now.'

'Two days?' Suiono was somewhat surprised, eyebrows warped. 'Why not take her to clinic?'

'It's not an ordinary illness, not the doctor's type,' Pegoa flickered.

'What's it then?'

'It's a custom one,' Pegoa added.

'Custom one? I see.' Suiono combed his hair with his fingers, unconvinced. In his native Malaysia, they also believe in *occult practices* but becoming less and less popular as western medicines overtook the shelf.

'She is treated with custom medicine.' Pegoa cemented his story.

'Wish her well.' Suiono revered custom medicine and switched topic. 'Our camps will spread out in two.' He looked towards Mendana, who indulged in puffing his cigarette. 'Food ration for different shifts.'

'We have enough food in stock.' Mendana continued nonchalantly puffing his cigarette as if nothing important is going on. 'Give me the schedule, shift hours, and so on.' He gazed at a distance. 'Who's that?'

The four heads twizzled and locked in one position as if run out of power, only to be cut short by Dan.

'A villager returned from his garden, I guess.'

A man approached the camp and swerved into the bush.

'Some operators saw a masked man,' Suiono revealed, eyes leveled at Dan.

'Someone told me, but I am yet to see one,' Dan rebuffed.

'Probably villagers.' Pegoa shrugged away his thought.

'Whatever it is, advise the locals to stay away from the main road,' Suiono advised. 'Logging trucks will work day and night.'

~

'How's the meeting going?' The Lieutenant has gradually attached to the whole of the operation.

'Sukulu got punched.' Atkinson shrugged, attesting not a big deal though, as he was at the wrong end of the discussion. Atkinson remembered the boys calling Chief Sukulu names, disrespectful ones. But to have a village chief being an inveterate gambler is ridiculously gross. It's like having a burglar for a police officer.

'He deserved that punch,' Atkinson said, the phone glued to his ear. 'Good news is, problem was settled, employed some more locals.'

'I guess that should solve their grievance,' Lieutenant assumed. 'They hate to see us. Glad you met them yourself.'

'What you got for me?' Atkinson enquired shifting the conversation.

'Bernard refused to surrender as yet. He made a point not to. He stands on his principles.'

'What principles?'

'Not to be involved in logging. Any logging for that matter.' He announced, thinking the young man has all the rights to stop logging on his land.

'Is that a joke? Why can't he join the operation, get paid, support family, and enjoy life like everybody else? That doesn't need damned principles.' Atkinson pondered on his words, much to his disappointment.

'We will not stop until we put him behind bars.'

'You said that weeks ago.'

'It's complicated.' Lieutenant weighed the thoughts in his head. 'Good news is, Australian Defense Force will step in soon to support.' He raised his hands to his chest, indicating a gun with fingers on the trigger. 'They will deal with the arrogant, with those who refused to surrender their weapons.'

Atkinson flicked his eyebrows.

'Nicodemus Kebe.' Lieutenant Kilua produced a photo. 'He was already given an order to surrender.'

'Who the hell?' Atkinson wrapped his thought around the issue, not the subject.

Lieutenant continued. 'Also known as *Steel Face*, still possess high-powered weapons, controlling the mountainous regions of Guadalcanal.' He waved the photo of a man in army uniform wearing an aviator sunglass with a navy green scarf on his head. 'He's an Ex-Field Force, so you know what he's capable of.'

'Field Force?' Atkinson assumed by the look in the photo, he could do devil knows what without blinking his eyes.

'Field Force are trained police officers specialised in field security. More like soldiers.'

'And what is his motive?'

'That's the question,' Lieutenant said, 'but one thing I can assure you, he killed more civilians than anyone I know.'

'Rotten pig.'

34

Jemes searched Merre's eyes. Her face was like a carved statue, with no glint of life in her. She had lost half of her weight over the course of three days, robbed of food and water. Her eyes locked on the ceiling.

Jemes saw the shadowed bald head figure at the entrance, a bottle cupped in his hands. With caution, he walked in and slowly knelt beside the bed. The interior of the kitchen is dim with minimal ventilation. The air is thick and drowsy. It's a practiced belief that minimising or closing the ventilation protects the victim from mundane spirits.

'Merre, I brought this for you.' Chief Ko'oga gently placed the bottle beside the battered mattress. 'This for dry eyes and mouth.' He looked around for support, 'can I have a spoon?'

An elderly woman appeared behind the partition and forwarded the utensils, allowing Chief Ko'oga to measure the prescribed volume to be used. The treatments have no prescribed dosage, only weighed the amount to be used based on the condition and age of the patient. It's a skill one has to borrow from age.

'Merre, can you hear me?' Chief Ko'oga looked with a general practitioner gaze, rubbing off the sweat from his wrinkled forehead. 'You'll be fine...'

'Merre darling, Chief is here to give you medicine.' With exerted effort, Jemes lifted her to an angle sufficient to swallow the medicine. He pushed the pillow at her back to wedge her forward. 'Easy, this will not take long.' Jemes assured his wife.

'Let us pray for the medicine. Shall we?' With permission granted, Chief Ko'oga prayed. Whilst everyone closed their eyes, Jemes examined his wife, with head dropped, holding the sick soul tightly to his chest. Her breathing is normal, except her body that has already lost half of her femininity. He touched her face and rubbed her shoulders and arms. He was disrupted when the word 'Amen' was chorused.

'Hold her still.' Chief Ko'oga shifted around to take his position. He knelt, facing the woman and slowly tilted her chin, and pushed the spoon into her mouth as if feeding a baby.

Merre coughed. Chief Henry levered her head up, assuring her with kind words. The women at the side attentively watched. Jemes smells the fresh aroma of the medicine; raw as fresh leaves being squeezed.

'I will give her another dose at midday.' Chief Ko'oga stood up and headed for the door.

'Careful, it's slippery.' Alo leapfrogged on the jagged surface of the boulders poking out of the stream surface.

'Wait. Where will this lead us to?' Bernard is unconvinced, anxious they may end up in the Rebel's nest again. He took out the Compass from his pocket. Glad he did not put it in the bag.

Alo dashed forward, utilising the time at their disposal. He looked towards the sky; the sun's rays penetrated through the foliage. He had used a lot of his strength, which indicates they had been running for an hour.

Bernard studied their direction, satisfied. They are heading northwest, away from the camp.

'Keep moving,' Alo mumbled, not even turning his head.

'Can we take a rest?' Bernard panted.

'Not now.' Alo ascended the adjacent steep slope, more calories burned.

Without further words, Bernard tottered behind.

The next half an hour was onerous, the walk became more tedious than thought. Only sounds are of heavy breathing and random spitting.

'This is it.' Alo reached the peak. He absorbed the surrounding scene. From their position, one can see the river snaking below. It's a perfect spot.

Bernard dropped his load, taxed out. 'This is our gift from Steel Face.' He propped the gun against a tree trunk.

35

Jemes was not educated, but he is a well-respected figure of the community, and his tribe. At age forty-one, his height and physique can be misinterpreted for what he is capable of. He is lean and stands 6 feet, an ideal candidate for a soldier. But as said, it takes years to get a soldier out of a man. But whatever his strength left; he lost it all to his wife. He walked towards Pegoa's house, subconsciously accepting it was one o'clock in the morning, obsessed about his sick wife.

At the door, he called. 'Pegoa, it's me, Jemes.' In a community, approaching someone at such an early hour only attested one thing, a call for help.

'Pegoa, it's me, Jemes.' Still no response. After a couple of seconds, movements were heard coming out from the house.

'Pegoa is not here. Who's that?' the voice queried sleepily.

'It's me, Jemes.' He was startled by the light that had switched on. The introduction of solar-powered lights is truly a blessing for the locals. 'I thought he's here.'

'He's gone to Honiara. Is Merre ok?' The voice queried inquisitively, followed by footsteps, probably the rest of the house is waking up.

147

'I need help. Merre is not getting any better.' His response was engulfed with distress. 'I want to take her to the clinic.'

No one speaks for a moment. 'I am coming.' Pegoa's wife assured her offer for support.

'No, it's fine.'

Jemes withdrew and marched out into the dark. He needs someone to talk to. In such a situation, he needs support from relatives or elders, empathetic support. That is all Jemes needed, and Pegoa is the man that fits all the criteria.

He strode towards his house and was startled by a group of boys.

'Suiono is coming. We'll take Merre to the clinic.' Toxic announced. Like everyone else in the village, the boys also have been monitoring Merre's condition. It's a simple act of kindness.

'Thank you, nephews. I kind of need help...' He sobbed.

'No problem. We are here to help.' Toxic silhouetted against the approaching light of a vehicle.

'Merre. We'll take you to clinic.' No movement. Jemes looked at his wife's eyes one more time, her condition is getting worse; the custom medicine did little. Chief Henry Ko'oga not able to complete his supposedly three days' treatment. Merre is too weak to swallow even water.

The women packed clothes, utensils and toiletries to be taken to the clinic. They stood away for space, allowing the men to carry Merre into the vehicle. Four boys levered support around the bed, slowly they picked her up with the bed and glided towards the vehicle.

Little Edna holds on to her dad, gripping her little fingers tightly. She has gotten little sleep. Like the elders, she prayed whenever the thought sprang up in her mind.

'Darling, please stay with your aunty. Feed your bird. Commandeer will be hungry if you leave.' Jemes comforted her. 'Me and mum will be back soon. Ok?'

Her aunty marched forward. 'Come, we will go to the river tomorrow. Also, with your bird.'

Wasting no more time, the engine gained life. Suiono switched on the headlight, ready to move. Like everyone else, he wanted to help the sick recover. Of which she will. All they have to do now is take the patient to the clinic, the doctor and nurses will do the rest.

'Look after our house.' Jemes told the women who stood around the vehicle. They nodded their heads and muttered among themselves. 'We'll continue to pray.' They looked to Merre who lie in the middle of the back tray, emaciated like a dried bean.

Suiono put the car in the gear and it slowly rolled forward. He could tell the woman needs urgent medical attention. *But why wait this long? They should have taken her to the clinic days ago. By now, this woman should have recovered.*

You cannot intervene into someone's belief. It's disrespectful. Worst if you want to deny it to their very eyes. That's why we are labeled differently, though we encounter similar problems on a daily basis.

36

T he yellow eighteen-wheeler logging truck pulled its trailer like a tortoise, slow but determined. The logs are packed and bundled firmly with a seamless iron chain. The Hino engine roared along with a whooshing sound, scaring the surrounding bushes to succumb to the annoying noise.

'Tighten up your belt Nimo boy.' The driver geared the engine up the hill. 'Speed up lady yellow. Speed up.' He grinned as the engine ignited its power. 'I like the sound of a new engine.' The driver is one of the more experienced on the island. Thirty years behind the wheel is enough to hone his skills for such a risky job. 'Driving a logging truck is not an easy job.' He coughed, pumping the engine energetically, causing the truck to vibrate vigorously.

'I want to learn how to drive,' Nimo admitted, vicariously admiring the old man displaying his skills.

'Of course, you can drive. It's easy.' He grinned with his tobacco reeking lips, displaying his betel nut-stained teeth. 'Not that hard like math you learned in school.' He sniffed long and hard, making a funny face, a habitual contraction of muscle-tic. 'All you need is courage Nimo boy. This is a risky job, and if you are thinking of taking your girlfriend for a ride, I guess you should consider driving a taxi.' The vehicle shook as if ready to capsize. 'Loose soil,' he mumbled, maneuvering the machine along the narrow road.

'How old are you son?' He sniffled another funny face.

'Nineteen.'

'Glory days owed you, my son.' With a stretched right hand, he changed gear. 'I was your age when I first drove, a plantation tractor.' He tightened his hand on the wheel. 'Started as a tractor crew and slowly climbed up the ladder.' He talked without taking his eyes off the road. 'Time flies son, I only have two or three more years on me and then I will hang my wheels.' Sniffed another reflex of the face.

The conversation gripped their attention for the remaining minutes before they reached Tuvu in no time. The vehicle moved at a reduced speed, releasing air like a train. 'Here we are son.' He pressed on the brake, slowing down the engine. 'Base one, over.'

'Drive through, offload at your left.'

'Raja.' He communicated to the forklift driver, who watched from a distance away. The sound of the engines is deafening so much that they will have to use a two-way radio, complemented with hand signs.

Nimo watched in silence. The log yard was flat and bare. The driver sniffed unconsciously. 'Our first trip for today son, we'll target to complete ten.' He smiled. 'Whenever you come to a stop, always pull up the handbrake. It's safety first - always.' He looked outside, trying not to meet the wondering eyes of curious Nimo. 'Good morning boys.' He waved at the security guards who watched from a distance.

The security officers watched in admiration as the forklift cupped the logs down. Like a crab, the crawling machine grabbed the logs, tightened firmly between its claws, and placed them on the ground with a crash. As cumbersome as the task was, the logs dropped with a thud, causing the ground beneath their feet to shake like a five Richter scale earthquake. 'I can watch this whole day.' One security said.

⌇

At the eastern edge, a navy-blue tent was pitched on the periphery of the camp. The second tent is only tied halfway. Dan is under the blue tent, talking to the microphone, with eyes outside.

'I got some news. Over'

'The bandits?' Lieutenant still drowned in the month-old blather.

'Lieut, bandits no longer exist.'

'You serious? I don't see them in my prison cell.'

'Bernard, remember?' Dan glanced outside; securities still slaved their thoughts to the machines.

'How can I forget?'

'Both his parents killed during the crisis.'

Response late from the other end. 'Both parents? Are we missing something?'

'Yes, his dad is from the island of Malaita.'

'I see, that explains it all.' Lieutenant paused. 'Poor boy.'

'I think he needs counseling, he's traumatised,' Dan stuttered.

The radio cracked and then dropped silent again. He eyed his security colleagues sharing a cigarette with another lad. He thought he recognised the face. One a member of bandits. The name slipped out of his mind. The logging truck was reduced to a mere skeleton. It mechanically folded its trailer on its back like a muddy scorpion and roared to life.

37

'We can't locate their footprint. They must have floated down the river.'

'Give your mother that lame excuse!' Not satisfied with the outcome, Steel Face metamorphosed into a monster. 'How come you don't see them, you blind? There is only one way out and is through the river. You idiot!'

'I - I will-ah-ah- find them,' the embarrassed watchman stuttered, assuring his leader in a worshipful tone.

'Don't bother,' Steel Face retorted, 'many ways to trap them, our eyes are big as these mountains.' He walked around restlessly, anticipating the unknown. 'They are not spies. They are nothing but hopeless kids foot lead about for nothing.'

The other members felt a sense of relief too. They have seen their leader demonstrate his anger in numerous ways, from torching houses, putting bullets to peoples' heads, and burying humans alive whilst they pleaded for their lives. His ill-disposed activities will surface when someone challenged or questioned his *Draconian* rules. And no one in his right mind will.

'The government calling for overseas support, like a crying baby,' he announced. To him the idea of peace is bleak. 'We'll fight to the last bullet.'

The interior of the clinic is spacious but lacks modern equipment to convince the public of its capacity. With no available option, Jemes accepted it, knowing the nurses were trained to do their job. With his limited understanding, to him nurses are synonyms for doctors, to care for the sick.

Merre lay on an adjustable bed, easing the options for feeding and treatment. The interior is hot, no essential appliances like fans and air conditioning systems. The clinic was only powered by two 100 watts of solar panels, and applications are limited to lightings systems and other urgent appliances as needed from time to time.

Jemes stared out at the corridor, which he'd been doing since he arrived. It's where the relatives of the sick patients waited. He scanned the faces for familiarity, but no one stood to greet them. For a long time, he glanced at random faces passing by - no familiarity. He only has his mind to communicate with and seems to be comfortable for now. The appearance of a face startled him. He dropped his head in response. Too late.

'Hi Jemes.' A broad face, thick grey beard and bushy eyebrows, furrowed.

'Hi Chief,' Jemes responded in a dry tone.

'Who is sick?' Chief Jonah slanted his head towards the bed. The tone became dull very quickly. 'I am sorry.' He paused as if trying to compose a sensible sentence.

'Merre's sick.' Jemes said.

'I do not expect to see you here,' Jonah growled with a sympathetic tone.

'We arrived last night. It's fever, also losing blood.' Jemes said. Chief Jonah is a prominent figure in Aola area, everyone knows him as a Chief and a *Thibo* tribe leader. Like Jemes, he is the head of his clan too.

Chief Jonah's eyes scanned the surroundings. 'I returned from my garden, and someone told me you are here.'

Jemes' eyes locked at the bed. Speechless.

'Fever and losing blood?' Chief Jonah observed valiantly. 'What about food?'

Jemes only turned his head. Jemes is Jemes. He had conventional views and was very conservative in his actions and thoughts. Even the clothes he wore are dated, that his wife had to take the liberty of purchasing new clothes for him most times - all the time. 'She is without food for two days now, only this.' He brought his eyes to the drips the nurse injected into her left wrist.

'Do you try any custom medicines?' Chief enquired.

'Yes. We did ...' Jemes left the response hanging, showing the suggested option had been crossed out.

'Little improvement.' Jonah completed the sentence for him.

'Yes.' The drip slowly passed fluid into his wife's body. If this drip is empty, another one will be replaced, common sense tells him. He looked around the interior of the clinic, it was all empty, except a couple at the far end.

Jonah cleared his throat. 'I remembered years ago. One woman had a similar illness. Passing a lot of blood, and the nurse said that her case was beyond medical treatment.' Jonah leaned forward to Jemes. 'I told her husband I can help. The husband looked at me, asking if I am a doctor. I said to him. 'Look, doctors may be trained in their field for six, seven or even up to ten years." But Western medicine does have its weaknesses too, that's why people died in clinics and hospitals.' Jonah continued relating his story. "I can help," I said to him.'

Jemes raised his head and contorted his eyebrows.

Chief Jonah continued, 'so, I asked the husband if I can give her traditional medicine, and he agreed. I gave the woman one teaspoon of medicine three times a day. Only a teaspoon.' Jonah continued without even blinking his eyes. 'After two days, the woman asked for food. She is now well in their village in the highlands.' Jonah content with his lecture, stared at Jemes as if expecting the same scenario to be repeated.

'You saved her life.' Jemes slowly raised his head and looked toward Jonah.

'I did.'

Jemes shifted his chair closer to his wife, widening the gap between him and Chief Jonah. 'I will have to wait for the nurse first.'

'Sure, I am just saying,' Chief Jonah responded, 'this is a custom-related illness.'

Jemes didn't respond, nor protest, eyes were locked still at the bed.

'You know my house.' Jonah pointed to the eastern end of the building. 'In case you need my help, come see me.' Jonah got onto his feet. 'We have a deacon here too. I will probably call him to come and pray with you. I'll be around in the afternoon.' He strode towards the door.

Halfway out, Chief Jonah stopped. 'Oh, one thing ...uh' He darted around momentarily and faltered. 'I met Pegoa in Honiara last week. He asked me to sign the *Thibo* land bordered with you for logging.' He darted around, the only person within an audible distance is the one on the bed but is too sick for such talk.

Jemes felt a lump in his throat.

38

The sun slanted over *Tuvu* bay, casting its final gleaming rays for the day. The nocturnal creeping creatures whistled their mandatory call, warning of the imminent darkness. A heap of logs swathed the western edge of the camp. A drab caterpillar forklift, mucky as a giant mud crab crouched next to the heap of logs.

At the eastern edge of the camp, two figures busied pitching up their tent, emitting small mumbling sounds under the nakedness of the evening sky. The other securities have gone back to their villages, waiting for their shift.

'The talkative one is your brother, right?' Dan enquired loudly, more of curious than an actual question.

'Thomas.' Osama tapped the butt of the cigarette to a tree trunk. 'Toxic for short.'

'Toxic, that's an interesting name.' Dan responded understandably though his instinct loathed the name. He signaled Osama to pull the other end of the tent.

'Hold it firmly.' He pulled and tied the tent to a nearby shrub.

157

'How do you come up with your names?'

'Names?'

'Yes, the nicknames.'

Osama hissed. 'How, I guess you mean why because it's easy as breathing in air.'

Dan grinned. 'Right, I mean why.'

'It's to do with growing up, I guess you know what I mean.' What registered in Osama's head is a different reason. They purposely invented an alias to hide their identity from police.

'I see.'

'But we are not abandoning our birth names. Those are the names we will go down to our graves with.' Osama said. 'Will be written on our gravestone, if they damned care about us.' Osama allowed the cigarette to glow between his lips, both his hands engaged.

'Pull,' Dan ordered, moving to another corner. 'Good, hold it.' He tied it tightly to a coconut trunk as if it would never be untied again.

'What is your name?' he enquired.

'Irvin. Irvin Boe.' He slapped his hands clean before he adjusted the cigarette between his lips. 'I see. Would it be ok if I call you Irvin?' Dan seeks permission, ducking into the tent, appreciating the shelter they constructed.

'Sure, that's my real name.' Osama twitched, he toyed with his thought. 'And you, what is your other name?'

The question was received with a fake smile.

'Daniel, eh -Daniel Bako.'

'Daniel Bako?'

Dan for the first time sensed the name sound exotic, especially for one who has both parents as Solomon Islanders. 'Yes, everyone called me Dan,' he said. 'My parents gave me that name.' a deliberate lie. In his profile at Tetere, he is born Peter Pai on the New Years' Eve of 1975. His father is from the western end of Guadalcanal Island and mum is from Shortland Island, bordered with Bougainville. His mum's trait gave him the pigment of a darker skin complexion. He is barrel-chested, stocky with a broad face which loosely matches his 5 feet 10 macho. A potential Mike Tyson in him.

'Your parents?'

'My dad passed away a decade ago. Only my mum is still alive.' This sentence was the first and only truth Dan spoke about himself. He felt a sense of comfort after spewing the truth, glad he's not a ghost after all.

Silence settled in.

'What about you-?'

'My dad used to work at a resort at West Guadalcanal.' Osama interrupted the silence. 'Before the crisis.'

'And now?'

Silence. '...passed away.'

'I am sorry.'

'Heart problem. He was a drunkard, probably the cause. We only live with our mum too.'

'Sad. Now we are friends.' Dan found a common ground to sympathise with his new friend. 'Bring your stuff inside.'

'Tell me about Ghombua.' Dan spread the mosquito net across the floor.

'What about it?'

'The People, land ...' Their discussion fascinated him.

'It's one of the biggest villages on Guadalcanal.'

Dan looked bored by the conversation, not what he was expecting. 'What tribe are you?' He swerved the topic.

'Ghaobata.'

'I see.' Dan removed his cowboy hat, feeling the sweat evaporate on his shaven scalp. The same tribe also existed in West Guadalcanal, but he is not part of any tribe, considering the matrilineal system, he will not inherit land from his father's tribe.

They were so absorbed in the discussion that they did not notice the approaching footsteps.

'Who's it?' Osama finally heard the noise and squinted outside; it was getting darker after each blink.

They both marched outside in unison. Dan took the lead, only to be welcomed by pitch darkness. 'Bring my torch,' he whispered. At first, Dan thought it was a wild boar, but the paces were distinct. It's of a man walking away.

They stared at each other in the dark.

39

Atkinson's eyes were glued to the wall as if it were a TV screen. Crumpled on his swivel chair, he smoked his tenth cigarette for the day. He smoked an average of twenty cigarettes a day, making it one packet a day. This is no surprise, as he started smoking when he was attending high school in Fremantle, Western Australia. With his buddies, they would sneak out-of-school compound during recess to 'recharge' as they called it. Bad enough for him, he still plugged into the power board.

He blew the smoke into the air and observed the smoke dispersed above him. A knock at the door got his attention without a surprise. 'It's open.' Atkinson rubbed his thick beard, assuming everyone who enters, or about to enter is a client. The *Yes, We're Open* sign at the door implies an open-door policy that attracts clients. That's his secret charm. In his definition of business, no appointment is required, as long as you have good intentions for business. The door slowly opened, and a man stepped in.

'Hi Pegoa. I thought you already left for the village.'

'I was late for my transport,' Pegoa said. 'This is not a different island; this is still Guadalcanal anyway.' He simpered.

'Right, this is still Guadalcanal.' Atkinson grinned, savoring the response.

Pegoa walked over at a chary pace across the room-attired in a white collared shirt with a suitcase in his hand. His experience in an office environment is now exhibited in his well-mannered approach.

'Have a seat.' Atkinson pointed towards an empty chair opposite him. 'Everything ok?'

'Always.'

'Brilliant. So how can I help you?'

'I am here to check you.'

'Check me for what? I am not sick,' Atkinson grinned.

Pegoa managed a ghost of a smile, then his face turned vapid. 'Jemes wife is admitted at Aola clinic. I received a phone call this morning, she's in serious condition. She's now in a coma.' He paused and continued. 'They will bring her back to the village.'

Atkinson was struck speechless for a while. 'Sorry to hear that. Is she...?' he dropped his question incomplete.

'Yes. She is admitted since yesterday.' He leaned back on the chair, 'Fever, worsened overnight.' As a village elder, he shouldered a huge responsibility.

Atkinson holds his cigarette high, burning. 'You need some help you said?' Atkinson read his intention like a book.

'Little assistance. This will mean a lot to Jemes and his family.' This sentence floated in the air for seconds, allowing some thoughts to settle on it.

Atkinson tapped the table. 'Not a problem, I will contact Suiono and see if he can help with food.'

Pegoa appreciated the response, though he expects financial support. He nodded his mild-mannered agreement. 'Thanks a lot.'

'You're welcome,' Atkinson said.

'Did you say something about the shipment? I must be hearing it from the grapevine.'

'Right.' Atkinson looked at the calendar on the wall. 'It's today. Right, thanks for reminding me.'

'The locals are looking forward to that. Especially Jemes and his family.'

'All of us. I am also looking forward to that shipment, though I will not have a chance to see it.' Atkinson beamed.

'I will make sure they provide security day and night.' Pegoa affirmed before he stood up, eyeing his way out.

'What's the hurry? Tell me something, how's the situation in the village?' He pried for more, anxious he might miss something.

'Don't worry bossman. Those boys will always follow whatever I say.' Pegoa bragged, which was vivified by a satisfied look. 'See, they now joined the company.'

'What about their leader?' Atkinson queried with enquiring eyes. 'Still bragging about his rules?' A contemptuous grin then said, 'rules are for fools.'

Pegoa slowly turned his head. 'Nonsense - all nonsense.'

They both laughed.

'Good news is, Australian soldiers are coming to rescue us from this mess.' Atkinson concluded.

Jemes slowly hung up the cloth partition around the bed. Two nurses attended to her, conducting their routine checkups. They took her temperature, blood pressure test, assessed the eye pupils. Whatever the outcome is, it doesn't mean a thing to Jemes. The report the senior nurse provided is sufficient. He prepared to leave.

'We're sorry. Nothing much we can do.' The nurse empathised with Jemes, reasoning her condition from the perspective of a nurse. Jemes can read from their faces they had given up their stride to proceed by any means.

'I understand.' Jemes nodded his head, not approval but accepting their empathy.

'It's beyond what we can do.' The nurses continued. 'She had a problem with her liver, disrupting the normal function of blood circulation.' This is all she could manage, nothing technical, of which

Jemes agreed. The details mean nothing to Jemes. The younger nurse, obviously a recent graduate from college is trying out the knowledge she learned from her studies. The supervising nurse responded a few words with her head tossed sideways as if trying to make a point.

After a long silence. 'You - you already arranged a vehicle for pickup?' The nurse queried pityingly with an austere sympathetic face.

'Company vehicle,' Jemes muttered.

The nurse cleared her throat and asked. 'Do you have kids?' This is a distinct question nurse would like to know more about. Especially female ones, they are more concerned about family affairs than men in general. That is the beauty of women. She looked at Jemes who slowly nodded his head before responding. 'A girl.' The silence fell at the bedside for a while and was disrupted by the sound of an oncoming vehicle.

40

'I am the one who signed, not you. Should I remind you?' Sukulu blurted out.

Suiono read the reaction well. 'The company has rules. You can't do whatever you wish. I don't have to remind you too.'

'I know what rules are.' Sukulu pointed at the ship floating outside, not even turning his head. 'I have the power to dispute the shipment and sue the company.'

Suiono is unconvinced and confused. 'I don't understand you people.'

'It's not about *us* people. It's about this company and its agreements – rubbish.'

'Agreements?' Suiono shot a gloomy look around the camp. 'What agreement you be talking about?'

'The access agreement.' Sukulu snorted, hands akimbo.

'There's nothing in the access agreement that says you can hire anyone, anytime.' Suiono stood his ground, he will not fall to the petty games.

But there is more than meets the eye. Mr. Atkinson is both a contractor and a licensee himself, which deemed any agreement with the landowners futile. According to the government code of logging practice, the licensee (person awarded with the logging license) will bear the responsibilities of the landowners' benefits and how the operation will be conducted as outlined in the document called the *coupe plan.*

Dan watched Suiono and Sukulu engage in an argument. It's becoming a daily routine. In all talks, there will always be finger pointing, it's an endless drama in both camps. More or less like a debate. If someone is as good as his word as said, then no one around here is good.

Dan eavesdropped the whole time from his tent. From what he heard, Sukulu wants to sign a contract in providing additional security. This has been received with apathy, as Suiono does not accept additional securities. This is a violation of the company recruitment protocols, and it's an extra expense for the company.

Sukulu is restless. He wants to enter through the backdoor with his ruce. He discussed with bossman, basing his reasons on the land –owning tribe privileges. But the land is owned by the tribe, not by individuals.

Suiono turned and walked towards the tent where Dan is standing. 'Can I use the radio?'

Dan jerked his thumb to the corner. It's the same radio he used to communicate to Tetere but on a different channel. 'Is everything ok?' Dan pretended he didn't overhear the argument.

'Fine-everything is fine.' He grabbed a microphone and started calling. 'Honiara base, do you copy?' The radio made some crackly noise, but no response. 'Honiara base, do you copy?!'

'Copy loud and clear,' came the response.

'Can I talk to bossman, over?'

'Sorry, bossman is out. Over.'

Suiono gawked at his wristwatch. He dropped the microphone.

Sukulu stomped towards the tent like a raging rhino, not satisfied with the outcome. 'Look. I already talked to Atkinson about this.' He shouted from a distance. 'Do you forget I am the landowner here?'

Suiono turned pale in a second – face dehydrated like a dried leaf. He felt a sudden rush of blood run through his veins, the feeling of punching someone in the face.

Sukulu looked hard at him, hands on his hips with shirt open exposing his shaggy chest. 'Do you know what it means to be a landowner here?' He started his induction. 'See what happened to this camp, always under dispute. Do you know why?' Sukulu exploded. 'It's to do with landowners.'

'I know. You already said twice,' Suiono snapped. 'Let me talk with bossman first. You know the company rules.' Suiono steps out of the tent.

Sukulu glared with brooding eyes. 'Rules are nothing without us. We are the landowners; you must respect us. You talked about respect; can you show it?' He commanded Suiono, stamping his feet on the ground. 'Do you want to see another roadblock?'

Suiono glanced at another logging truck that arrived with its load.

'Power is in my hands.' Sukulu slapped his hands together, loud enough that the securities stole a few glances towards them. Embracing his strenuous thoughts, he reversed out of the tent. 'I give you six hours. Six hours!' He waved five fingers instead. 'If nothing happened, I will chase you out from this camp.' He picked up his paces and marched away in haste. 'Bernard is my boy,' he bragged.

⌇

Alo's house is a small, low thatched roof with two rooms. It's not even rooms, it's partitioned into two equal parts. Alo uses the other half, and his mother occupied the other. A small veranda extended out where Bernard sat, dangling his feet. Alo and his mum reside at the foot of the hill, with the closest houses separated by some bushes.

'Just returned from Jemes' house.' Alo's mum responded in a fairly shaky voice. She walked over, old and frail. 'Where have you gone boys?' She gazed at Bernard and uttered in a soft tender voice. 'You have to come home. A lot of young girls around.' She positioned herself next to Bernard, feebly levered herself up. 'I told Alo many times to construct a ladder,' she complained. 'He never listened.'

Bernard listened subtly to the murmuring of the old woman, nothing to say.

'Boiled potato inside.' She disappeared behind the wooden door. 'Alo, why don't you bring something for your brother to eat?'

'Already. And could you stop that noise?' Alo snapped, bored by the old woman's jaded talks.

'I am just saying,' She cooed. 'Poor Merre, she is not getting any better.' The talk about Jemes and his series of misfortunes had swept through the community like a tsunami. It's unbearable not to comment.

The old woman continued mumbling. 'If Alo's father was alive, he would have been part of this. Thank goodness, he'd been called early.' She mawkishly added. 'His uncle Jemes shouldered the responsibility of the tribe.'

Bernard gawked at the chickens and hens pecking and scrabbling the decayed waste. For the first time in a while, missing his parents gained weight inside him. His deceased parents did not have proper burials. He pondered on his life, his dream. As a kid, he always told his mum he will be a police officer one day. To fight the bad guys.

You have to study hard. He recalled her words. *Only boys who attended schools can be recruited as police. Uncle Jemes can't be one because he can't write his name.* The scenes replayed in his mind.

A knock at the door. It's not a knock though, it was butt-ends of guns and heavy boots. Band of men came rushing in through the door, five, six... ten. They searched all the three rooms with torchlights. They grabbed my father by the shoulder and threw him to the floor. I watched in silence from afar, helpless, as I could not do much to defend my father. Sixteen years old and still depend on my parents. They took my father away, the last time I saw him. The one that marched him out had the voice of a machine, loud and croaky, leaving my mum pleading helplessly. The house was then torched in flame, with doors locked from outside. Lucky enough, I would rather say our blessing, I managed to push my mum out through the back window.

'Ready?' He was startled by Alo's voice.

'Ah-yes.' He twitched, turning his head hastily as if to clear his eyes from distraction.

'Come on man, cheer up.' Alo tapped his shoulder. 'Ironggali, the god of the mountains.' He impersonated the posture of the brigand leader. They both laughed.

'See this scar, I bruised myself falling into the toilet.' Bernard fueled the fun.

'And we have guns with no bullets.' Alo burst out another throaty laugh. The hilarity subsided after seconds of uncontrollable frenzies.

The old woman still mumbling something to herself. 'What's all the laughter boys?' came the question, out of curiosity.

'None of your kitchen talks.' Alo fired back.

'Logging ship is loading -,' Bernard jumped to his feet.

Alo turned towards the house, and hefted the bag on his shoulder, 'mum, see you tomorrow.'

41

*O*pen the damned door! I am a Landowner. He gawked around; nothing seemed to be moving, and the receptionist is nowhere to be seen. He touched the knob, but a subsequent thought forbids him. *You have to knock first. Respect, a first impression seducer.* He flicked off sweat from his forehead.

'Hi mate, you are early today.'

Sukulu was startled by the incoming voice.

'Hi yes, good morning boss,' Sukulu said. No further talk.

Atkinson unlocked the door and bade Sukulu to follow him inside.

'Take a seat,' Atkinson said, and proceeded with his morning routines. Turn on the switches, open up the windows and clear the table space, before dialing the office phone.

Atkinson cupped the phone to his ear. He looked towards the door, nodded his acknowledgment, and continued talking. Chief Sukulu takes the liberty of finding himself a comfy place to sit.

Sukulu riffled through the newspaper at his disposal, looking for no particular news. The front page covered the arrival of the Australian and New Zealand army led intervention. He was impressed by how the fifteen neighboring countries teamed up to restore law and order, from Papua New Guinea to Niue. A Pacific way as they said. He flipped through the pages, a paid page on Non-Communicable Disease tickled him awkwardly and uncomfortable somehow. It's cancer for the Pacific region, claiming thousands of lives annually. A lifestyle disease results from improper diets and lack of physical activities. He studied the line graph for a few seconds, illustrating a soaring trend.

'Sorry mate, chat with a friend in Brisbane. Wow, you are early today.' He tapped his shirt pocket, looking for his pen or a cigarette. 'Yes. So ...?' He took out a cigarette and lit it instantly. 'How's everything?'

'Good.'

'Just good?' Atkinson choked out the words, coughing.

'Everything is going well. The ship arrived yesterday morning, a huge ship, enough to load ten houses.' Sukulu responded with a reserved tone.

Atkinson has elevated their conversation topic to the right height. Like a pilot, he slowly brought the plane off the ground. From that height, he can now relax; the seat belt signs off.

'I spent the whole day there yesterday. *Whew.*' Sukulu face lighted up, glad he witnessed the show.

'Logging ships are massive.' Atkinson agreed. 'That one is not really big. I saw one in Panama, an oil tanker. It's massive, the biggest I could remember.'

'Metal structures float.' Sukulu's face beamed with a child's surprise.

'It's science.' Atkinson summarised the details. 'Science enables a metal structure to float, fly, dive and drive.' Atkinson recalled as a kid he wanted to be a pilot. In the 1960s, technological advancement had swept across the major continents, America, Europe, Asia, and even Australasia. The end of the Second World War created a lot of opportunities, a technology boom in telecommunication, medicine, agriculture, and transport. Atkinson grew up in those days, a dreamer in his own world.

'The landing area was crowded,' Chief Sukulu continued. 'People postponed going to their gardens to watch the loading.' He snorted.

Atkinson managed a weak smile. 'So how many boys you said you hired?'

This question sprung Sukulu from his box of thoughts. He gawked at Atkinson, who puffed his cigarette. 'That's what I am here to talk about,' he growled. 'The Operation Manager forbids me. I told him I got permission from you, but he never listens. What is he, anyway?'

Atkinson smelled the intention; he placed a packet of cigarettes on the table. Sukulu grabbed one and lit it. After his first puff, he continued with his sulky talk.

'Yesterday we had an argument. A close one - almost ended up in a fight.' He puffed vigorously. 'That Malaysian tries to act smart. He freaked me out.'

Atkinson smiled at the outrageous tone of the news, assuming it was news. He'd already been informed twelve hours earlier. For the sake of the conversation, Atkinson perceived it as if listening to a kid complaining he received fewer sweets than his elder brother, but hilarious like that of a female comedian ridiculing her failed love affairs. First, Sukulu already received his portion and still wants more. Secondly, his grievance or which he claimed, was supposed to be dealt with through the right channel, not hurling it to the world as if someone cares. It doesn't work that way. Not for Atkinson, he cannot be easily fooled by such pity stratagem.

'I want him out. Sack Suiono, he's a rotten tooth in the company,' Chief said. 'Let the locals do the job.'

Bernard gazed at the horizon lying naked in front of them. The incoming waves created tiny pockets of air under his feet, giving him an inkling of what is coming. This is what he will do, he chose to be. Live a simple and good life is a necessity for many, not him. He got to work his way out of this puzzle of life.

'Whoa - see that.' Alo marveled and pointed towards the ship.

'That's a monster.' Bernard squinted. Next to the ship is *Vulelua Island*. From their position, he calculated it will take them an hour by dugout canoe. 'Funny - see big countries come to us for logs.'

Without a word, Alo strode towards the canoe. He eyed around the vicinity for a moment, picked up a paddle, and threw it into the canoe. He glances around, satisfied of what he saw, and proceeds to action. With exerted effort, he pushed the canoe out to the sea, causing a splash when it hit the waves.

'Let's go.' Alo gripped firmly to the tail of the canoe, whilst Bernard glided along, watching the incoming waves.

Bernard continued mumbling into the spyglass. 'Loggers need another planet for their cravings.'

'They already have one, it's called a desert.' Alo chuckled.

Before they realised it, the canoe swiftly drifted on the waves 'Good day for fishing.' Alo tossed the paddle into the water twice and scooped out a handful of seawater, feeling the saltiness raking his hands. The canoe generously moved forward with its momentum.

Bernard too was occupied, feeling a gram of gravity inside his chest. 'Aim for the island. We'll rest at the island till lunch hour.' He spied the island and swerved his focus to the ship. Searching the surroundings, his binoculars came to a stop when the black structure came into view. 'It's a floating mountain.' Silence seized its queue. 'I don't see anyone moving?' he queried in a crispy voice, for a moment he thought he was duped by the size of the ship, a mirage.

Locking the island at the seam of the canoe, Alo paddled. He looked towards the east, Aola community gleamed in the distance, then out to the sea, a lone fisherman in his canoe.

Bernard squinted; the shimmering lights played with his eyes.

Alo watched the birds gliding around freely, occasionally dive and dip their beaks into the water scattering the forage fish, some lucky with a catch, some not, and the routine continues in a circus. 'Can you identify the fisherman?' Alo curious about the canoe.

Bernard swept the binoculars ninety degrees east. After seconds of examination, he responded. 'It's ...' he stuttered. 'It's empty.'

Alo stretched his eyes if it will make a difference. 'Drifting -.'

Bernard is more anxious about their arrival than what he initially envisaged. 'The deck officers will be freak out to see us.' He took out his binoculars and spied on the ship from front to rear, top to bottom, and repeated. Two crew members are chatting at the deck, pointing to the mainland. A couple of heads float about like *pac-man* game.

Alo steered the canoe straight towards the island. 'You see anything?'

'"Pacific Will". That's the name.' Bernard announced as if reporting back to an army base. *Pacific Will? Does not look like Pacific Will to me? It's not our will to log our trees.* Little to their knowledge, this Hong Kong based vessel has been previously registered under three different names, under different logging contracts.

He recalled reading an article that illegal logging is a big business, and it's surging. The Loggers' eyes are global, and their hands are equatorial. *These damned pigs study geography too.*

Alo threw the paddle, two to his right, two to his left. The canoe bobbed along with the waves.

'Floating giant.' Bernard wondered. *That is one good thing about technology. It makes things we thought impossible become possible.* He thought to himself. He learned in science classes that *any matter with a density less than or equal to the equivalent volume of water will float.* Simply put, a ship floats because it weighs less than the ocean of water below it.

The loaded barge approached the ship with a determined speed.

'Check the camp.' Alo wondered suspiciously. 'See if you can spot Osama.'

Bernard goggled around, playing with the figures in the scope if he can stamp a name on any. 'It's all blurred under the shades.' He turned the binoculars to *Vulelua* Island, then to the scrum of birds, shifting further out to the ocean. The drifting canoe still toyed about by the current.

Little did they know the canoe is manned, by a dead body.

The rising sun perforated its rays through the clouds and glistened the sea surface across the bay. Villagers decamped from their respective dwellings and rushed toward the beach to answer the call of nature. As their centurial survival instinct, diurnal birds wake up to the rising sun and start scavenging for food. Birds are endowed with their unerring acuity, enabling them to sense food sources miles away, even in foul weather. For seabirds, fish is an integral part of their food chain, and are well adapted to the marine environment - the mangroves, beaches, brackish lake, estuaries, and of course floating debris.

The villagers heard a seagull that resonated a screechy sound. It glided across the bay and abruptly landed on floating debris. It's an evocative call that something is happening, something unusual. This bird has been around these waters for years and is well versed in the routine of the locals.

Seabirds are human navigators for as long as humans are around. The ancestors to these islands landed safely, aided by this *symbiotic* relationship. As they sailed across the cosmic oceans, they caught fish for food. The discarded remains were scavenged by the seabirds, which then showed them wind directions and the position of the islands.

A curious villager paddled out to check the drifting object, he could only guess by the look of it. Moving closer, he was right, it was a canoe. He recognised it; it was owned by one of the villagers. Whoever used this canoe must have left early in the morning for a fishing trip. But why abandon the canoe and let it drift? Or was the morning tide washing this canoe out to the sea?

In displaying its instinct, the seagull flapped its wings and glided away. The boy paddled closer for a quick glance; his heartbeat fluttered from what he saw. The flies started feasting on the body, and swarmed the mouth, nose, and ears like bees in their hives. It is the dead body of a relative. His uncle.

A man plunged a blood-stained bayonet underwater. It's a crafty practice he had mastered in concealing all possible clues. Besides the bayonet, he also thoroughly rinsed an elastic rubber and meter long 12 mm steel rod sharpened to kill. At last, he could breathe a sigh of relief after all the torturing work. For the past twelve hours, he hardly had no time to close his eyes, vigilant for his diabolic mission, to ensure his execution goes as planned. Happy that all went well and uninterrupted, he felt a spurt of adrenaline, satisfied with his vices.

The man found walking from his garden hut to the river estuary was taxing, especially for a semi-conscious victim who lumbered clumsily like a wounded rhino. His timing was right as planned, the night quiet and dark and the crescent moon wan. With the power of *Vele*, he hallucinated the victim under his malign spell, and tortured the victim the whole night, doing all the things hell prescribed. He had all the time given to him by the devil to do his masterstroke. Before dawn break, he was already at the beach, choking the last breath out of his victim. Placing the body in the canoe was not a big deal, just ensure the load was evenly distributed to balance the weight. He tossed the canoe out to the sea, beyond the breaking waves, and bade his diabolical goodbye to the victim. The tide did the rest of the work, cleaning up, washing away all footprints and whatnot.

Five hours later, two boys came and pushed another canoe out on the same spot. Inhuman as one can get, leaving no trace behind is every serial killer's goal. And we witnessed one.

42

Night fall crept in silently. Jemes is sitting at the verandah, staring at the tent that has been pitched to accommodate those who will come to pay their last respect. It's a centurial form of practice inherited from their ancestors. A couple of men chatting in the dimly lit tent, and darkness claimed the surroundings.

Jemes glanced around briefly then produced a written note. The thought of it flustered. It's a page torn from a student exercise book. Whoever wrote the letter asserted two things. One, he has a colossal interest in what is going on. Second, someone is hiding somewhere, watching, waiting to act at a proper time.

The note was discreetly folded and scribbled on. He carefully unfolded the page, eyes darted around sagaciously. It's a whole page of writing, filled with black ink scribbles. Whatever the message it bears, it means to disturb Jemes' attention. *Letters, words, what does it amount to?*

43

The weather is always unpredictable. More bizarre, the changes in weather patterns created confusion among locals, even scientists too. It affects the yearly cycle for planting taro and yam, which substantially delayed the harvest time. These changes if continued to decadal scale, it's what they called *Climate change*.

But Climate change is not the topic of discussion under the pitched tent. Merre passed away at 5:00 am sharp. Someone registered the time.

The group of men scrambled for comfort as the drizzle started to drip. Among the group of men, Chief Ko'oga wore a green lava lava, with no shirt on. He leaned against the post of a make-shift tent, tilting his bald head sideways. He was subdued by his thoughts, his medicine did little. But that's traditional medicine, sometimes it works, sometimes not - one just had to do something about the illness.

Next to Chief Ko'oga is Pegoa, wearing a blue Polo shirt and white shorts. Their discussion is sketchy. They jumped from one topic to the other. But more on logging operation than on any mild talks.

⌣

Jemes leaned towards the body, still could not believe his wife was gone. His solace is his comforting thoughts – *this is life, it's short but precious. Short to have decent dreams and precious that sometimes we forget that one day we'll die. What an illusion.* Probably the very reason some people entertained a dissipated life. Some devoted their time and money to food, drinks, and entertainment. They want to enjoy life to its *fullest* before boarding their coffin, where one's flesh will eventually decompose and become nutrients for the plants.

Jemes holds tightly to his daughter; they already missed a beloved member. 'Edna, your mother was gone. She's gone...,' Jemes cried. In his mind, he can still recall the days when Edna was a baby, and he would carry her on their way to the garden.

Seven-year-old Edna will have to live without her mother. Though her father is alive, life will lose its balance, like a bird with a broken wing. The ordeal of losing a loved one will be a lifetime scar.

⌣

The canoe slowly approached the wall of the ship from the western side of the ship to avoid being spotted from the mainland - which they tried. Speechless, mouth agape, they felt so small by the size of the ship.

'Largest structure I have ever seen.' Alo was amazed as if he just seen a giant – sinister. The only largest structure he could relate to is the six-storey building in Honiara city. But this one is different. The size is massive, and the fact it floats is even more bizarre to imagine, especially for Alo who never had a chance to study basic science, let alone the *Archimedes principle*. This 75,000 deadweight tonnage is not huge by standard comparison. There are specially designed bulk carriers that can transport up to 400,000 DWT.

'How will we land?' Alo anxiously queried, felt so small by the size of the ship.

'Move closer, move closer.' Bernard directed him with no clue of how and where to dock.

'Over there.' A deck crew leaned on the parapet of the deck, and pointed towards the metal frame. They steered the canoe, trying not to ram the canoe into the wall of the ship. To their comfort, the canoe bobbed along with the waves.

'See. The ladder is there,' Bernard said. 'Slow-slow.'

Slowly the canoe aligned with the lustrous metallic flank of the ship.

'I got it,' Bernard said. He caught the wrought iron frame and maneuvered the canoe to a berth, timing the oscillation of the waves. As soon as the canoe ascended to the desired height, he leapt off. Hands gripped tightly at the metal frame like a frog.

'Pass me the bag,' Bernard said. He grabbed the bag and ascended the ladder. A head protruded from the top of the stairs.

44

Dan watched out to the sea. Two approaching figures distracted him at a distance. He stood up, stretched his shoulder, and spied closely with heightened interest. As they moved closer, he could tell they have something important to say.

Dan kept an eye on them as they approached. 'Good morning boys.' The two boys stopped as if hitting an imaginary wall and stared at each other for a second.

'You come for someone?' Dan scanned their pallid faces. They are both in their early teens.

'We want to report to Tetere Police,' One of the boys said.

Hearing this, Dan continued to study their faces for resemblance. He glanced one more time before adding.

'You two from?'

'Aola.' The other one responded, and swallowed, ready to spew out the details.

'Follow me.' Dan led them to his tent.

With no time to spare, one boy blurted out. 'A man was killed. Just this morning.'

'What-where?' Dan's face petrified, at what he had been expecting from the faces.

'Chief Jonah.' The other added as if competing to give out details.

Dan begged them to continue, which they did.

'Found his body out in the sea, floating in a canoe.'

The revelation of this mysterious death raises the hair on Dan's back. *Killed? By whom? And why? Do they know he's a Police officer? Crap, no way. If they knew who he is, it's a game over.* Somehow, he is right. Nothing hides, especially the devil bird that patrolled the night like an invisible drone.

'Chief Jonah? Aola?' Dan tried to register the name.

'Yes.' They responded thoughtfully. Eyes locked on Dan, probably shocked to see how black he is.

Dan never met Chief Jonah before, and in his job, he is obliged to know all the key characters around the area. Church leaders, tribal leaders, youths, and of course, village chiefs. As the rule of thumb, everyone has a story to tell in any happening. Police know this well. That is their strategy - they see through many eyes, as they said.

'I am glad you report, 'Dan said. *That's what everyone should do. Report any incident, isn't it that simple? Report to the local authorities, be it the police or other private companies like Pacific loggers.* But that is not the case here, locals are scared as a cat to involve the police directly. Police usually learned from a third party. Oftentimes, their presence is simply to verify and make proper report for the incident. Especially in these areas, where tribal feuds are common, reporting to the police is perceived as putting oneself in a trap.

'We want you to report it. To the Police.' Knowing that the company is equipped with a two-way radio. On top of that, it has a direct line of contact with Police.

'I will. Give me some more information. This will help the Police to speed up the investigation. ' Dan looked at a distance, where security guards banded together, trying to get the gist of what is going on. 'Has the body sustained any injuries? How did he got killed?'

With eyes at each others face, they both rapped details out at different course. Sensing this gawkiness, one stops, leaving the other to continue. 'Don't know but suspect someone is responsible.'

Dan studied the reactions of the two faces, trying to extract the details from them.

'Pierced his neck with a knife.' The other completed the sentence.

Dan turned pale instantly. It's all bad news. Sorcery at Ghombua, killing at Aola. Damn it. *What's this place going through? A devil intermediation? Are these nuisances coordinated? If so, then there must be a mastermind somewhere. Smiling his best now.*

Dan jotted something in his notebook, no time to hide his true profession as police, prompting his colleagues to wonder.

'They should report it to Tetere Police, not here.' The other security rationalises the urgent call.

'They call for help,' Dan responded vaguely.

'A man killed?' Lieutenant stammered for detail. He glued the microphone to his mouth, his bulky structure stood out of the swivel chair.

'Someone from Aola. Yes.' Dan answered. '*Chief Jonah Pelu.*' He allowed the message to establish in Lieutenant's head, while he spied around the vicinity of the camp. Osama and the other security guards chew betel nuts and share cigarettes. A routine practice that occupied at least half an hour after every two or three hours of work.

'Chief of Aola?' Lieutenant Kilua's radio is dead silent for a while. He pondered on the news, how the events turned out overnight. 'Have mercy on us. We need help here.'

'Found dead this morning. Stabbed at the neck.' Dan looked at his watch which registered 10:00 am sharp.

'I am taking this report seriously. A team will dispatch soon.'

'It's a murder case.' Dan stooped down.

'We'll do an autopsy,' Lieutenant interjected. 'I will call Colonel McColl to be part of this mission.'

'Tell me.' Lieutenant voice echoed again. 'How's the situation there?' Paused, followed by 'the bandits, sorcery, roadblocks?'

'It's like a tropical cyclone every day, one cannot go to sleep and dream in peace.' Dan exhaled tediously, staring out at the ship. He squinted to see clearly, seeing one canoe approaching the ship.

45

I t took Tetere Police forty-five minutes to reach *Tuvu* bay. The phantom black 75HP Mercury engine powered the white ray boat, tearing waves apart like a zipper, trailing a stream of spume.

Officer Brian slowed down the engine, 'Adeade village,' he announced. Next to him is Officer Julie, occasionally shoved as the boat hit the waves. Two IPMT officers occupied the seats in front of her.

'*Tuvu* logging camp.' Officer Julie felt an urge to talk, pointing to the shore.

Colonel McColl looked around, balancing his wide brimmed sun hat from being blown off. He wore a blue life jacket vest, buckled tightly around his torso. 'Your colleague based here?'

'Right. Officer Peter.' Julie cautiously nodded her head, looking towards the shore, then to the rolling mountains inland. *Coward.* She thought to herself, regretting the scar on her shoulder.

'This would be more of a vacation than a vocation.' McColl grinned, eyes leveled with the shoreline, observing the smoke billowing from the camp, a scene of an abandoned battled field replayed in his mind.

'*Vulelua resort*. Used to be packed with tourists.' Julie orientated her first-timers. McColl and his female colleague lingered to admire the abandoned beaches.

'I could spend my remaining life here,' the female IPMT officer said.

'Closed down,' Julie said.

'Crisis halted everything, a good lesson for this country.' McColl raised his eyeglass for a clear look. His colleague is busy snapping photos from her Nikon *Coolpix* at all possible angles she could manage.

'Aola. 'Julie pointed into the bay. 'We will land at the clinic.' Officer Julie instructed the driver. A small crowd formed, expecting their arrival. Officer Brian maneuvered the boat towards the wharf, then throttled down, leaving the boat to bob on the waves, aiming towards the landing site.

'This is it,' Julie announced, scrutinising the faces, eavesdropping on the local dialect. Her spine stiffened when she saw a man with a black scarf on his head.

The interior of the ship is sophisticated, despite being commodious. The corridors extended out to different sections of the ship. Bernard scanned the empty corridors, and then picked one with an arrow pointing to a kitchen. He was halfway down when a voice called.

'Stop!' A Chinese man in a white uniform rushed forward, a deck officer. 'No go, no – go – ok?' He looked suspiciously at Bernard and then at Alo. 'What you here for, you?'

'We want to sell something,' Bernard said, tapping the bag. 'We have fruits, bananas, and Papayas.'

'Come, I see?' The Chinese ordered in a monotone that is less appealing.

Bernard raised his eyebrows and signaled his colleague to open the bag. The Chinese lunged forward for a look; he took his time as if unsure what he is looking for. He finally nodded his head, satisfied with what he saw.

'O'light, follow me.'

The mess is partially filled. The tables are set up in three rows, facing the kitchen. From the numbers placed on the tables, there are more than ten tables. He saw a table tagged with the number 12.

Asian aroma filled the air. If one thing to know about the Chinese, it's their ingrained passion for food. The moment they sat down with their soup and chopsticks; they lost concentration on what is happening around them. This is the magic of food every culture around the world embraces in different ways. Food is more than filling up the stomach with starch and fibers, it weighs its own social-cultural values in all traditions. It's reasonable and proper why different cultures kept their recipe a valued secret.

He led them to a compartment behind the mess. On their way in, they overheard distinctive language spoken noisily as if debating who will finish his food first. Whatever they are saying, it must be about the food or the work. They furtively strode past the mess; trying not to get the diners' attention.

They were ushered into a room, more like storage, a table blocked them from reaching the wall. The room is unattended, giving Bernard an ounce of confidence to negotiate.

'Nei hou.' A voice echoed in Bernard's ears, hello in Cantonese. He darted around for the source of the voice. A flabby-face figure in a similar white uniform appeared behind the walls. The walls are partitioned, splitting the room into two tiny compartments.

The second Chinese turned towards his counterpart, talking in distinguished language, detailing the intention of the visitors. They exchanged a few words, heads nodded in unison, followed by glances towards them. This caused Bernard to feel edgy about the content of their conversation.

'You want these?' Bernard intervened to cover the awkwardness, pointing towards the bag, but they continued with their conversation, ignoring their presence. Bernard scanned the interior of the room, drab and lifeless, at least, that's what he is thinking. A note was pasted onto the wall, written in Chinese. Not sure if it is a notice or a to-do-list. Either way, it doesn't matter. They need to deal with these people on the sly and get the hell out as soon as possible.

After a lengthy discussion, the one who ushered them spoke, 'Noodles o'light?' He shared his prompt look between Bernard and Alo, and tried to coax them with cheap junk.

Not a word. Bernard adjusted his jacket on his shoulders.

The Chinese cleared his throat and continued. 'You give us - we give you noodles. O'light?' He tried to break it down as if they don't understand his first response.

'No o'light-ok?' Bernard looked at him quirkily, knowing his colleague doesn't speak English. Or worse if he's deaf.

Bernard peeped towards the door, then at the other Chinese. 'You want this? 'He gestured an ILY sign with his hand. The Chinese looked agitated; something is going on. Something valuable or illegal. But the beauty about the latter is that - they are like hotcakes. Pornographic materials, guns, drugs. It's all illegal to trade without a license, but before we realised it, these vices transformed into fortunes.

'Me see again?' He took a step forward.

'Good stuff.' Bernard opened the bag slightly wider. This time, the other Chinese nodded his head and talked to his colleague. Probably he smells something fishy going on. They both nodded their heads and agree on a point. The other talked in Chinese and rushed back into the room where he had appeared from.

This created a rotten feeling for Bernard. A cold sensation started to weigh down his poise. *Stay calm - stay calm.* He assured himself, maintaining his composure and alert. It's a dangerous game they are playing.

'What's happening? Where's he going?' Bernard asked, suspicious.

Alo hadn't spoken a word since they entered the ship. Bernard handles all that.

The sounds of incoming footsteps prompted Bernard to weigh up his duffel bag and ensure it is properly closed. Two Chinese rushing in with determined steps.

Hell no.

46

Bernard peered towards the door and saw the second Chinese appear again. He is carrying a black nylon briefcase. Whatever in it, it denoted one thing for Bernard. The interest is there, he just needs to nurture it like a seed. No rush.

Bernard eyed the other Chinese closely; short, stout, with hair meticulously trimmed above the ear line like North Korea's totalitarian leader, Kim Jong-un.

'You give us what we want, we give you, Ok?' Bernard pictured if he could strike a good deal with these people. It would be a lot of money knowing these people spend most of their time travelling around the world, and no time to spend. *A classic job*, he thought. The incoming footsteps disturbed his thoughts. The Chinese pointed to the briefcase. Bernard took a step closer to have a look inside.

He pried the briefcase open.

'Yes - open. Open.' The Chinese face melted into a smile, trying to beef up the conversation.

Bernard shuffled his fingers through the pile of glossy magazines and DVDs. Some in English, but most in Chinese, which they barely understand. He could tell from the pictures; it's all erotic stuff. Bernard stood up and glanced at the two. At least one of them can speak English well. *Damned porn-addicts.*

'We do not want these stuff,' Bernard blurted out. 'We want money. Money-ok?' He looked at Alo who remain silent, posing a suspicious look.

'Let's make a fair deal.' Bernard stepped forward. These people need visual explanation. A kind of product promotion talk. They knew the actual value of the goods as their craving for it is profound. It's just they do not want to spend money, no one gets broke on this floating island. Or maybe they tried to play petty tricks on them, so they can get it through some trivial arrangements.

Bernard looked boldly at the one whom he thought had a genuine interest. His English is terrible though, forget the English lexicon, drug dealings, and illegal activities do not require one to be fluent in English. Chinese and Russians had been involved in this lucrative trade for centuries-dealing with addictive drugs, cocaine, heroin, opium, methamphetamines, and a battery of other illicit substances. They ride on the laws like a bicycle.

Bernard stooped motionless; he felt something itchy with a numb sensation. Like a mosquito bite. Or is he being pinched from the back? His vision quickly blurred which also noticeably drained his energy. He wriggled to gain his strength, and turned towards Alo, but the feeling is irresistible. His feet gave way to his weight. The content of the 50cc syringe content plunged Bernard into a coma.

The Toyota Cruiser came to an abrupt stop. Suiono jumped out and marched towards the scalars who were busily jotting down in their tally sheets-inspecting the logs. Seeing Suiono, they switched off the chainsaw.

'Can I see?' Suiono turned to the one holding the clipboard. He flipped through the list repeatedly.

'1-3-2-0.'

'That's what already loaded.' Came the response. 'Eh-we- we still to load about five - five hundred.' The one with the sheet explained, looking to the remaining piles. He is the chief scalar, swiftly running his pen down the list.

Solomon Islands government exported round logs on an average of 800,000 cubic meters round logs per annum, exceeding the sustainable harvesting rate many times over. That is not what Suiono had in mind, he is more interested in dollars that will be converted from the numbers.

'Can I talk to the stevedores?' Suiono requested. He turned and saw Deve busily running a tape measure along the heaps of logs. 'Hi Rasta!'

Deve returned a grin.

'Call Mo,' the one with the radio announced, handing him the microphone of the two-way radio strapped to his waist.

'Tuvu log pond, over.' The radio made some noise, and a voice cracked a response.

'Copy. Go ahead.'

'This is Suiono, Operation Manager. Can I talk to Mo?'

'Speaking.'

'Hi Mo. How long will it take to complete loading?' Suiono held down the radio to his chest and waited for a response. After a second or two, the radio breaks into a responding voice.

'Twenty-four hours, depending on the loading.'

'Including the night shift?' Suiono questioned in a demanding voice.

'Yes, Sir. We only have one badge, otherwise-.' The voice from the radio continued. 'The ship will only berth for three days.'

'I know. Let me know if you need our help.' Suiono lowered the radio. As an operation manager, he has to ensure the loading of the logs meets the targets. The ongoing disturbance from the surrounding communities is counter-productive, and Suiono is anxious about the loading time, to complete before another dispute surfaces.

'Will ensure loading completed tomorrow - am, over.' The radio dropped silent.

'Excellent job boys.' Suiono praised the scalars. He stopped when he saw a boat speeding across the bay.

'Police.' Someone said.

47

The body was placed on a wooden bed, the height of a kitchen table, covered with a white cloth. Ambient heat and moisture had done punitive work on the body - a pale ash color and dry due to excessive loss of blood. The lifeless eyes were wide open, and the mouth crumpled sideways. The limbs were dislocated from their sockets and probably strangulated with an elastic material such as rubber to restrict the flow of blood. It's a sorrowful death to imagine.

Nothing left that signifies life. Words have been shared about the killing, leaving only lurking fear and anger. The autolysis-*destruction of cells*-promptly took its natural course of breaking down the cells. The process usually starts in the liver, then the brain before the rest of the body.

Taking his life away was not all; his scrotum was also missing, his tongue chopped off; the incision was precise and clean. The killer took his time to demonise the victim before finishing him off.

Colonel Addam McColl gently fitted a pair of latex gloves into both hands, and meticulously tapped the body. He observed the

193

skin; he tapped the chest and side of the corpse, as if to check any remaining cells that may still spark life. It's an external autopsy, he is not qualified to conduct an internal examination. The pathologists and medical doctors are trained for that, and which often the case, involves surgery and removing affected organs for minute analysis. Or even cutting open the scalp of the head using the vibrating saw, removing the brain from the cranial vault. A tedious technical job. Heaven forbids, he is not going into that detail.

Addam McColl flicked the eyes, clueless as death. 'He was strangulated. Lost a lot of blood.' Colonel McColl frowned. Scenarios played in his head. *How did he get killed? What type of weapons were used? How long does the struggle last?* An hour, by the look of what remains.

A female colleague looked quizzically at the body. She took photos and zoomed at different angles of the body. The scene engrossed her thought, and she soaked her IPMT white polo shirt with sweat.

'Looks like rubber, stopped him from screaming for help?' Colonel McColl observed the mouth, sunken as if he had no gums. 'Involves some struggle.'

Gently, Colonel McColl examined the head. To his surprise, there was a mark on the back of the skull. 'This is the cause of the death.' He pointed at a depressed spot, with a trace of blood that oozed out slowly.

'Looks like some metal,' Officer Julie said.

Colonel McColl assumed, from the appearance of the body, he must have been killed twenty-four hours earlier and immersed underwater to clean out any possible trace of bloodstain. The killer is smart; he knows what he was doing, and could have written a classic book entitled-*how to torture your victim like the devil.* It's truly the work of the devil, they can smell his sweat.

'The relatives said he constructed a canoe.' Officer Brian informed Colonel McColl. 'That'd take days and weeks.' Officer Brian has been talking to the relatives, comforting them followed by a bunch of questions. Unlike Officer Julie, Officer Brian is not a talker. They assigned him as their driver, which he is very good at, both on land and at sea. And like Officer Julie, they are Lieutenant Kilua's right-hand officers. They have the right ingredients of what police officers needed. *Smart and committed.*

Colonel McColl darts around, a single eyebrow raised, an engaging look. 'Can I talk to -?'

The faces were not moved by the words.

'Any relatives we can talk to?' Officer Brian stressed, knowing well there is more to the cause of death. The killer might be around, listening to every word they said. *Sociopath.*

A woman stepped forward and started, 'he said he will return the next day. But he's gone. My papa.' The woman burst into tears, 'he had nothing-no enemies, why-why him…?' She sobbed.

Colonel McColl pointed at the feet. 'Look at his toes.' To their amazement, all his toes have been removed. From his experience as a former Police officer, he never experienced such a level of torturing. Most of the murdered victims he came across were killed and disposed of to be found or decomposed.

Colonel McColl continued. 'Did he talk about any plans, or visit to someone?'

'Yes, he talked about going to Ghombua.' Came the response. The name *Ghombua* dropped a bomb.

'Ghombua? For what?' Colonel McColl queried profoundly.

'He has relatives there.'

A radio call from the walkie-talkie startled Officer Julie. She rushed out through the door to answer the radio call. It's from Officer Peter.

Bernard's eyes blinked. His focus blurred with transient images, buzzing in front of him. *Are these human beings? Where Am I- Am I dead? This place is …where is this?* He blinked, and tried to open his eyes, he was struck with anemia. Some kind of chronic *fatigue syndrome*, but he is too young to be diagnosed with such eccentric diseases. His muscular physique prompted the Chinese to dose him averagely with a narcotic that put him to sleep for an hour.

He trampled forward, semi-paralysis, waving around to gain his balance. He lunged forward one more time, with a strenuous effort. He opened his right eye, left eye as if testing the indicators of a vehicle. He engaged his limbs by shaking them; try to stand up, but his feet won't allow it. They tied him to a metal bench with lockable fittings bolted to a wall. *Stupid. Who are these idiots? What on earth do they think they are? Lunatics.*

'Let me out!' He screamed at the empty walls of a small cubicle, the size of a bathroom. *Am I in jail? Do these people send me to Tetere?*

He studied the interior closely. Only one table and the rest are boxes. This is not Tetere, definitely not. 'Alo!' He regained his composure, 'Alo! Alo!' His voice drowned in the small room. He shouted one more time. 'Alo, you there?!' The louder he shouts, the sillier he looks, hearing his own voice bashing back into his eardrums. This is terrible, no one wants to be trapped in this cubicle like a prisoner.

He seized on the approaching footsteps, 'Alo?' The footsteps were of a man, no mistake of that. It took five seconds before he recognised the face, he was the one they were supposed to strike a bargain with. Memories slipped off his mind. He felt dizzy and black out into a coma.

He glared at him, which he defiantly ignored. 'Where is my friend?' The Chinese winked his eye.

Idiot! Bernard hated the figure and his pretentious act. He wore short khaki trousers, without a shirt, exposing his oversized tattoo, which extended from his right shoulder through to his chest. A creepy crawling creature with scales, which he presumed to be a dragon. He's Chinese, it's not a coincidence.

In a befuddled state, Bernard examined him suspiciously. 'Where's my friend?' Bernard scowled. No response from the Chinese. Bernard recalled him as the one who doesn't speak English.

'Where's my friend? And get-me-out!' Bernard attempted to use sign language to send the message. The words seemed to have landed on a concrete wall. The Chinese disappeared in haste from the room with an *-I don't care* look.

They restricted his movement with a seamless chain- hog-tied to a metal frame. The Chinese disappeared without a word, and *probably going for a key. Or is he checking me out before injecting another dose?* The mere thought is annoying. *What time is it? How long am I in this cage?*

The footsteps approached the room again. Two figures appeared behind the door. *Great, now release me.* He recognised his friend at the very instant.

Bernard hissed. 'Hey, what is going on?'

The Chinese funneled towards the door, produced a key from his trousers pocket, and free Bernard. 'You go now, go!'

'You speak English?' This annoyed Bernard more, hardly blinking his bleary eyes, furious how the Chinese pretended not to understand English. *You are such an ass.*

'Shhh-.' The Chinese interposed, commanding Bernard to shut up. 'This way!' They are ushered towards the exit door, one that faces the mainland.

Bernard traipsed as if he lost ten kilograms from his body-drained and disoriented. 'Our bag?' He inarticulately stated, but the Chinese keep walking like an earless ghost.

'Stupid snake eater.' Bernard cursed; the whole thing is in a crimp. They walked past a group of Chinese crews busied talking in an incomprehensible tone. Their usher led them along the deck of the ship, prompting Bernard to enquire. 'Hey, you, where's our bag?'

'Come-here...' came the mass of confused response.

Gaining extra energy, Bernard fast-forwarded. 'Hey, our bag.' He raised his hands to indicate a load on a shoulder.

'Here.' He open a door and produced a canvas duffel bag, as if already pre-planned their exit. 'Go, go-quick.' He ordered them, pointing towards what looked like a metal frame. A ladder by random guess.

Upon reaching the metal ladder, Bernard looked down only to see the menacing surface of the choppy ocean waves splashing against the wall of the ship. 'Where's our canoe?'

'Down, down.' The Chinese stood back and pointed out in a showy pose.

'I don't see it.' Bernard fired back, regaining an iota of energy. *I'm going to punch your damned slitty eyes.* He shot a furious look that prompted the Chinese to beam a vacuous smile. Chinese are not good at smiling, but whenever they managed one, it's either the sweetest or the bitterest. The smile of this Chinese is that of the latter.

Without a word, Alo stood helplessly, accepting whatever the outcome. Not for Bernard, he is the guy who does not tolerate defeat, not in his trait. Eyes scanning the sea like a bird, he saw a canoe drifting meters away.

'Pull...' the Chinese ordered, pointing at the rope that have been replaced with a longer one to avoid the canoe from ramming the wall of the ship.

Without wasting more time, they strode for the ladder. Bernard took the lead. He was on the fifth step down when a voice roared in his ears.

'Bernard!' The voice dropped a bomb, prompting Bernard to peep up the ladder. The face is not of Alo, it's whiteface in a blue-hued uniform. 'You're under arrest!'

48

The mourners positioned themselves around the grave. Elder Moses limped forward and sobbed his introduction, 'we gather here today, to farewell to our loved one -,' he wobbled. 'Death is human's mystery, our common enemy, whether you are rich or poor, young or old, your time will come. It's human's oldest question, why death? Why?' he looked at the mourners, wiping off mist from his eyes.

The normal proceedings followed the sermon; life sketch and eulogy were read out. This prompted the mourners to nod their agreements. Some lamented how little Edna will cope after losing her mother. Some sentiment for Jemes as he will now have to live as a single father. Or if possible, he can remarry somehow, but life with Merre was over.

Many pondered on life's oldest wonder. *Life is short, it's a lie. All we have done under the sun is temporary. Like mist, here today and gone tomorrow.*

A few meters behind the mourning crowd are Pegoa and Chief Ko'oga. Pegoa is wearing an island shirt, arms across his chest. The

199

topic had little relevance to the funeral service. It's about the logging operation. As the operation progresses, more forested land will be combed out, and Pegoa knew well. He was looking forward to engaging more landowners to sign up for their land.

'We missed one of our members.' Chief Ko'oga looked toward the grieving relatives.

'I felt sorry for Jemes,' Pegoa sympathised.

Chief hushed, considering how bad life could get. Unspeakable. "Chief Jonah of Aola also passed away.'

'I heard they found his body floating out in the sea, right?' Pegoa asked.

'Yes, in a canoe. He is a good craftsman.' Chief Ko'oga admitted.

'It's sad to see good people die without being aged.'

'I will leave for Aola after this burial. I should have left this morning, but you know, we also lost one member of our community.' Chief Ko'oga exhaled loudly, shook his head as if to say *what more of this life?*

'I remembered him visiting you last month, isn't it?' Pegoa queried.

'With his two grannies, right.' The sentence was followed by a long silence; tears formed in Chief Ko'oga's eyes. He turned towards the mourners.

'Elder Moses is good at his job, his sermons are short, lively, and touching.' Chief Ko'oga, added, then he tweaked his grey beard. They both admired his sermon; he talked about soul and body when a person dies, life after death.

'Jemes already received the first royalty payment.' Pegoa added with a diversion of the topic.

'This is news. Sad, he received the money and have to go through this loss. It's a pity.' Chief Ko'oga looked at the flowers thrown into the grave. What a coincidence. Flowers symbolise life, bloom in the morning, and fade with the setting sun.

A hymn was sung as the coffin was lowered into the grave.

Pegoa continued after a break. 'First lot he received is the entry fee.'

'How's the issue with the landing fee?' Chief Ko'oga queried out of interest.

'Bossman discussed with them. They received their demand.'

'That's good news. The company can now operate smoothly.'

'Just between us, the company is planning to expand southwards, you will be fortunate.' Pegoa announced it buoyantly, seeing the potential logging grids in his head.

'Umm-that is what I am about to ask you,' Chief Ko'oga said, glancing towards the grieving relatives, weeping uncontrollably and louder. Jemes put his hand around his daughter, he wept out the loudest and is comforted by his relatives, moving him away to clear the space for those shoveling the ground to cover the coffin.

'The company provided the coffin,' Pegoa interpolated.

'Only a man with a noble heart can do such thing,' Chief Ko'oga said.

'Of course, he has a heart for the people.' Pegoa continued, then swerved to logging again. 'We had a brief discussion about that. He wants to see landowners around the logging consent area.' Pegoa bends down to chase the flies from his legs.

'This is a chance to benefit from our land,' Chief asserted. 'I will talk with my relatives at Aola first.'

They watched as the crowd slowly dispersed. At the distance, a boy with a bag ran towards Jemes' house with a group of children in tow.

'Commander,' someone shouts.

A group of children compete for space, running with a bag. Inside it is a parrot, heads tilted sideways, and eyes protruded. It had been choked, placed in a bag, and thrown into nearby bushes.

Bernard felt his throat dry like scales, mouth voluntarily opened, arms gained weight, and he gripped to the metal frame. The sound of the outboard motor engine added weight to the gravity. He turned to see a boat, blue and white checkered.

Bernard considered options of jumping into the sea and diving like a dolphin, emerging somewhere they cannot see him. Or better still, hide under the breaking waves. All the wistful thinking added up to nothing. Left with no option, he gave up to the Police.

It took Bernard forever to reach the boat. The female officer snapped a handcuff and clicked to its lock at a breakneck speed. 'You will plead your case at Tetere.' She pushed him down forcefully.

Bernard convulses into defeat. Worst, the smell of the sea fused with his sweat is excruciating to his nostril.

'Remain silent, or we will charge against you every word you say.' Officer Julie's eyes locked on the most wanted man - the bandit leader. 'You are going to jail, that's where a loser like you belongs to.' Officer Julie snapped a derogatory line, an act of subtle revenge.

Bernard ignored the order, and turned sideways towards the shore, a barge racing with time. A canoe is toed and rolling on waves behind the barge. What he saw is annoying still. A man in a cowboy outfit waved with a taunt. 'Have a great day.'

Bernard recalled what the rebel leader said about the man.

49

A new day dawned. As an embraceable practice, the villagers started their day as usual. Say their morning prayers before committing more sins, be in the gardens, playground, or at the river. For Jemes, the day entails a series of days he will miss his wife. He sat at his verandah, staring vacantly at the heap of fresh soils forming a grave. In his hand is a written note, it contains a sinister code.

It's a one-page letter, written in a blue pen. He can read nothing besides recognising the letters that represent himself. The writer signed off his identity. Receiving a letter from an unknown individual could brew mixed feelings, and if the content is not known, it's irksome. *Is this a compliment or a threatening letter? If it's the former, then why not directly come to him.* In most cases, the latter is the one that usually involves hideous intentions. He meditated upon it for a while, as if the meaning will appear on the wall.

Forget it. A lot of important things to think about. Not this worthless piece of paper. He flipped the page over, not surprised to find it blank. He tapped his fingers on it and studied the letter by counting the lines of writings- twenty-seven lines, with few lines skipped. The words are all connected, in spidery shapes, round, strokes, vertical lines, some dropped lower than the average lines. It's like a non-Chinese seeing the Chinese script for the first time, it's all symbols clamped together.

For Jemes, like everyone else in the community, reading is a foreign prodigy, it's only introduced to them, and it's reasonable to say it's not embedded in their culture. Like money, it's extraneous. Superfluous. Locals have survived centuries without being formally educated in foreign ways. That's naturally accepted. Reading and writing are seen as a foreign concept, and always lash out on the imposed threats as experienced with the missionaries, traders, blackbirding, and recently loggers. But that is where literacy gripped its fingers deep.

If one cannot find the meaning of formal education, what's the point of sending children to school? Besides, to be educated requires money, a lot of money. In a parallel context, money is a foreign medium for exchanging goods and services. Jemes parents were averse to foreign systems, including formal education. If they sent one of their children to school, it would be only for a few months, and would not spend a single dollar on tuition fees. Only their daughter completed half the primary school curriculum, which was only guaranteed with the support of a local teacher -who'd later become her husband.

To Jemes' parents, man will have to work and sweat, not sit idle like a tethered pet. They valued their resources more than anything else-revered nature in place of divine being, and it does work perfectly well for them. They inherited a big fertile land, abundant with fruit trees, flowing rivers and streams, and a culture that defined themselves.

Plant taro, yams, build big houses, and raise a family. That's life. Jemes recalled the exact words his father used to say. *We only do things we survived on. So why attend school, it's a waste of time.* Jemes stared at the floor, replaying the scenes in his head. He leveled the letter to his face, and locked his eyes on it for seconds, still, it makes no sketchy difference. It's like staring at a starless night for solutions, you only got lost in it. *Who should I talk to?* His thoughts tick the list of his relatives' database.

Bernard? He sighed. *Why chooses that life?*

Sister Jenny, tears formed in his eyes. *I miss you, sister.*

Head bow, tears beaded down his cheek. *Merre why, why?*

Problem is like an arrow shot at you, either you survived it or got killed, whichever way, that's life. Jemes just got hit by an arrow, and he survived.

Rumors are like food, delicious when shared. But unlike food, rumors can spread like a virus. That's what happened in Ghombua after the death of Merre. Everyone was talking about an *unknown* man seen around the gravesite a couple of times.

A few eyewitnesses came up with their versions. Many agreed, that the perpetrator was somewhere watching. A group of women doing their laundry in the river, like everyone else, also swamped with the rumors.

'Jemes saw a man, tall, with big beard.' A plump woman started and seemed to be obsessed with the fluff. The others looked on, bidding her to continue. 'The night of the burial, he was seen close to the grave, mumbling something before stamping his right foot on the grave.' This statement raised eyebrows.

'The killer is reclaiming his power,' another woman added.

The other women listened with heightened interest.

The plump lady continued. 'He walked away quickly into the nearby bushes and disappeared in the dark.'

'Tall with a beard,' one woman said, which obviously anyone can fit the description. Jemes also is tall with beard. So is Chief Ko'oga also have a long grey beard.

'But why Merre?' came the query that got everyone's attention.

'I bet you don't want to know, because it can happen to anyone,' another woman said.

They looked towards Jemes house. 'It's the logging,' someone whispered. 'They tried to kill Jemes, but not succeed.'

'So, they killed Merre instead?'

'Something like that. It's possible, who knows.' The plump lady continued her role in chairing the discussion.

'But Merre was a different tribe. Why?' More questions than answers.

'It doesn't matter.' They looked around with unsettled minds. 'And the talking parrot too.'

'Yes. Commander,' One woman intervened.

'Sorry. They killed it the day Merre was buried.' They sat speechless as if paid respect to the bird.

'They have relatives in Aola.' Not sure to make a comment or ask a question.

'Yes.' Came the ambiguous response queued in another incident. 'Chief Jonah was killed the night Merre died.'

Eyes projected towards Jemes house. They stopped talking and began calling their children's names when they saw Jemes sitting at his veranda.

50

Little Edna takes her time to sweep around her mum's grave, admiring the flowers she placed at the head of the grave. It has been four days, and she already felt the prospecting emptiness that she will bear for the rest of her life without a mother.

'Dad, can we call church elders to come and pray with us?' she sensed the need for divine intervention.

'Yes, my dear. They will come this evening.' Jemes looked at the grave, coconut trunks are used to construct a rectangular pebble-filled bed. For seconds, he was lost in thought.

'And for commander too?' she carefully places flowers on a heap of white pebbles —a miniature grave of the bird.

'Yes, and for commander too,' Jemes assured, could not express his feelings any longer. He stared at little Edna, thinking how she already missed her mum and her talking parrot. He was deep in thought when his daughter riddled him with another question.

'And when will I resume classes?' Jemes is not ready to talk. The question put Jemes in an awkward position. He has no answer to the question. Or any question of that nature.

Sensing the lack of response, the girl pushed on like an adult. 'We will sit midterm exam week after next week. My friends said they will help me with my classwork.'

'Good. That would be helpful.' Jemes responded without even thinking. Not bad for a standard one kid to talk about education. Jemes don't have those memories to relate to-it's like he has no past with classroom talks. It's not on the list of 'to- do' things as his growing up. He will not continue to live an ignorant life, not for his daughter. He wished he attended school in his young days. He studied his little girl; he can see the face of her mother in her eyes. Smile and sweet as always. That is all he could remember, she was gone.

'Fine, my girl. You must attend school. It's very important.' All he can afford to say, for he doesn't know what school is all about—more like church, maybe. He tightened his grip on the yellow envelope he is holding.

'It's a hot day, isn't it?' Elder Moses twitched around for some comfort.

'It is. The heat of the clouds.' Jemes agreed as if he's interpreting the weather.

'Who could predict the weather anyway?' Elder Moses kindly pushed an empty chair forward. 'Looks like it's going to rain.' Elder Moses eyed his visitor compassionately and folded his hands across his chest.

After a long silence, Elder Moses started. 'Life is a borrowed dream. It belongs to somebody else.'

Jemes nervously dropped his weight, exhausted like an old tractor, which is reasonable for what he had gone through.

'When I lost my first wife, it took me three years to get my thoughts back.' Elder Moses breathed in slowly, 'Prayer is my secret. I prayed over it and slowly everything falls back in place.' The weight of his thought contorted his face. 'It's like a scar that gradually healed, but surely it will keep reminding you of the past.'

Jemes took an eternity to absorb the words. He had a feeling that time heals wounds. And yes, one will have to pray too.

'How's little Edna?'

'She's with her aunty,' Jemes briefly stated in an arid tone. 'I always pray with her. We pray together.' It's been three days after the funeral. He recalled the exact words Elder Moses said at the funerals. *This world is not our home.*

'I am always with you in my prayers. The whole community is.' Elder Moses created a warm, assuring smile as if he tried to say all is well. 'I know it's hard.'

'Thank you. I feel like nothing inside me.' Jemes looked squarely at Elder Moses. The scar on his forehead speaks volumes about his young days. Short and aggressive. Now in his sixties, he committed his life as a devoted church leader. Some villagers marveled at him for holding on to the position without being paid a single cent. It's a sacrifice.

'Time will heal our broken hearts.' Elder iterated. 'Heaven is our home.'

Jemes looked at the scribbling on the walls with pictures -like passing scenes replayed at the back of his head. His eyes settled on a pinned note, scribbling resembles what he had in his hand.

Seconds of silence, 'Well, how can I help you?' Elder Moses moved to the point; his thick eyebrows contorted.

'I – I have one thing.' He produced an envelope from his hand.

Elder Moses studied Jemes for a while, then to the envelope, as if to try to find the right word that connects them both. 'Let's go inside.'

'I know- it's hard for you to accept life now.' Elder Moses sympathetically added, balancing his hands on the rail of the stairs, and slowly limped upward. Elder's house is a two-storey building. Corrugated iron roof and timber walls alternated with sago palm leaves. The ground floor is spacious, enough to hold a conference for twenty people.

'Take a seat here.' He pointed to the chairs in the living room. Elder Moses is a retired school teacher, and so had the opportunity to afford a semi-permanent house. What Jemes still dreams of having.

Jemes struck in wonder, fretted like a child. He handed the envelope to elder Moses. It took elder Moses forever to study the envelope.

JEMES TOKI, GHOMBUA VILLAGE. The blue handwriting was marked on the envelope.

'What is this?'

'I don't know. That's what am here for.'

'Oh, I see.' Elder apologetically accepted. 'Sorry, who gave you this?' Elder started, asking with the tone of an interrogator.

'Nurse.'

51

'I will now smile.' Atkinson puffed his cigarette.

'Yes, you deserve a big smile, 'Lieutenant said. 'Depressed face brings you illness, not healthy for your liver.' He advised as if reading a quote from a Tibetan Dalai Lama's book. He could imagine the smile on his face while cupping the phone to his ear.

'We need to cheer to this great achievement with a few beers.'

'No problem, anytime you want to talk,' Lieutenant agreed. 'I am working on their case now.'

'Brilliant...' Atkinson can now put the thought of bandits to rest. A spark of adrenaline rushed through his thoughts. He put on a deserved smile, knowing it is also the medicine for the heart. Accomplishing a smile involves dozens of muscles, it's a natural cure. It transformed one into another state of human existence as experienced during meditations. That's another book, anyway.

After seconds in cloud number nine, Atkinson enquired. 'Excuse me, did you say someone killed?'

'I guess I shouldn't spoil your day.' The line dropped dead.

The news of the killing got Atkinson's mind revolving as if having a terrible nightmare.

He produced an opened envelope from his drawer and studied the undersigned. The letter is only a week old. Atkinson recollected his dad's advice. *The ground can be damned slippery at times.*

He's lenient enough to stare at the letter. It's a page and a half long, thick and dense with paragraphs. *The logging operation will not move eastwards, only if my eyes are closed....* This is the sentence that got Atkinson's mind exploded. *Only if my eyes are closed.* It's a local proverb, when someone says it, it means NO with capital letters. A synonym for never.

Atkinson revolved his thought on the prospects, the letter is more of a threat than a dispute. He produced a cigarette and lit it up, puffing madly as always when he is under pressure. *But why worry?* He comforted himself. *All threats are now gone. Bernard is in jail, and the writer of the letter was now gone.*

For a minute, Elder Moses' lips moved magically, not a sound. After digesting the content, he blew his cheeks in an unpropitious gesture. 'This is a call for a land hearing.' The words finally vented out with pounds of queasiness through Jemes' body. He peaked at the note indifferently.

'Who? What?' Jemes couldn't even decide on a single word. His eyes lighted up with dry emotions.

Elder Moses checked the door and continued. 'I don't understand. No date, fake name.' Elder Moses thinks over the name. For his sixty plus years, he had not come across such a name. 'Ghani Bua?' He switched his stare to Jemes, their eyes met.

Jemes skewed his head. "Ghani Bua? Can't be. I mean...,' his stomach churned like boiling water. 'Ghani Bua.'

'Sorry, who handed you this letter?' Elder Moses posed the question again.

'The nurse.'

'You should have asked her.' Elder frowned. 'Whoever wrote this letter knows you.'

Jemes gave an unconvincing gaze, brooding with silence.

'One, he knows you. Second, he used a third party to conceal himself. It's obvious.'

No response from Jemes besides ambiguous nodding of the head. He gawked at the wall, more writings. *Heaven help me.*

The vehicle exited the main gate and sped up along the highway. Sensing the emptiness in the car, the driver turned on the radio. A live coverage on the Australian and New Zealand soldiers led intervention dominated the air. The vibration of his mobile phone snatched his attention.

'Addam McColl's phone, hello'

'It's me, Lieutenant Kilua.' He paused for a cue from the other end.

'Right, Lieutenant, how's it?' Addam McColl confirmed the voice, heavy as stone.

'I had looked through the report.'

'Lieutenant, I am driving. Give me a second.' Addam McColl pulled over instantly.

'I have looked through the postmortem report, and I have a question.' He paused; pages flipped. 'You mentioned the killing occurred six to ten hours before pushing him out to the sea.'

'Right. No trace of blood on the body. Even the canoe was clean.' He eyed a passing vehicle. 'The killer somehow knows the victim.'

'Excuse me?' Lieutenant Kilua's voice twirled like a tornado.

'He was led out from his garden hut, by someone the victim trusted-away from his comfort zone.' Addam McColl glanced at the passing vehicles and continued. 'This gave the killer time to execute his anger.' Another vehicle passed, a white pick-up truck passed by, overloaded with passengers.

The response came forth with a long sigh. 'You're right, this killing is not an accident. It is well-planned and executed like a professional.' He used the word *professional*, though he thinks a better word should be used instead. 'Scrotum and penis cut out.'

'Know what?' Addam McColl responded with eyebrows flicked apart. 'It's very unlikely to transport a dead body four kilometers down the river.'

'Meaning?'

'That's it. He was alive and walked down to the coast. I am convinced the murder scene was somewhere near the river mouth.'

Silence popped involuntarily before Lieutenant spoke. 'River mouth? You could be right on that.'

'Lieutenant. I have an appointment with the Foreign Affairs office in fifteen minutes' time, I need to rush.' He gave a ghost of a smile, knowing his time in the Solomon Islands is coming to an end.

'Ok, thanks for the report, at least we have something to bite on.'

'Lieutenant, can you talk to the landowners,' Addam McColl gave voice to his suspicious thought.

'Sure.' Lieutenant agreed. 'Good news is, we have one here in jail to start with.'

52

'Someone reported them to the Police.' Toxic whispered and darted around at the others.

Stonie was crushed with defeat. 'They were caught while trying to trade for guns.' Eyes locked on the magazines he leafed through.

'Dan reported them.' Toxic spit it out solicitously. The members looked at Osama, as if he was the cause.

'Dan only reports the killing at Aola.' Osama said.

'Whatever you say, it was because of him they were arrested.' Toxic implied.

'Seriously? Is that what you think?' Osama rebuked.

'Who else can? Dan knows the police at Tetere.' Stonie cast his eyes around for seconds, then settled on the glossy page of an *adult* magazine. The statement caught the attention of the team members.

The following seconds were swallowed in silence, staring at the flickering fire, illuminating their shadowy figures. Like the people in the village, they indulged in the rumors about the killings too. But the apprehension of their fellow friends is a different story they are not willing to accept. It's a disease to their thought.

'Someone reported them.' Toxic unwittingly scavenged for details. 'Someone from the company.'

'They entered the ship. Is it that simple?' Osama justified.

'Pee on the Chinese.' Toxic snapped.

'See this Chinese.' Stonie waved a nude photo, laughing guiltily. The laughter lasted for a moment, no words, but that is not all.

Unbothered by the pleasantries, Osama continued. 'You just can't go inside the ship without being seen. Unless they are *Vele* or something.'

Sensing the austere tone of the conversation, the laughter voluntarily vaporised. Eyes compromised, looking at the fire, finding the next word that may bring consolation. As often is the case, extroverts will say the first and the last word in any argument.

'They saw a group of men during the night of the killing.' Toxic swerved the discussion a little. 'They strangled him in his garden hut.'

'Someone saw a group of men?' Deve queried.

'That's what I heard,' Toxic said.

'Killing was at a different location and later paddled the body out to sea.' Nimo reasoned it out. It's a rumor, anyone can throw in his thought like dice.

'And why push him out to sea?' Toxic queried.

'True, why push him into the sea?' Osama adds taste to the thrills and spills.

'So that someone can find him?' Stonie guessed. 'The killer at least has some sense.'

'But leaving the dead body in the garden hut, people can still find him.' Stonie visualised the possibilities. 'Someone will find him after all.'

'Yea, he cannot just disappear, his family will look for him,' Nimo said. Finally, after weeks of working, they managed to sit down together again.

'The corpse is clean, no trace of blood.' Osama adds more thrill to the story.

'Soaking the body in the water overnight will play that trick.' Nimo paused for a puff. 'Smart fool.'

Pitch darkness encompassed them in silence. The machines silhouetted in the dark like monsters, giving him goosebumps. 'It's no ordinary killer, he's a slayer.'

'They suspected Bernard,' Nimo said.

'Bernard?' Stonie queried considerably. 'Not the Bernard I know.' He disputed, knowing Bernard has no enemies, only opponents.

'No one is perfect, circumstances can change things around.' Deve intervened. 'Even ones who fell from the sky.'

'Who falls from the sky?' Stonie lost the lines.

'Lucifer. What do you learn in going to Church?' Deve scoffed.

'Love, not the devil.'

'Well, Church not only taught us about love. Remember Cain and Abel?' Deve said.

Nimo sighed away the argument. 'If the body was soaked in the water, what about crocodiles?'

'Crocodiles don't feed on dead bodies, they only feed on what they killed.' Deve questioned his thought. 'I've learned that from somewhere.'

'Seriously, I don't think vicious creatures can be that selective?' Nimo queried in a probing tone. 'Next time, we'll hear those crocodiles don't eat red meat,' he smirked.

'What do police say?' Toxic interrupted with a twist.

'The white man is said to be an expert,' Stonie added.

'Police just take photos. Funny, they don't even go up to the garden,' Nimo sneered.

Silence crawled into the conversation, except for the flickering fire. The silence was broken when a devil bird flew past straight above them. *Koa-koa-koa.*

'*Vele*, pee on you! We're not scared of you!' Toxic shouted.

Aola community is quiet. The body was buried as it started to emit a putrid odor. As expected of his chiefly status, hundreds of people turned up to pay their last respect. The people came from the surrounding communities, some as far as the eastern tip of the island. No longer will they call upon him for his sagacious advice and the running of the community. As said, heavy is the head who wears a crown, and only a few dares to wear one.

Late Chief's house is a high building. Same size as Chief Ko'oga of Ghombua. But as a Chief, it is not something to mumble over, besides bloodline, one's status in the community can qualify him to the chiefly title. It's not restricted to a specific elite group or tribe. This changed when Christianity was introduced in the early 1900s.

Under the high building, there is a group of men. The elders, who have been endowed with respect to almost reverence. And as the tradition goes, the privileges are in surplus as they were given priority when it comes to accommodation, food, usage of toilet and all essential necessities. Pegoa is part of that group.

The lament tarried on hours end. *Where, how, what, when* and *why* dictated their thoughts. In respect to the chief title he bears, the body would usually leave for days. Acceptably up to four days. Or when the body started to decompose and giving out a fetid smell. For late Chief Jonah's body, they had compromised to one day as the body had been severely wounded, creating multiple openings for decomposition. The *autolytic enzymes* sensed the absence of life and started to destroy the cells.

The villagers have been staying vigilant for the past two days. They left out whatever their tasks were, not even going to their gardens. Mostly it's a form of benevolent respect but fearing the killer who might be moving around with his lethal weapon was intriguing still. The killer isn't stupid; he is smart. He probably stayed with his family at home, assisting his wife in doing the usual house chores. Or maybe disguised himself among the relatives of the deceased, also wondering what he was thinking.

The relatives shared sentiments about how the perpetrator could supposedly plan out his scheme. Like the police, they too speculated their own conclusion, how the scene might have been unfolded. Maybe not one killer, could be a group. This thinking of a band of killers further terrified the women, who discussed among themselves, how scared they are to go out in their bush gardens.

No clue was noticed at the garden hut and the surroundings. The bed was not even folded, as if he would still be there for a few more nights. But something raised suspicion, some of his items were missing. They cannot locate his bush knife. Probably snatched from him before his killing. Who knows, only the killer and the devil know.

The more one thinks about it, the more tangled one's thought get. More questions than answers. Does the incident happen at night or midday? Many claimed the devil possessed man-*Vele* killed him. Others argued it's not *Vele*, a group of killers involved. Whatever the devil was, the question remains.

His three daughters are all married. They knew well how he usually spent his daily life. As he usually told his grandchildren, 'Work till the end of times.' He talks like an evangelist, though he reached only standard three in a Methodist church-operated school.

They knew too, that he will normally spend a week or two working in his garden or crafting a new canoe. Usually, he took his grandsons with him. This time around, he went alone, the reason heaven forbids. Sleeping in his garden hut was not uncommon. It's a practice to console himself after his wife died of pancreatic cancer some years ago. He had gotten used to staying by himself. And recently, without a glimmer of suspicion, he had been watched closely by someone. The killer.

53

Lieutenant Kilua flipped through the printed photos; his jaw dropped. It's a police job, though they already buried the body, the investigation will go on until they pinned down the culprit or are convinced that they exhausted all possible clues for any suspect. Lieutenant Kilua committed himself to that, he can't get enough from the photos scattered on his table, for no obvious reason, he scanned through the photos he filed in his archives. A burnt vehicle at Ghombua, a drowned woman at Ghombua. *Are these events linked to a single perpetrator?* He slumped back on his swivel chair, cupping both hands at the back of his head.

Late Chief Jonah was strangulated and tortured to his death. This is no ordinary killing, it rooted out from one's indignation. And if so, *who? Enemy? Rival? Or an act of revenge? But what was his past life like?*

Like an artist with his paintings, the killer tried to convey a message, but in a vicious way. The neck was pierced with a sharp object the shape of a bayonet, diagonally right through the brain. Similar to the woman that claimed to be drowned a year ago. *Is this a trademark of a single killer?*

The photos were zoomed in from different angles. One photo that robbed his attention is one of his toes, removed from their base. *Scalpel. A sharp surgical knife or blade sharpened for such.* He sighed, so loud that his subordinates turned their heads in unison. 'This is cruel. Satan truly did have a son, and his descendants are nuts.' He was obsessed, googling his memory for past time incidents of equivalent nature. The search came up with no match. He wished they should also take shots of the crime scene. Nothing was heard from the locals about any such suspicious scene that might trigger an investigation. Not a clue.

Addam McColl is right, the perpetrator is a close ally, relative, disgruntled friend - someone he knows and trusted. Who knows, could be a fellow church member who usually sat rows away during services. Whoever he is, he is smart and stupid alike. Smart in a sense that he left no trace behind. Stupid enough that his involvement is obvious; torture is a bold signature of cold-blooded murder.

Land disputes occurred between tribes, and blood relatives who in many cases are family members. Lieutenant Kilua wondered to himself. *The deceased is also a Thibo tribe.*

~

'We have Judas, thieves, opportunists, whatever you wanted to call them.' Elder Moses' words repeated in his head. *'They will always look for opportunities to enter your life. Like a virus, they cannot survive without a host.'* The words resonate more religious than logical to Jemes who knew little about a virus.

Sitting on his veranda, he gazed at the river. It flows with life. There's life in the river. Children are full of life, it's no surprise they enjoy swimming, even if it takes a whole day, ignoring the multiple reproaches chorused by the elders to get out of it. His attention spontaneously switched to the letter, relieved he knew what it holds, still fretting over its implications. Elder Moses revealed the content of the letter but did little or nothing to solve the puzzle. It's like a Guru reading his fate from ancient codes and then handing it back to him undisclosed.

He called for a land hearing. He claimed the land as rightfully his. The letter renounced Jemes right to the land, and claimed the land was stolen. *I am not a thief, who are you to label me one? And no date? What if it's an overdue letter written some ten years ago? If so, what is his motive?* He recalled the words Elder Moses uttered. *'Everyone wants to be a landowner because of logging.'* He sighed longer than usual. *Ghani Bua.*

Jemes gripped the envelope tightly; it was much heavier than when it was sealed. He hated it like a snake. He cannot stomach the prospect of announcing it to his relatives. *If he wants to call for a land hearing, then why hide behind the veil of an alias.* From Elder Moses perspective, of which Jemes agreed, it's not even a name, *Ghani Bua* means *chewing Betel nut.*

The house is empty, little Edna has gone to the river to do the washing with her aunty from her mother's side. *Your family is cursed because you stole my land.* He leaned against the old wooden door, wondering. *What tribe are you?*

Melancholic thoughts crushed Jemes' thought. Parents were long gone. Now he is the head of their family. His wife was recently passed away. His only sister was also gone-drowned. He looked at the river again, shimmering in the sweltering sun. *Is it possible?* He still cannot accept the cause of his sister's death. *Is she truly drowned? Or was it all set up to make it look like drowning?*

Sister Jenny, tears formed in his eyes. *I miss you sister; you are the one that should translate this letter.* Eyes locked on the graves.

Merre, why leave me alone behind. He bends down, tears beaded down his cheeks.

The letter spread open on the floor.

Dear Mr. Jemes Toki,

Land Hearing - Ghombua Land.

This letter is to inform you that the <u>Thibo tribe land</u> you signed is under dispute. From now on, I have to remind you that the above-mentioned land is rightfully mine. You have disrespected my tribe by signing the land for logging without my tribe's consent. According to the law, you are a thief, claiming what is not yours.

Also, I do not know where you originated from, what devil you stand for, or where your sacrificial grounds are. You have no right to Ghombua Land.

If you want to challenge my ownership, I suggest you call for a land hearing, and honestly, I am not afraid to face you in local court.

Mind you, stealing is sin, and the Bible says, the wages of sin is death. If you do not give up the land, your family will be cursed. Let's respect each other and not steal others' land.

Thank you

Yours faithfully

Ghani Bua.

54

I t took Lieutenant Kilua precisely ten seconds of wordless scrutiny before he started.

'My name is Lieutenant Kilua, I am a Police Chief here at Tetere.' The Lieutenant processed the details in his head. 'Sons, we want to build a decent society. A society where mothers and their children, boys, girls, the elderly, and everyone is free from criminal activities. Police alone cannot do it. Police need the support of the communities; chiefs, elders, church leaders, women's groups, youths...' He stopped with a sigh, realising what he said is supposedly relevant to the communities. Not in this interrogation room.

No response came from the two suspects, eyes floating around the bleak room. The size of a twenty feet container, and is scantly furnished. One table and three chairs, ushering in awkward isolation for Bernard and Alo.

Bernard's eyes darted around uncomfortably, depressed as the room itself. At the exit, two security officers stood their guide, unsure if it was part of their job to block the doorway. *Why not just close that damned door, that's what doors for.*

'You two are young fellas. I could call you two as my sons.' Lieutenant Kilua examined the subjects before signaling the guards to close the door. Alo is anxious and worn out, and like Bernard, eager for the discussion to be over as soon as possible. In nineteen years of his life, Alo never came this close to a police officer, worse facing one in a closed room. 'Listen, none of us want to go through this whole thing. If we can cooperate, then it would be over in no time.' The Lieutenant opened his red Manila folder. 'These are reports received from your community.' Eyebrows twisted, try to be considerate like a leader. 'I felt sorry for the community, that's why I must work on this. I have relatives in Ghombua too.' This is his first card. Acquainted himself. When they buy his trust, he will strike like a cobra.

Bernard maintained his composure, a little nervous about the unfathomed outcomes. What would become of them. Definitely jail, but how long? He weighed the prospects in his head. The thought of it is more intimidating than sitting in the room, facing the oversize figure. He can tell Lieutenant Kilua's words portrayed ambiguity. Even his astute pose lacks conviction. Who knows, maybe part of the scrupulous process - a pretentious feat.

'We all want to enjoy life. Not with guns. Don't you?' He shot the question into the ceiling, letting it hang there like a drop of water, ready to land with a splash. 'That's why we sacrifice our lives for this work. Policing is not an easy job, especially on Guadalcanal.' Lieutenant fiddled his fingers on the table as if he could lure them into talking.

You are not sacrificing your life, Lieutenant; you get paid for that. And talking of risk, I love taking risks. Bernard pondered on the words but couldn't find the right note to strike on. He cleared his throat. 'May I ask a question?' cutting the dull talk short.

'Sure.'

'What are we arrested for?' The question though surfaced prematurely, it's on the right stance. And for Bernard, it makes a lot of sense to ask, they had been apprehended forty-eight hours earlier. Since then, nothing was said about their case, besides boring *to remain silent* orders. That begs a question, after all, one cannot docilely remain in silence forever. It doesn't make any sense, *Homo sapiens* are social beings as far as human nature is concerned.

'Good question. We will get to that later.' Lieutenant shot a contemplating look; the question is the least he expected from the members of the group that hit the media like a heatwave. 'I cannot say a thing. It's all in here, the files will speak for themselves,' He responded with a reserved tone. Of all the things in the file, looting and burning of the vehicle is not mentioned, probably its periphery to the killings. But crime is a crime.

'Oh good, because we also have thick files in our head too and might help you with your investigation. Speed things up -.'

The response caught Lieutenant Kilua with repulsion. Lieutenant Kilua managed a grin, sensing an oddity in the tone of the conversation. 'Not sure, but what are you boys doing here in my office?' He remained calm, knowing that he must conceal his frustration by any means. And like weather, Lieutenant Kilua is unpredictable in his approach. His mood is fluid. 'I have forgotten peace because of you boys.' He grimaced, like a master to his servants. 'We all suffered the consequence of the past crisis, it's tough. Not your fault, not mine either.' He candidly advised. 'Time for the gun is over, now it's time for the hoe and shovel.'

Bernard continued examining the interrogator, with muscular arms that can do horrible damage, and someone would have been blind to undermine his potential. Silence follows its natural cue. Lieutenant leafed through the pages. 'See this?' He produced a photo, waving it like a flag. 'Recognised this?' A photo of a dead man. After seconds, they put a name to it as the late Chief Jonah Pelu.

'This killing happened before you entered the ship.' He shot them a penetrating gaze as if expecting a tunnel to form out of their pupils. But that's what police do during interrogation. While making them talk, they drilled into their minds. Eye movements were observed, a vault of a zillion pieces of information if executed well.

'It's a brutal murder, it takes more than one person to do that evil.' Lieutenant briskly stated. 'He's been strangulated, then soaked in water, I guess.'

The two suspects shared hint-less glances. No words.

'Involved some struggles too. See the bruises.' He waved the photo. 'Where were you two before entering the ship?'

'In the village.'

'Village, after the village?'

'We walk to the coast and paddled to the ship.'

'And whose canoe you used?'

'Someone, we don't know -.'

Lieutenant Kilua knows they stole it. 'What time was that?'

Silent. Glances shared. '6 AM. Around that time.'

'On your way to the coast, do you meet someone or saw something suspicious on the beach?'

Delayed response. 'No- we saw no one, nothing.'

'What time do you leave the village?'

'Four, five o'clock maybe.'

'Both of you?'

'Yes.'

'Before departing the village, where were you?' He leveled his eyes at Bernard.

'Sleeping.'

Lieutenant Kilua studied the two subjects, eager to extract something valuable out of them.

'Both of you?'

Heads nodded. 'Look, we know nothing of any killing, trust me.' Bernard said, sensing the Lieutenant tried to wedge them into the scene as if it's the only option.

'What about you?' Lieutenant Kilua shot Alo a disparaging look, noting his impaired sight.

No words. They are not going to answer preprogrammed questions like robots.

'You need to think correctly, son.' Lieutenant Kilua produced a second photo that almost made them faint. 'How's about this?'

Bernard felt his body convulse, not sure whether to run or fight. Taking revenge in a locked room is not an option. Tears formed in his eyes. Seeing this, Lieutenant grinned, assuming his work was a success. 'It's ok, we all made mistakes.' The manipulation of suspects into talking is the key. Every word said can be weighed, and once the suspect starts telling the truth, it's no going back.

'No!' Bernard deranged, banging his hand on the table, not wanting to see the face talking.

'That's his mother.' Alo responded unreservedly

Lieutenant was shocked, as if mistakenly addressing the Pope, Madam. 'I am sorry. I am sorry; I don't mean to ...' Lieutenant observed the reactions. To some extent, he realised, he should not have produced it first. His instinct triggered him to do and to see the reactions.

Bernard nodded understandably. 'Don't believe everything you hear, Lieutenant.' He precipitously got the courage to face him. 'Some village elders are corrupt, heart black as soot, and to hell they are doomed.' Bernard looked with an uncompromising face.

'She was not drowned. She was murdered.' Lieutenant discreetly announced, eyes still at the photo. 'She was poisoned with chemical, causing the veins to splatter.'

'I know.' Bernard interrupted, fed up with the stories. 'I saw it all.' *And how the hell you are not doing your job? Office Police.*

What will become of me? All have gone. All hopes are gone. Jemes stared across the village, only the voice of kids playing at a distance. Birds flying across the village prompting him to recall Commander.
Why do I have to go through this life. He dropped his head and gave a heartfelt cry. This is the life I dreamed of as a child. To be the tribal leader. The weight of the crown he wore is getting heavier each day.

Who should I trust? Jim Pegoa, Chief Ko'oga, Elder Moses. Ghani Bua popped voluntarily. The name made him want to punch the door. He lingered over the name, unsure where to start-- a person with no history, no records, and worse if he even existed. He holds back his anger, knowing he shouldered a responsibility, the leader of *Thibo Malaghai Kiki tribe.*

The passing figures distracted him. A group of men walked past his house, competing with their different paces. He sensed something is brewing, he can tell by their jarring look. Whatever it is, it has to do with the logging operations. A practice that has become ingrained in a few locals taking advantage of the circumstance.

'They are from *Adeade*.' A voice came behind him. He looked to see Stonie standing behind. 'Nephew, what is it?'

'They asked compensation from one of the operators.'

'Compensation?' The word smells like puke to Jemes. 'Again?'

'He took one of their girls,' Stonie continued. 'They demanded five thousand dollars.'

'Five thousand?' Jemes turned pale. The entry fee he received was the same amount, but that was reasonable considering the size of the commodity. 'That's too much for taking a girl.'

'You know those people, known for breaking all records.' Stonie shrugged his shoulder, knowing they were the ones who plagued their communities.

'They brought us a lot of problems. Disputes, compensation, roadblocks...'

The group disappeared behind the bushes. 'It's too much,' Jemes said.

'Crap, I saw that girl vamp the operator,' Stonie said. It's trespass in a broader sense, but when girls are involved, common sense is ruled out.

'You looked tired, uncle.' Stonie puckered his face, pulling his nose.

'Fever. Very bad.' Jemes contorted his face, expressing his condition. 'Come take a sit.'

Stonie is a nephew from his father's side, which means he will inherit a different tribe. But despite the complexity of the tribal systems, Stonie finds comfort in associating himself with the *Thibo tribe* than his own - *Thogo tribe*.

'One just needs to stay comfortable indoors,' Stonie advised as if he were a doctor, pulling an empty chair behind him before dropping his weight.

Jemes has been hibernating for the past days. That's all that makes sense.

After a moment of contemplating, Stonie announced. 'I felt sorry for Merre.' He looked at the grave.

'Life is short, nephew. Death is what we will all go through.' He turned sideways, avoiding Stonie's eyes.

Breaking the awkward silence, Stonie continued. 'Bernard will miss his aunty.'

No response from Jemes, he felt what the sentence implied.

'Dan is not a security,' Stonie continued. 'He's undercover cop.' Stonie exploded it.

'You think so?'

'Everyone knows it.' Stonie darted around suspiciously. 'Bernard and Alo will soon be released. They committed no crime.'

Jemes twitched without a word.

Stonie continued his monologue. 'I am the one who spent most time with him. He only talked about protecting our trees. Our land.' Another side looks. 'Not killing people.'

'They suspected him as the mask man. 'Jemes teased his own confidence.

'I am happy to be a witness for him in court.' Stonie swallowed firmly. 'I am with him at the time of the attack. Someone is framing him up.' He reiterated, as if Jemes is a jury.

Jemes weighed the details in his head.

'I've lost my trust for our big men.' Stonie sneaked another look. 'Uncle, we will weed out those dirty ones. They are pests to our community.' He produced a piece of neatly folded paper and passed it to him. 'This is the report of your logs.'

Jemes ran his eyes at the sheet, speechless. Over a short period, he developed a hatred toward letters. Or any writing for that matter. *Another words-filled page?*

After considering the odds, Stonie read the content. 'One thousand eight hundred and sixty-one cubic meters.'

With mouth dropped open, Jemes beamed. 'And?'

'This is what you expect. 1-8-6-1.' He tossed the paper forward as if it could make any difference. 'Got this from the Log Scalars.' He lied; he sneaked into Deve's tent and stole a working copy.

Jemes turned livid; he leaned forward to take a glance. He understands digits, but when combined with letters, that's when it became a nightmare. 'So how much...?'

'It's sixty-five dollars per cubic meter. Stonie calculated in his head. At least he reached standard four so understands basic arithmetic. He picked up a stick and started scribbling numbers on the ground, before rounding it off in his head. 'It's hundred twenty thousand. That's big money.'

'Belongs to the tribe anyway.' Jemes pondered on the amount. 'I am sorry, I only gave our women the entry fee.' He added as if to say, they are the inheritors of the land. Besides, he wants all to take a piece of the cake.

'Roughly what you expect,' Stonie said. 'Nimo also provided the cubic meters from the logs transported daily.'

'One hundred and twenty thousand?'

55

A bird flapped its wing and crumpled onto the ground as if hit by a bullet. *Wait, it isn't the ground after all. It landed on the water, splashing. With a strenuous struggle, the bird fluffed its wings, only to be pulled down by its own weight. Soaked like sponge.*

A group of men in dark suits walked over with unregistered faces. They mumbled to each other; it took longer than one could comprehend. They tramped with blatantly glaring eyes, he could feel their animosity, it's written on every inch of their faces.

'You.' One of them stomped forward with tornado force. A hand flung for his neck, odd is that he is about to be stifled.

Bernard attempted a voiceless scream. Limbs frozen. They are the ones who killed his parents. He can sense the fear inside him, developing like an embryo.

'Who are-?'

'You will never know. Never.'

'Hey, what do you want, go away.'

'You are the last one. We are coming for you.'

They approached him, closer and closer, cornered him with their glary look.

'Help--!' Bernard felt the loss of breath rushing out of him, as the pain crawled up his spine.

'Bernard.'

Much to his relief, he sensed that he was being rescued by aliens. He awoke to the pitched darkness absorbing him like water.

'What's' all that snoring. We are not sleeping on a six-inch mattress.' Alo murmured in the dark, cuddled tightly to the opposite wall.

Bernard snuggled himself against the wall for comfort. 'I hate these people!' Bernard barked.

Alo does not bother to ask; he can only presume. 'Lieutenant is a pig.'

It's their third day in jail. The thought of their fate is daunting. How many more days will they be in the stinky cell? The interior is merely three steps on all sides, all concrete. The only ventilation is from the roof-high window. It's not even a window, it's a slot.

'We are not criminals!' Bernard begged, only to hear his own voice resonate back in despair. He bashed his head against the wall. 'Go and catch stupid Steel Face!'

Alo absorbed his acuity, observing Bernard, who had already given up all hope to the questionings that yield little or nothing.

'Lieutenant is right. My mum was murdered.' Bernard punched the wall again as if it were going to open apart. 'Revenge is in my hands, and it will be done, I know it will happen, just wait for the right time.' He recalled the scene when his mum was found at the bank of a flooded river. Of all the things he could remember, the whole community searched high and low for days. After all the searches, the body was found on the third day when a wader flew up and down the river, screeching in high pitched sound. The locals read the sign and followed the bird. To their surprise, the body was covered with debris on the river bank, half-decomposed. For a month or two, the locals were scared of the river like a ghost.

'Somebody there?' Bernard kept thumping the wall. No response, it's obvious the adjacent cells are empty. No one gets to prison these days; you are either part of peacekeeping side or joined the ex-militants. In between is not acceptable, it's cowardice to be sitting on the fence. The mere thought of it ignited raw anger inside him and wanted to blow up. 'You all good for nothing!' His throat gets dry the more he shouts. Worse, the stagnant smell of urine, vomit, and faeces is unbearable, they just have to accept it. But for how long, it's just going from bad to worse? Trapped in the mountain cage, drugged and locked in the ship, locked up in this prison.

'Who is it?' Bernard can tell it's the dawn of a new day, the ambient temperature is picking up.

Like a parasite vying for space, Lieutenant Kilua needs information. For convenience, he now shifted the meeting to his office, only with Bernard. He produced the battered file onto his desk and put on his reading glasses. Slowly and carefully, he flipped through the reports. This makes one wonder how he even goes to sleep at night after reading those daunting reports. Photos alone can cause *chronic insomniac*. But whatever one thinks, Lieutenant is enigmatically proof of such conditions, he still sleeps six hours at night. Page by page, Lieutenant reduced the file size, and spent a few seconds on each like a ritual.

'Morning Bernard.' He growled, heavily breathing that Bernard could hear as the air rushed through his windpipe and vaporised into his lungs.

'Morning.' Came the grim response.

'My officer is also attacked.'

No response.

'Such a coward.'

No response.

'I have considered your case.' He looked at Bernard, reading him like a book, eager to reach the end page. 'Something is missing in your story.'

Bernard felt the pressure mounted on the words that made him want to scream out his lungs. 'We have no story, there's nothing you can get from me-*us*.'

Lieutenant gazed at Bernard as if reading subtitles of a Chinese movie. 'Let's be honest son.' He reminded him as if talking to a pre-class pupil who doesn't know how to differentiate between bullying and fun. 'Police are there to embrace law and order. And you people attacked them, gracious.'

'Who else is with you?'

No response. Bernard stared at the wall behind the Lieutenant. Bible verses posted, but there's one that Bernard is meditating on.

Be sure your sins will find you out.' Lieutenant read from memory. 'That's one of my favorite texts you saw on the wall. You cannot escape from your crime; it will always find you.' *All mysteries will be unraveled.*

'Yeah, if you commit one,' Bernard said.

'Do you know what that offence weighs?'

'I know what's the consequence of a crime, but what do you expect me to say, to admit that I did? Let's stop wasting each other's time.' Bernard gathered his wits and responded firmly.

Lieutenant paused, unimpressed. 'How can I believe you? You need to show me the evidence.' This is the approach to stimulate the subject to talk.

'Evidence. I am the evidence; do I look like a psychopath who killed people left and right?' Bernard said.

'No. I am not saying that. It's what happens, doesn't matter what one looks like. A priest or a pastor can be a killer.' He breathes for a question. 'Where were you during the attack?'

Bernard said nothing.

'Where were you?' Lieutenant slammed the table.

Bernard is silent.

'Lucky for officer Julie,' Lieutenant said. 'Committed and stronger than before. What doesn't kill you makes you stronger.'

Bernard remains composed, he's ready to talk to the core of things. 'I know, she is the one who hand-cuffed us. Can you ask her what the assailant looks like?' A question well directed and regarded. 'I am sure she can tell you.' It did not even occur to him that anything like the Lieutenant exists in the Police force, bald head, and thick eyebrow with thick lips. He should be with the Fire department, where such a muscular man is needed. Police need officers who are fit to chase criminals, not heavy set like fuel tankers.

'Of course, she will.'

Bernard looked towards the door, two male officers standing their guard. Turned toward the subject, still scrutinising.

Lieutenant continues. 'She had the details of the man who attacked her. Maybe any of your members who attacked, who knows?'

'Now you fall to someone's trick, good luck.' Bernard crumpled onto the chair, allowing the thoughts to establish in his mind, *is Chief Ko'oga a member of the masked men?*

Lieutenant Kilua's eyebrows arched in response, obviously no cue to strike with venom as yet. 'Son, I hear what you said,' He discreetly added. 'Whatever it is, I am yet to learn about forgiveness. Not now, maybe later.'

'I guess you will not until the masked man is captured,' Bernard concluded.

56

A ceiling fan revolved around its axis, creating microturbulence of the air in the room. The creaking sound of the fan concerned Atkinson very little, smoking a cigarette, staring at the tally sheets. Content with the first shipment, but not happy with the excessive spending. Entry fee, landing fee, compensation, goodwill payment. 'I have spent my entire bank account on this.'

'Operation on Guadalcanal is *damn* expensive. A lot of demands, unnecessary ones,' Suiono added in a distorted tone. 'Compensation for landing fee, access fee, gravels, girls, everything.'

Atkinson jerked his head, 'They have a price tag for everything,' he smirked and diverted his attention to the calendar. 'Will double the cubic meters for next shipment.'

'Not a problem.' Suiono posed with unruffled composure- an exceptional commodity for his job.

'Let the locals deal with themselves.' Atkinson grabbed a cigarette from his pocket. 'This is how we'll run the operation. Never tell them what to do, they hate to be told. Rotten pigs.' He lit his cigarette

237

and puffed impatiently. 'Use their tribal leaders in negotiation, put them in the frontline, and you cover under their shadow, this is called *transference of liability*,' He added cunningly, recalling how he used Sukulu with the tactic, it works. But he said nothing about the demand to remove Suiono from the company.

Suiono sighed his prejudice. 'The locals don't see the benefits in the operation, they keep demanding compensation and complaining. Lazy people.'

'Let's not waste our precious time trying to correct them.' Atkinson passed Suiono a pay cheque. 'Brilliant job, you deserved a medal from the Queen.'

Suiono grinned. 'Thank you,' little did he know the logs have been shipped on the sly-without the knowledge of the government. From government statistics, between the years 2000-2003, Guadalcanal recorded no round logs export. Corruption at its best.

'I almost forget about the payment arrangement.'

'What arrangement?' Atkinson asked, taking a drag of his cigarette.

'Royalty payment. They agreed to deposit fifty percent of the royalty to their tribe's account.' Suiono passed the note.

National Bank of Solomon Islands
Account Name: Jim Pegoa
Account #: 2000184446

Jemes hands shuddered with discomfort and frustration. He received a cheque with the amount devalued, as is what he was told. He walked to the door, then back inside, body tensed. He wanted to scream, but his reason was denied. At one point, he wanted to tear the cheque in half, straight and simple as that. 'You're a conman!' he shouted.

Little Edna came running inside with flowers in her hands. 'Daddy, Daddy, you look different today.'

'No, it's still me.' Jemes moved about as if losing his responsibility of being a father. He is restless. 'I want to see the paperwork. Evidence. Numbers.' He talked, only to find himself facing the forlorn face of his daughter, staring.

'Daddy, can we go and pray with Elder Moses.' Like her mum, Edna acknowledged the power of prayer, especially in situations beyond one's control, as the one she now witnesses.

'My girl, go outside with your flowers. We will see elder Moses later.' Jemes sat down and dropped into tears. Regretfully realising the ones he trusted were barbarically eating him like cancer. Worst was that he learned from someone he considered inferior in the community. Of all he could possibly think of, he knew numbers, and he can't be wrong on this - there's safety in numbers as is said. And just because he cannot read and write doesn't mean he has a dysfunctional brain. He can read and write, just not English words.

Jemes slumped onto the wooden chair, stooped with both hands locked at the back of his head. Logging crushed his life with unspoken problems, family members gone. Worse still, deracination to a larger extent, streams polluted, fertile soil eroded, vegetation disappeared and community fragmented.

Jemes is convinced that changes come about with educated minds. To Jemes, education is nothing but the adoption of faraway land beliefs. It's the domestication of individual minds which alters behavior and lifestyle. With good education comes money and good life, as he sees in his fellow village men. But like all things, it comes with a promiscuous package containing good and bad. Bad was what Jemes saw and felt, more bitter than malaria tablets.

'I expect more than this amount,' Jemes spit it all out like plaque.

Pegoa flicked through the log tally. 'Look Jemes, we can't argue as they are the ones who do the payment.'

'They have the money; I have the land.' Jemes felt the sourness of his mouth, prompting him to implicitly spit in front of Pegoa.

'I understand your disagreement, this is the first shipment.'

'First shipment? I am not paid for shipments, I am paid for the trees,' He argued with eyes popping out, echoing the hidden knowledge in him that struck his opponent surprisingly.

'They tallied the logs and paid according to the numbers.'

'What numbers?' Jemes demanded.

'Number of trees cut.'

'I know the number of trees cut, and where they cut from.' Jemes flicked his fingers on his forehead, finding the next word.

Pegoa exchanged a glance between the tally sheet and the cheque he was holding. 'Look, I only provide what's signed. If you disagree -.'

'Signed?' Jemes is hysterical. 'Who-what is signed?' His legs were hardly planted on the ground. 'I did not sign the damned paper, if that is what you mean. Atkinson only read it to me.' He growled at the figure in front of him.

'That's it. You agreed to the agreement.' Pegoa said.

'I did not sign. No, never.'

'Not my fault, go and talk to Suiono.'

The response was not well received. 'You are the Land Coordinator; you are the one who deals with these things. You know it.' Jemes eyes darted around, looking for advice from elsewhere.

Pegoa weighed the resentment in Jemes' voice, but an angry man is a stone you don't bother to turn. 'You right.'

'Of course, I know my rights,' Jemes' grievances multiplied.

'Listen, I am the one that negotiates for logging from which you now benefit. And for you to come and accuse me with that tone, it's unacceptable.' Pegoa said.

'I am not accusing you Pegoa, I am speaking the truth. I need your help, not arguing.' He spoke. 'True, you negotiate for the logging, but I do not agree to sign. Not my tribe, no one, it's all from you.'

'No, you misunderstood, I am not the one responsible. If you disagree, then sue the company.' Pegoa rightly stated.

The word *sue* means little to Jemes, but he knew it's a process that means a load of nuisance. 'Pegoa, I understand it clearly, that's why I raised my concern to you.'

'Yes, but why can't we discuss this in a respectable manner.' Pegoa glanced behind him, his wife watched with an open mouth, as if ready to jump in at any moment.

'I have to say this in front of your...' He nodded to the staring wife. 'Now, I know who really you are,' Jemes unguardedly announced and walked away in haste.

57

'You still not answer my question.' Lieutenant Kilua's face turned dull like a fish. 'You have to give me something convincing, and that you will.' Lieutenant knew well he could not jump for the big murder cases. If he could solve misdemeanor cases first, the scenario would collapse in a domino sequence, giving a whole picture of the puzzle.

It's been a week. Six days to be exact. Three interrogation exercises for the suspects. The passing days are taxing for Bernard and Alo. They have been deprived of necessities, and just want to get away from the place. Seeing the police officers day-in day-out has its own discomfort. They were irresistibly struck with uncertain fear--*how long will they be kept behind the cells? Weeks, months, years?* The mere thought of this *brain-numbing* exercise is painful. The interrogation is pain itself, besides the trite remarks and repetitive questions.

'I know, it's a mistake, we all knew that.' Lieutenant threw in a bait, relentless still. 'If I were in your shoes, I will do the same.' He stared at the two expressionless faces, with no clue to find. Blank stares like a mummified statue. This prompted Lieutenant to speed up the process by putting a little more pressure on the exercise.

'Tell you what, you are wasting your time.' Bernard blurted, in an attempt to fend for themselves from the strings of questions.

Ignoring the statement, Lieutenant Kilua involved Alo in the discussion. 'What were you two doing in the logging ship, anyway?' Lieutenant diverted the questions a little.

'Trade for stuff.'

'What- what you want to trade for?'

'Appliances, solar panels, anything worth it.' Bernard said

'I see.' Lieutenant has no further interest in the discussion. 'Such a coincidence, a killing taking place prior to you entering the ship. That very same morning.'

'We know nothing...' Alo finally got the gut to speak, his finger pointing upward, finding heaven through the ceiling. Like Bernard, Alo wants to get out, away from the clanging sounds of metal gates, the x-ray- like probing eyes of the police officers, and the *seemingly* endless chains of questions like going through beads of a rosary.

'Come on, don't tell me you don't know what I am talking about?' Lieutenant tossed his head forward, leveling his eyes with those of Alo, of which he shot back with his only functional right eye.

'We were up the river and walked down to the beach in the early morning.' Bernard cannot stomach his contempt any longer.

'I am talking to your friend here,' Lieutenant continued. 'Where exactly were you, you know it, don't you?'

Often in the case, the subject answered with an alibi, so it's hard to get the facts right.

'Up the river,' Alo said and hit the silent button.

Lieutenant smiled, sensing a gap in the conversation, 'you said up the river? Who else is there?'

'Just the two of us.' Bernard intervened, trying to help.

'I am talking to him, not you.' Lieutenant locked his eyes on Alo. 'Tell me who else with you?'

'Me, Bernard...'

'And?' a bridging question.

Alo cast Bernard a nondescript look. 'That's it.'

'That's it? Don't give me that crap, son.' He raised his voice and studied Alo for a few seconds. 'Do your parents still live?'

The sudden switch of the conversation aroused Alo.

'Your father?'

Alo slowly turned his head. 'I live with my mum.'

Lieutenant's eyes still on Alo, expecting more, enjoying the flinching cues.

'Big brother already married. Also, two sisters.'

'So, you are the last born of four, right?' Lieutenant connecting the details for himself. He has been through this process a dozen times. He knows how to make the subjects talk.

Alo only nodded, nothing more to say.

'Look, your mum will miss you. She expects you to be with her. Don't you miss her?' Lieutenant's voice lowered, enough to get the attention of Alo for a brief moment. 'You miss your mum, don't you?'

Alo nodded.

The Lieutenant nodded too, assuming a sympathetic manner. 'The truth is, amnesty period covers whatever activities you were involved in. All militant related activities were pardoned. I am an ex-militant too.'

Seriously, so why are you asking stupid questions? You know during the height of the crisis, everyone is a potential killer, you can't trust anyone. It's crocodiles in the water.

Bernard cleared his throat, enervated by the process. 'Sir, we respect you as a leader and your role as a Police Chief. To be honest, we have nothing to hide, nothing relevant to your investigations.'

Lieutenant managed a slight nod, accepting the compliment, but not the admission.

'The masked man. Look for him.' Bernard wittingly added with gruff voice. 'I guess you may need our help.'

A call from the phone was made by the Lieutenant, which he accepted without a word. He left the files scattered on his table and bend over to accept the call.

'Lieutenant speaking.'

'Hello Lieutenant.' The voice sounds engrossing.

'Who am I speaking to?' Lieutenant enquired; a bit anxious, like a student that's not been informed about a quiz.

'It's me, Dan.'

'Oh, Dan, how on earth you...?' He paused, finding the next right word. Knowing that he is talking to a phone, not a two-way radio.

'This is a company's phone. They gave me one, so I want to try it out.'

This is a breach of the protocol. 'I see. It works eh-?' Lieutenant Kilua responded with reserved thought.

'Yes, it works.' A brief silence follows. 'How are we doing with the suspects?' the phone hushed. The news is channeled the other way round.

'Good. I mean, we are getting there.'

'Great.' Dan now can talk freely, avoiding the unnecessary cues in the conversation, telling who should talk, and who should listen. But at least some orders are in place, unlike mobile phones. 'So...?' *Is there anything I should know?*

'Atkinson now knows what we are capable of.'

Damned right. 'We are more than capable.'

'Interrogation progresses well, but not as I expected.' Lieutenant breathed in with a delayed exhalation, figuring things out in his head. 'Will have to vamp things up a bit. The only response I get is rubberneck stares, nothing much as yet.' Lieutenant adjusted his position on his chair, body lunged forward awkwardly over the table. 'Bernard's smart, he got some education.'

'Form six dropped - out, I guess' Dan intervened.

'Not dropped out. He escaped the crisis, so he did not sit his university entrance exam. What a shame. He even mentioned something about the people involved in the killings. I reckoned, we may need him, he's an asset.'

'You think so?'

Lieutenant continued, 'as you rightly mentioned, Bernard needs counselling.'

'Correct, but problem is, we do not have professional counsellors here. We can only discipline,' Dan said.

Lieutenant Kilua summarised his thoughts. 'Both parents brutally murdered. No proper burial. No support from elsewhere. No place to call home. The boy is lost. Those are the cause of all the traumas.'

'So, what you are saying is-?' Dan suspiciously enquired.

'I am not saying, it's logic.' Lieutenant Kilua interjected. 'Addam McColl also thinks the same.' Lieutenant Kilua is no psychologist, but he understands a little about post-traumatic effects on people. It's post-traumatic reactions after the tragedy he went through. It's a hard life for him, especially with no brother or sister. A rare kind of *melancholia*. Severe depression.

'Both parents killed. A great loss,' Dan said.

'Let's wait and see, if peace is restored in Ghombua now that he's in jail. Otherwise, he has nothing to hide. No lies, no alibi, I read it all,' Lieutenant said.

After a silence. 'I guess, the root cause is still not solved,' Dan cued in brusquely.

'Pardon me?'

'Suspicion of killing is still ongoing.'

'Killing-what- who?'

'Jemes, the principal landowner went missing since yesterday.'

58

'My wife is having a baby.' Atkinson announced jubilantly. The least Lieutenant expected as an introduction to a business meeting, but he accepted it for a start. Big men need some family talk too.

'You are the happiest man of the moment.' Lieutenant Kilua congratulated him.

'This is my second child, a boy.' He paused, contemplating the father's role in marriage.

'You will have another man to deal with,' Lieutenant said.

'Absolutely. My son from my Australian wife is now in college.' He looked toward the waitress, signaling her attention.

'In college?' Lieutenant Kilua responded in a surprised tone.

'Yes, you think I am still a teenager?'

'No-no, I don't mean that,' Lieutenant explained. 'I mean you are lucky to have a son already in college.'

'Anyway, enough of that.' He was obstructed by a waitress standing next to their table. 'Can we have?' He looked towards his colleague.

'I will get wine, red.'

'Ok, get two red wines for us,' Atkinson ordered.

For seconds, they both eyed the skirt of the waitress that swayed entrancingly as she strode away.

Atkinson turned to face Lieutenant. 'I want to thank your office for the enormous support.'

'It's my pleasure to see the operation rolling.' Lieutenant Kilua summoned up a broad smile.

'Honest, I am quite impressed how you handled the situation from the rough beginning.' Atkinson's face beamed with gratitude, wondering if Lieutenant dies tonight, who will replace him? Seeing most of his officers are half his age.

'It's teamwork, without the team, nothing will be achieved,' he said, 'we have a lot of challenges as well. I do not want to spoil your day.'

The clinking sound of the wine glasses is gripping. They both looked towards the waitress, mouths water-as the wine sparkled in the glasses.

'Here you are.' the waitress placed down the glasses with a trained posture

'Thank you.' Atkinson accepted the apparent hospitality rendered.

A few seconds were very much appreciated in silence, sipping pints of wine.

'May I ask about the interrogation?' Atkinson managed a question.

'Sure, I guess you will not want to hear the outcome.'

'No harm, Lieutenant.'

Lieutenant Kilua collected his thoughts from the hit of the wine, thinking about where to start. 'Bernard is not all we are looking for. It's beyond Bernard, Bandits, or whatever we'd called it.' He cleared his throat, gathering his response for the staring eyes probing him like a textbook.

Lieutenant Kilua gazed around briefly. 'It's more complicated than we think. It's like we are entering a rat tunnel, a mess.' He took a swig from his glass.

'Something we don't know?' Atkinson sensed the complication of the situation.

'Yes, something, many things we don't know. And it requires overhauling the whole community for the big fish.'

'Big fish?'

'Correct; chiefs, village elders, church leaders, they are the big deal.' He paused. 'I know it's hard to digest, but that's where things are heading.' He swayed the wine glass in his hand. 'Slowly but surely, the scenario will unfold.'

They were interrupted by heavy thudding; a wall of camouflaged uniformed men entered the restaurant-what everyone had been long waiting for their arrival; Australian Defense Force.

59

'I don't believe in *vele*. This is a kidnap.' Suiono doubted.

'Kidnap by whom?' Mendana had a squint-eyed pose, hands folded across his chest.

'I don't know, landowners who disagreed, maybe.' Suiono brusquely added, eyes glued on the pages of logs tally.

'This is Guadalcanal, boss.'

'Yes, so?' Suiono's face puckered.

'The island where they practice *Vele*, in case you forget.'

'I don't believe *vele*. It's only some kind of night bird that pissed me off.'

'Whatever you think, I respect your views.' Mendana frowned, leaning against the post of the tent. 'I guess witchcraft is also practiced in your country, right?'

'*Vele* is not a witchcraft.' Suiono explained his line of reasoning. 'It's sorcery, someone had an intention to kill.'

'I can't tell the difference. Witchcraft, sorcery, *vele* or whatever are possessed human beings with magic powers.' Mendana argued.

Seeing the argument between two non-Guadalcanal men, Toxic felt obliged to intervene. '*Vele* are normal humans. Anyone can be a *vele*.'

'Normal?' Suiono scoffed.

'Yes. They are not vampires or some sort like you see in movies. They are real humans, they eat and drink, shit and pee like us...' Toxic stammered.

Ignoring the rationale of the explanation, Suiono queried. 'But how can we prove if someone was killed by a *vele*?'

'You don't want to know, eh?' Toxic smirked.

Suiono dragged on his cigarette. 'Go on, how?'

Toxic chuckled. 'It's obvious. *Vele* usually faked their killings to resemble mishaps.'

'Meaning?' Suiono enquired.

'Like falling from a tree, drowning in the river.'

Suiono looked squarely at Toxic with a bubble of doubt. 'But how can you tell it's a *vele*? What about if someone really fell off and break his legs and left to die? Or drowned and never to be found?'

'You are right, but that is where the trick is.' Toxic continued, eyes an inch wider, he furrowed his eyebrows to make a point. '*Vele* killings always leave behind marks.'

'Like?' Curiosity seized Suiono by the neck.

'Part of his body removed. Late Chief Pelu was more likely a victim.'

'Damned stupid,' Mendana rebuked. 'So as Jemes?' he engaged his mouth to clear his curiosity, not his brain.

Toxic continued. 'I am not saying Jemes was killed by *vele*, but we could only assume since it's been a day since he went missing.'

Mendana watched eerily, allowing Toxic to continue.

'Can you tell if someone practiced *vele*?' Suiono enquired, curious to learn a bit more about enigmatic practice.

'Simple.' Toxic continued. 'Usually, they don't sleep at night. They're not scared of the dark and can travel miles when everyone is sleeping.'

'For what?' Suiono contorted his face, tried to make sense of the situation, 'people are sleeping in the night.'

'Spy in the night and kill in the day,' Toxic simplified.

'They can travel around the *entire* island in minutes. Right Toxic?' Mendana put a gist to the details.

'What?' Suiono finds it hard to believe his ears.

Toxic continued. '*Vele* possessed a supernatural speed, even faster than a jumbo jet if you consider pre-departure routines.'

'And what if...?' Mendana posed an incomplete sentence, digesting the details.

'You can't see a *vele*, they are invisible.'

'Invisible?' Suiono flabbergasted.

'Yes, like air,' Toxic said, leveling his eyes at Mendana. 'Only *vele* can see *vele*.'

Suiono firmly added, 'tell the boys to assist the community in the search. I believed he is still alive somewhere.' He darted around the camp, expecting to see his ghost transiently appear.

60

The search continues into the second day. Rumors had it he must have been attacked and left to die a torturous death somewhere. Suspiciously, the past nights have been raining cats and dogs, which convinced the locals to conclude beyond doubt it's a *vele*.

Chief Ko'oga called on all able-bodied village people for a community briefing. He must play his role as a community leader. His trombone voice once more commended.

'I want you to move in groups. Not alone.' He announced croakily, drying the tears from his eyes, and rubbed his wrinkled face, then his baldhead. 'I believe with all my heart; Jemes is alive somewhere.' The villagers nodded in agreement, little to deliberate on. Somewhere at the back of everyone's mind, Jemes was already dead, for his chance of surviving is weightless.

'The team from the logging camp will assist us.' He nodded to the boys who joined. A crease formed between his eyebrows. 'I'd like to say here, whilst we're not sure of his whereabout, or what was happening to him.' He paused. 'I do not want to hear rumors fly around until we know the truth.'

'Why can't we call the police?' A voice queried at the back.

'Pegoa is currently in Honiara. Will confirm the news first before we report to the police. Will report it as a *missing person* after three days lapse.'

'Three days? He will not survive it if trapped somewhere.'

Little was known. His daughter is the only one who last saw him, said to collect firewood along the logging road, and never returned.

Silence crawled in like a ghost; everyone could sense it. Jemes house was empty and virtually lifeless. Little Edna now lives with her aunt.

'I would like us to cooperate,' Chief continued. 'We 'll pray over this during our church service this evening.' The rays of the sun fiddle among the foliage of the trees, creating iridescent shadows on the ground, implying life is shaky and fleeting.

'Is there any note?'

'This is not a suicide.' Someone responded.

Days passed and hopes grew thinner with each passing day. Lieutenant remained unconvinced, reluctant to accept he's got little or nothing from the interrogation.

Bernard overheard boots thudding on the concrete pavement, melded with the clanking noise of a dangly bunch of keys. The cell door opened, producing two uniformed police officers.

'Follow me. Both of you.' Came the order.

Bernard and Alo staggered out of the cell, squinting their eyes. It took them a minute to reach the interrogation room, despite it being only a block away.

Again? When will all these ends? They entered the room; the setting is the same. A table, three chairs, and an exhausted-looking figure wearing a reading glass. It's almost a *never-ending* routine. Same questions, same answers.

'Welcome back again.'

No response. No good words to address the interrogator that will make him jump-*you're free to go!*

'Take a seat.' Lieutenant Kilua studied them for a few seconds as it was his first time. 'You mentioned the masked men. Who are they?'

Bernard glared with contempt. 'Why? Why do you care?' He glanced at Alo, taciturn as always.

'Can you tell me more of the masked men?' He studied Bernard for a moment. 'What are they? Are they real or something you just imagined?' The Lieutenant gave an undecided look that produced an awkward silence.

'Can you give us something to eat first?' Bernard diverted the discussion. 'We are starving, biscuit and tea is not enough for one to survive on.'

'What do you expect in prison?' Came the wry response, and he slumped back in the chair. 'Remembered what I said, you scratch my back, I scratch yours.'

'I swear by my mum's grave, we have nothing to say.' Bernard's face ruffled, realising that his mum's burial was nothing to fuss about. They conducted no proper funeral service, no life sketch, nothing. They just buried the body. He felt tense and cold from his feet when he recalled the scene. The putrid smell of semi-decomposed body, skin peeled off, and the body soaked like a sponge. The disguised faces of the crowd were struck with fear as the body was wrapped up and placed in the coffin. The images were still intriguingly vivid in his mind.

'Give me something, then I will release you.'

Another trap?

'Why do you need to know?' Bernard senses something is missing, or probably he misunderstood it all. 'So, you can complete your made-up report?'

Lieutenant Kilua cupped his hands and placed them on the table. 'I am afraid to tell you. A man went missing in your village three days ago.'

The eyes of Bernard and Alo met briefly, expecting more. 'Who-what?' Bernard felt a knot in his stomach tighten.

'Who are the masked men?'

Bernard shrugged. 'What difference will it make?'

'Sons, I am just a human like you.' He responded in a calm voice, knowing they already got hooked in the throat.

Bernard took his time to study Lieutenant with a spark of confidence. 'The mountain rebels, brigands. Did it ever occur to your mind?' He partially responded, still fear of the unknown. 'Did you say someone went missing?'

The radio made a cracking noise. Lieutenant Kilua bade them silence as he grabbed the microphone. They watched him reciprocate the overused responsive words. He locked his stare while talking, this made them nervy.

'They found the body.'

The body convolved in a lumpy heap. At a distance, one cannot tell it's a human body that was covered under the dead leaves. Three days had crumpled the giant swamp taro leaf to parch and collapsed around the lump of putrid flesh. A plague of flies feasted on the disembodied lump of body parts.

The leaves were removed to expose the body parts. 'Dear - have mercy on me.' Elder Moses recoiled, he couldn't bear the scene and the fetid smell. 'It's-it's a body, him.' He gawked at the heap of flesh as if displayed for sale, lacerations are obvious and smothered in pus, brutal. Limbs warped and distorted, separated from the main body. He was decapitated. The disembodied head is positioned upright next to its torso. The mouth was distorted, exposing the blood-stained white teeth.

Brutal, what an unpardonable crime.

'Precious—I can't see this.' Chief Ko'oga was baffled, the scene sent ripples of nausea through his body. 'We need --- stretcher.'

'For what? This isn't a human body, not anymore.' Deve shot a penetrating gaze, making sense of the situation. 'We need a sack. The smell attracts flies.' He wafted the air in front of his face.

'Deve, this is a body, it's Jemes.' Elder Moses interposed, recalling the three dimensions of humanity. Soul, spirit, and body. 'Put him in a proper stretcher.' The soul and spirit long left the body days ago when the killer choked the last breath out of him.

'Elder is right.' Chief pawed his stomach. 'Wrap plastics around your palms.' He glanced at the mutilated body parts, too much for his eyes to bear. No reasonable explanation, he stood in silence, watching the shuddering faces moving about around him, absorbed in instant disgust.

Elder Moses limped forward with an empty copra sack. With strenuous effort, he spread out the sack next to body parts. 'Poor Jemes.' He mumbled, recalling the letter he translated for him. *Ghani Bua.*

Deve took the leading role. In response, the group coordinated themselves, forgetting the murder scene for a while, though it registered in their memories as the worst killing that ever occurred in their village.

'We need another sack.' Elder Moses requested. Next to him stood Chief Ko'oga, wordless, unsure if what he saw was real. He watched the boys step in to assist Elder Moses, slowly they constructed a stretcher out of bush materials. The crime scene is open like a playing ground, with no cordon, no forensic team, no investigations. It's different from the sophisticated crime scenes as seen in the movies.

'Look!' A young lad shouted at the distance. 'Footprints.'

The others rushed towards the boy. Whoever the killer is, he chose the right spot for his vices. First, he picks a swamp, the least trodden area in the bush. Secondly, blood is easily soaked into the waterlogged marsh. But weird to say, not much disturbance around to denote a struggle. Another perfect murder scene.

'It's a wide foot-' the boy tried to interpret the footprint.

'Shush-' Deve hushed him to shut up. 'Don't say a word.' Everyone agreed knowing that the killer could be nearby, listening to every word they said, and the least silly mistake one can do is to mention his name. It means putting your name on his *killing list.*

Deve is not a superhuman. But given the odds, he guessed it right. The assailant is watching at a distance, cowering behind the roots of an uprooted tree. He triumphantly watched all their moves, listened to their exchange of words, and ill-founded postulation of how the victim was killed. That is not the question the killer is interested in; the question is if the rain has washed all his footprints out.

The killer has extramundane power to cause heavy rainfall, or hailstorm, one that even seasoned weathermen run out of words to explain. But some things are not meant to be disclosed - the unidentified flying objects and the aliens. The *Vele possessed man* is getting stronger after every killing, *and who can stop him? Police? IPMT?* He accomplished his wicked grin when they put the body parts together and carried the body away in a stretcher. Mission accomplished.

61

Atkinson looks dull as if he just got diagnosed with Malaria. 'Heaven help us.' He collapsed back on his swivel chair, puzzled, 'Solomon Islands is said to be a Christian country.'

'Christianity for many is only when they enter the church building,' Sukulu said. 'I felt sorry for Jemes, it's not even a week after his wife passed away.'

'I heard there's a group moving around killing people.' Atkinson groped for details. 'What are we dealing with here, idiots?'

'Hope we are not fantasising about movies,' Sukulu teased.

'Serious, that's what I heard. They came up with rules to stall the operations.' Atkinson blurted out indiscriminately.

'Maybe it's just a rumor. You know communities, they love to spread rumors like sharing food.'

'Bernard is already in jail; we are dealing with an unknown killer here.'

'Right, Bernard is related to Jemes,' Sukulu reasoned out.

'He's been framed. Someone used him as a scapegoat.'

'Scape-?' Sukulu just cannot pick out the words. Though he is fairly literate, his education is limited too. Worse off, his hearing deteriorated after being punched. But as Sukulu is, he does not fuss about it.

'They used him. It's a planned move.'

Sukulu turned his head, more in disbelief than surprise. 'Whoever did it, he's smart.'

'I guess you mean stupid,' Atkinson rebuffed.

Sukulu managed a beefy grin, revealing his tobacco-stained teeth. 'Yes. He is stupid to take another victim when the suspect is already in jail. The police now divert their search.'

'Maybe the killer is not aware of Bernard being captured...' Sukulu still does not get it, not sure what he's trying to pose- a question or a comment.

'It's possible, no one knows the whereabouts of Bernard the whole time.' Atkinson tossed forward for a cigarette.

'Looks like revenge.'

'Revenge for what? Jemes was not the kind of fellow who tangled with all kinds of problems. You know him well, yay?' Atkinson lit his cigarette, recalling the day when he first met Jemes. He can almost feel his presence, manly tall and black, casual haircut with beard. 'Some said *vele*. But what I saw was cold blood murder?'

'Possible for *vele*.' Sukulu also lighted himself a cigarette.

'I don't believe *vele*,' Atkinson debated.

'You don't have to bossman,' Sukulu interjected. 'Many people doubt if *vele* truly possesses that power to kill.' Smoke emerged out of his mouth and nostril. 'It's like questioning if the devil has the power to kill,' he paused. 'Well, nobody knows for sure unless you proved it yourself. For me, I will not bother trying.' He grimaced on the sly.

'But if *vele*, how can we tell.'

'No sign of struggle. A normal murder scene usually left behind indications of tussle.' He puffed, looking straight at Atkinson's face. '*Vele* will paralyze the victim with its power, causing the victim to look as if electrocuted. The fun part follows, when the victim become submissive to all his commands, torturing began.'

Atkinson's mouth dropped open.

'Power is in the small finger.' Sukulu continued.

'Small finger, what is that?'

'Shooting malign power at the victim by simply twirling the small finger.' Sukulu folded his right-hand fingers, leaving only the baby finger pointing, he then revolved it in an anti- clockwise direction to illustrate the devilry.

The incoming call distracted them. 'A minute.' Atkinson grabbed the phone. He rubbed his forehead as if to clear his mind of all the mind-throbbing revelations. 'Hello, Atkinson speaking.'

He looked towards Sukulu then to the phone, with eyes locked on the table.

Sukulu froze in deep thought. *Is this good or bad news?*

'It's Pegoa. He requested for a coffin.' Atkinson dropped the phone.

62

Five kilometers east of Pacific Loggers' office is Henderson International Airport. Six helicopters hover over the airport with their menacing dragon look. The choppers propagated a churning sound, causing the ground to vibrate every inch as they flew past. The impact is adequate to scare the enemies out from their hiding place, wherever they hide.

Two of which are Bell UH-1 Iroquois helicopters, a model that has been widely used in the Korean and Vietnam wars. *Huey* as soldiers preferred. The other four are modern NH90 twin-engine, multirole military helicopters. Unlike the round-shape *Huey*, the NH90 is more compact with a pointed nose. The model was used by the NATO Peace Keeping missions in Iraq and Afghanistan. Their presence at Henderson Airport might be overrated, but they have a significant role to play. To transport food, fuel, and other logistic services essential for soldiers who will be deployed to the identified hot spots around the Island.

Detachments are well organised for sea operations. Anchoring at the iron bottom sound is *HMAS Manoora*, a 159-meter *Kanimbla* – class landing amphibious ship equipped with two LCM8 light landing crafts. A kilometer west of HMAS Manoora is *HMAS Whyalla*, an Australian patrol boat that can speed up to 56 km per hour, specially designed for maritime surveillance. But that's not all, in Cairns, Australia, three more patrol boats are preparing to depart. These boats are designated for military bulky logistics and operations. The presence of the Australian-led military intervention is astoundingly welcome – but not for everyone. Steel Face is one.

~

'They set a deadline of five days.' Steel Face squeezed the note into a ball and threw it away. 'Five days, this is total nonsense. Who are they to come and tell me to surrender?' He placed the gun over his shoulder, the news felt like a boulder landed on him - a heavy blow. The letter is straight to the point, to surrender. No option is provided or a Plan B if he refuses. It's an ultimatum. One does not have to be a military expert to understand the second option, seeing the capability of the intervention soldiers is intimidating to one's bone marrow.

The members remained still and speechless. To them, life without Steel Face is unimaginable. For the past five years, they lionised him with colossal regard, as if he is some kind of god. He is the source of life, pride, and dignity. They revered him as the true hero of the Island, like a promised rescuer. Little did they know that his days are numbered. And it ends today.

'Ten days?' He configured the date. The date was ten days passed, and whoever was tasked to deliver the letter had delayed generously, for reasons we do not want to know. 'They are coming, anytime. Prepare ourselves, team.' All the anxieties bred paranoia, which is worse than fear itself. Steel Face is restless, he walked around the camp, bellowing on like an about-to-erupt volcano. For the past years, he rarely reacted that way. Hyperactive.

'Where are captured pigs? Bring them to me,' he ordered.

'Sorry, you mean...? There is no one left in the cages.'

'Don't tell me a lie.'

'You already killed them all, and the other two uh...'

'Who the hell brought this note?' he came to a sudden stop, all sweat. He surveyed the faces one, one more time.

The members cast their eyes around for assurance before one announced. 'One of our messengers.'

'Which one?'

'Ghombua.'

63

Bernard almost jumped when the words, *you are free to go,* echoed in his ears. He nodded at Alo, then eyes settled on Lieutenant Kilua. Released on the 1st of August is ceremonial. It's Guadalcanal Second Appointed day, a double celebration.

Lieutenant Kilua is a good man, he provided them a hot meal and a chance for a shower to clean themselves up. He was satisfied with the interrogation and its outcome.

For Bernard and Alo, they can't wait to get away from the brick-walled cell, free from the staring eyes of police officers, and away from the fetid cells, where one breathes his own urine and feces for almost, like, forever.

Bernard wears his black kiwi windbreaker jacket, a free man again. Despite being set free, he is sad to learn his uncle was brutally murdered. His feelings metamorphosed from joy to despair. No family, no uncle, no one he's looking forward to seeing, only his second Cousin Stonie whom he treated more like a first cousin.

Standing a few meters away from Bernard, Alo is looking forward to seeing his mother. Besides, Alo thinks of his friends, the river, he missed his home.

'Before you leave, I have one last request,' Lieutenant announced. 'Actually, it's my only request.'

Bernard's eyes popped out. 'Sure, what is it?'

'We need you to help bring Steel Face to justice.'

'What? Who do you think will...?'

'They are here.' The ground vibrated under their feet.

Bernard looked around as if the world had come to an end. He has no time to talk or even think. 'Who is here?' He felt his mouth dry, swallowing his savourless spit, he spun around and noticed moving objects swarming the western sky. Attention-gripping.

'Son, thank you for your patience,' Lieutenant said. 'It's been longer than we've expected. I know what you have gone through, all your files are now in my rubbish bin.'

The timing is perfect. At 2.00 PM sharp, the skates of an NH90 chopper hit the ground at Tetere Police station, the other five choppers circling in the air. The noise and the turbulence of the landing chopper is menacing. Bernard ducked to take a good look, making sense of the situation. Two uniformed soldiers jumped out from the landed chopper and marched out elegantly.

'Hi mate, you ready?' One soldier forward his hand for a handshake, then threw him a safety vest.

Bernard gave an austere nod, terrified by the daunting sound of the spinning rotors. He swallowed hard, accepting the role of a soldier as much as possible in thought and action. A fake posture can reveal his amateurism. *Be strong boy, this is your dream.*

He marched towards the chopper with heightened energy, more than he could ever imagine. *Flying in a helicopter, across the island?*

Awesome. They assisted him to his sitting position and buckled him up for safety. He marveled at the interior, it's compact and roomier than he presumably thought. 'Welcome on board.' One of the soldiers announced, the matured one of the four inside. The pilot with another in the front seat, doing what the pilot is employed to do. Pressing buttons, talking to the microphone, turned back to get an 'ok' gesture from the colleagues. The engine gained force, causing the rotors to ramp up with a roar, bobbing the chopper a bit. Without Bernard realising, the helicopter was already floating in the air as if blown up by some kind of monstrous gale.

As the chopper ascended, Bernard felt a sense of accomplishment. Lost in the sudden switch of circumstances, he didn't grasp Alo also boarded the same helicopter. He turned and managed a naive nod. The chopper glided to a thousand feet then headed eastward at 85 knots. Bernard gazed down the window, absorbing the passing scenes from the top. He put names to the rivers slithering to the sea. *Matapono*, brown as tailing of the gold Ridge mine, *Mbalasuna*, the debris-covered banks, *Mbarande* the torrential river, *Mbokokimbo*, the black stone river, and then the White Stone River, *Mongga*. The chopper swerved in the southerly direction, causing Bernard to slide sideways, still focusing on the village below.

'The murder scene is clean. No sign of struggle, except drips of blood.' Dan said. He looked around the camp, mostly empty except for a heap of rejected logs and offcuts. The fire has charred the heap of logs, creating annoying smoky air.

'The killer must be the devil himself.' Lieutenant Kilua frowned, leaning back into the chair.

Without giving time to absorb the response, Dan continued. 'Cannot get a clue from the murder scene. But I am thinking the killer is from another place.'

'Probably.' Lieutenant questioned his thought, 'you think they used him?'

'Not necessarily that. Perhaps a relative, not happy with the logging, whatever.' Dan analyzed the situation. 'I don't think anyone from Ghombua can do such an evil act.'

'You never know, a wolf can mingle with sheep.' Lieutenant Kilua tapped his fingers on the table, analysing the details in his head. He stared towards the prison block, which from a distance looked dull like a concrete tool shed, except that it has high walls and is secured with razor wire.

Dan continued, 'I don't understand.' The phone went silent for a second, disturbed by a sigh. 'This village has the largest Church building I have ever seen. I would say whole of the area, yet what happened here does not reflect the building.'

'It's only a building, having the biggest church does not guarantee one is righteous.' Lieutenant paused, 'it's the heart that matters.' He advised like a preacher of some reformation movement.

'The funeral is in the afternoon,' Dan said, glancing up at the sky; the sun is at its peak.

'What do the village people think?'

'Everyone keeps their lips pursed,' Dan said.

'Same as Aola.' Lieutenant intervened.

'Aola, right, same,' Dan stuttered. 'All I heard is *vele*, but as you know, when *vele* involved, the case seemed to disappear in thin air - hopeless.'

'Not this time round,' Lieutenant rebuffed. 'We will apprehend the culprit, now that the Australian Soldiers are here, I have all the aces.' Lieutenant added with firm assurance. 'I want you to attend the funeral service. The fate of your mission will be decided this afternoon.'

64

Steel Face was unsettled. Anxiety crushed his cognitive ability to make any decent decision. He had a feeling of a bloodsucking leech crawling up his spine, and his heart dropped to where his stomach was. He walked around the camp shouting and swearing as if the entire world had abandoned him. Pressure is bottling inside him, no way to be released.

'I am fine, no big deal. The Australian soldiers know nothing about these mountains.' He comforted himself with illusion, without taking heed of the time. 'Why will Australian soldiers have to come this far? It's a rugged track which took a day to trek.' Marching around, he sensed the surrounding emptiness. As expected in such a situation, most members had abandoned him with a good heart. Dominant is the fear that the Australian soldiers will capture and torture them. The thought of it is intimidating, considering the soldiers' level of training and high-tech ammunition.

The body was already placed in the coffin. Chief Ko'oga, Pegoa and Elder Moses kept a distance from the gravediggers. Elder Moses was flanked by two taller and lean figures, which he occasionally glanced up at in their conversation. They watch the gravediggers doing their job. The earthy smell of the fresh soil posed unsettling feelings in their nerves.

'I am afraid this community is losing its people like flies,' Chief Ko'oga cried. 'When will be the next one? And who?' He spat it out before he even realised its implications to his fellowmen.

'Sad.' Pegoa added, eyes at the loose soil that were continually thrown to the surface. Jim Pegoa was well-groomed for the funeral service. He combed his hair into a neat mushroom shape.

'I am sorry for this family,' Elder Moses sympathetically added. 'It's like within a week, Jemes' family just disappeared. Gone.'

'As a community, we must work with the police.' Chief Ko'oga continued. 'We cannot continue to tolerate such evil.'

"Will they release Bernard to see his uncle?' Pegoa wondered.

'It's possible if the community request it.' Elder Moses responded, glancing up at Pegoa. 'With a genuine reason like this.'

'He was already in--' Chief Ko'oga coughed. 'Informed.'

'Bernard?' Pegoa enquired.

'Yes, he will attend. The police will be here this afternoon too.' Chief Ko'oga continued with an aura of authority. 'Talking about the police. They are looking for the rebel leader, Steel Face.'

'I heard he is ready to surrender.' Elder Moses intervened.

'That's what I heard too; they wrote to him.' Pegoa cast his eyes around.

'A letter? He received a letter?' Elder Moses begged for more.

'Yes. A summons to give up his arms,' Pegoa said, eyes locked on the boys digging the grave.

A prolonged silence. The story floats in the air, draped with the fabric of rumors.

Looking around, Elder Moses added in a squeaky voice. 'Talking about the Australian soldiers, they are well-trained and fully equipped. I saw in the newspapers, huge ships, helicopters too...' He stopped in dead silence as the sound resonated in his ears. 'Helicopters?'

Seen from the sky, Ghombua village resembles the alphabet letter V. The village hinges at the church and branched off with two arms. Bernard grew up in a house located at the branch of V that cuddled up along the river. The birds -eye view brings the entire village into his scope, the area that was once his home now a barren lot, only charred remains of the structure can be seen bathed among the competing shrubs. Lined up the river, uncle Jemes' house, Jim Pegoa's house, a playing field then Chief Ko'oga's residence. Three houses up the river from Chief Ko'oga's house is the Church.

There is one thing that caught Bernard's attention. It's the newly constructed logging road. From the sky, it looked like a giant sleeping snake, slithered across the river, into the village, and headed into the hills.

Bernard remained silent, eyes down the window, tears voluntarily beaded in his eyes.

Bernard cleared the mist from his eyes, glanced at Alo then looked out the window again.

'Your village?' A soldier queried.

Bernard nodded his head.

The choppers sped along as if contending for space. Military-wise, the two choppers are sufficient for the mission, the other four only served as decoys, in case of any unexpected retaliation. For the past fifteen minutes, Bernard lost in his own thoughts, speechless which to some extent, it's reasonable as the noise of the vibrating rotors is overpowering. Only nods and empathic yes are engaged. Time will give him words to say.

'Logging.' The soldier spoke briefly, glancing at the newly cut roads crisscrossing the bushes like termites' tunnels.

Bernard recalled his friends, and comrades. What will they think? He wished they knew their two friends were in one of the choppers flying above them. He imagined how they would react. First time flying anyway.

He felt the thickness of his safety vest, sitting among soldiers. Huge and tough in their uniforms, armed with guns that he only saw in movies. *Only boys who attended schools can be recruited as soldiers. Uncle Jemes can't be one because he can't write his name.* The words ran through his mind one more time. Tears trickled down his cheeks.

'Mountains have grandeur from here.' One soldier talked to his colleague, eyeing the approaching mountains. The GPS on the dashboard of the chopper displayed their fast-shifting coordinates. The chopper decelerated to 70 knots and started to descend like an eagle, glided with claws ready to lock its grip. The soldiers peeped out the window, to make all possible efforts to get a sense of the mountains that zoomed closer and closer every minute. The mountain ranges are particularly serene from the top, but one must not be fooled by the scenery. Who knows what is under those impenetrable canopies.

'We are closer.' Bernard oriented himself with the river, stretching the hippocampus of his brain for hints. 'Still further up.' He recognised the river, but the camp as far as he knew is located at a confluence, where a stream merged with the main river. He imagined how rebels would react to the noise of six choppers. The face of Steel Face flickered in his memory like a flame. Expecting the unknown is terrifying. *What will he do? Hide, runaway, retaliate? But he surrendered. What about if this is a trick? To lure us to its web, like a spider.*

65

The choppers circulated the mountain ranges for about fifteen minutes, giving adequate time for the leader to show himself. Looking from the top, the camp is situated on a plateau between the river and a sharp cliff. The view is stunning from the top, a mosaic of foliage sprouting like giant broccoli. But under those trees you don't have to be reminded, it's creepy. Slowly, one of the choppers dived onto the cliff to get a closer view.

'Show yourself at the river bank now.' The commander of the troops announced in a loud hailer, looking across the mountain, assuming where the camp is. The mountain ranges are remote and formidable, without a helicopter, no one can easily access the camp. It's almost inaccessible. 'Sir, give yourself up.' No response from the camp.

After minutes of nerve-itching watch, CHOPPER ONE dove to the river bank. 'CHOPPER ONE is landing,' the pilot reported.

'Watch the bush track. Expecting him soon.'

273

'Copy.' Instantaneously, four well-equipped soldiers tactfully crouched out in position before maneuvering out at different angles. The movement of the soldiers got Bernard and Alo's attention. They both sat back in the landed chopper and watched in awe, feeling a bit edgy about the imminent outcome. But this is the work of soldiers, to fight the rebels.

A minute later, CHOPPER TWO and CHOPPER THREE landed, a distance up the river. Producing uniformed soldiers crawling out like cockroaches. Three choppers still fly high, surveying the entire mountain range. Another one dropped lower and flew only a few meters above the canopies. The scene is intimidating and worse, the noise propagated is unbearable.

'Halt, I see movement,' the two-way radio announced the progress. 'Is he armed?'

'Can't tell.'

'Hold your position. Don't shoot.' The commander ordered.

'Copy.'

The silence of the radio is numbing. *What is happening? Is he armed?* Bernard looked out the window, all soldiers took position in engaged posture. CHOPPER FOUR landed some distance down the river, leaving the two Huey helicopters to fly the space.

'Here he comes.' The radio announced. The pilot sat in silence, as if his job is nothing more than ready to fly the chopper away.

'Armed?'

'Positive. But hands raised.'

'Any company?'

'Negative.' Steel Face is a dead man when he reached the river bank.

Bernard craned his neck towards the window and saw an approaching figure in a gleam. He tried to establish the face that bore the name Steel Face. The radio conversation went on for a while, but was trivial to the ears, as the eyes do the rest. Bernard is sweating, seeing the face makes him want to cry, but held it back. A feeling of anger and anxiety overwhelmed him, but no time to express it. The soldiers have taken care of it all.

With both hands raised, the brigand leader staggered forward. His attire was all white, what a symbolic way to surrender. The presence of the soldiers had reduced him from an aggressive military commander to a docile troll. The soldiers approached him in calculated steps, executing all safety procedures in the process. With both hands cuffed, they led him towards the CHOPPER ONE, one Bernard and Alo boarded. Mission accomplished. It's the moment Bernard and Alo have been waiting for. They beamed with joyous triumph.

The brigand leader ushered inside like a sheep ready to be slaughtered. He has chosen his master, it's not nature, nor the mountains as he always vaunted, it's his submission to foreign troops.

~

The brigand leader belted onto his seat right in front of Bernard and Alo. He was all smeared with sweat, probably from descending the mountains or from the quagmire he's now in. Or both. He is speechless. No time for bragging about the mountains.

Bernard was startled by the unannounced ascension of the helicopter. Just as they took off from Tetere, without him realising, they already floated in the air.

Steel Face glanced around and met Bernard's eyes. 'You bastard. I am going to kill you!' He glared at Alo. 'Bloody traitors!' The scar on his face stretched wider, attesting to his anger for the unsuccessful chase. But with both hands handcuffed, it's pointless to devise an argument. Besides, he was flanked by two muscular soldiers, heavily armed.

Bernard's eyes are still on Steel Face, just can't get enough of him. Thinking of spitting some tart remarks, but his judgment rules it out. He is engrossed in his own thoughts, recalling the face that stormed into his parents' house, captured his father, and torched the house into flame. That's the *damned* Steel Face.

66

T he crowd dispersed as CHOPPER ONE landed. Two uniformed
soldiers jumped out in a practiced feat. After scanning the
vicinity, the leading soldier twitched a thumb up to Bernard and
Alo. Slowly, Bernard triumphantly jumped out of the chopper, and
nodded at the soldiers, communicating their appreciation for landing
safely at home. For Bernard, it's a triumphant relief, knowing that
some damned crooks will be soon thrown in jail. The big fish, as
they said.

'Your bag.' One soldier passed Bernard the duffel bag. They have
already forgotten about it. But one thing is obvious, it's empty. The
damned Chinese already scavenged its content.

As soon as Bernard and Alo strode off, the chopper ascended and
joined the other five.

Of all the thoughts registered in Bernard's mind, the toll of the
bell in a succession of strokes is attention-gripping, it thawed his
mind. It announced the coffin is about to be lowered. It tolls for
everyone, a way of saying a final goodbye to a deceased member.

276

Bernard was crushed with a sickening feeling of emptiness, a vacuum inside him deepened after each breath. He thinks of his parents, but what registered for a brief second was the face of his smiling mum. Always smiling, and when he returned home from school, his mum was the one he longed to see. With a broad smile, she would embrace him, 'My boy has arrived. A college student,' which Bernard was always proud of. He felt a warm tap on his shoulder, prompting him to turn, only to see an empty space. He looked to his right, Alo walked slowly, a step away.

The crowd moved uniformly towards the graveside. He put names to a few faces- Chief Ko'oga, Elder Moses, Pegoa, and Osama. Some faces turned to look as they marched towards the grave. A dose of nausea overwhelmed Bernard, unsure to cry or punch someone in the face, knowing the death was a torturous one. He absorbed the memories of his dead parents, first his father, then his beloved mum. The nostalgia is getting heavier in his mind; he thinks of auntie Merre, and then his uncle who is now placed in the coffin. Who will be next on the list? The thought is mesmeric.

'The helicopter dropped you?' Stonie startled him.

Bernard only managed a feeble nod. 'I am sorry for my uncle.' He sobbed onto Stonie's shoulder.

Stonie led him towards the graveside. The crowd parted as they approached. It is such a heartfelt scene, seeing someone arrive only to find his uncle is ready to be buried.

Bernard stood at the graveside, watching in silence as the coffin was lowered. It's a wooden-brown coffin provided by the company. The hymns were sung, sentiments shared, and the flowers placed on the coffin. Such a despondent scene to imagine someone you loved passed away. Especially for the person the tribe highly respected, a leader and an uncle.

The funeral proceeding was taken by Elder Moses. Just as everyone thought, he delivered a profound sermon about the mystery of death. Why death? Why this life is full of pain? When will all this be over?

Bernard saw little Edna wailing sorrowfully, consoled by her aunty. She is now an orphan, with no brothers or sisters. She is his only cousin's sister around. The more he thought about her, the more he sees himself—a shattered image. He took a step back to allow space for those shoveling the ground. Scanned around the sea of faces, he recognised Nimrod towered over Toxic. A distance behind is dreadlocked Deve.

Bernard darted his head around hesitantly and cleared his voice. 'Excuse me everyone-.' The heads turned automatically as if they had been expecting something from him all along. 'I am sorry, truly sorry for what ...' He sobbed, prompting Elder Moses to limp over and stood by his side.

'Go on son - go on.' Elder Moses bade him.

'We've been through a lot. I know, community mistook us for criminals.' He paused to wipe his eyes. 'On behalf of the boys, we accepted the negative talks, and to be honest, we are innocent. We had nothing to do with what was going on in our community. It's true, we are the BANDITS, but it's only a name.'

The crowd slowly convened again. Even those shoveling the ground slowed down and peeked over to hear the gist of the speech.

'They called us criminals...' he looked around, 'maybe for other things, but we are only humans. We made mistakes and learned from them - that's what humans do.'

The apologetic speech brought tears to Elder Moses. Even Chief Ko'oga was also touched by the words, standing at a distance, catching every single word.

Bernard was induced with empathy and took a noble stand, 'To our village leader...' He locked his gaze. 'Chief Ko'oga, I am sorry, apologise for what we'd done. Please forgive us.'

Chief Ko'oga broke down in tears. He stepped forward, prompting heads to turn in his direction. He positioned himself next to Bernard. 'Granny, I understand. I wholly understand what you've been through...'

The funeral service transformed into a reconciliation ceremony, and as a community, it was a memorable moment. Tears were shed and words of forgiveness and encouragement were shared.

Jim Pegoa stood at the back, detached himself from the crowd. He too was touched. He has been observing Bernard the whole time. From the moment he disembarked the helicopter. Wondering why he is not handcuffed. *Or is he released on bail?*

'The boys.' Bernard glanced around. 'We'll call the community for a communal reconciliation.' While they were still sharing comforting words, the approaching noise clamored for their attention. The choppers were long gone, but the sound is too gripping to ignore. It's the sound of approaching vehicles. Two white cabin land cruisers with blue and white checkered patterns. The word printed on the side was unmistakable as supposed to be - POLICE.

The people scuffled about, wondering what is happening. Four uniformed police officers approached the village - composed and determined. They marched straight up the village, Dan taking the lead in his cowboy outfit. They nodded to the staring eyes and continued walking.

Everyone is wondering. If it is Bernard and Alo they are after, they are heading in the wrong direction. Someone tried to intervene, but he was plainly ignored. And as Bernard wished for, they approached Pegoa's house.

Pegoa sneaked his way out in time. The funeral service was over, and Bernard, on behalf of the BANDITS had apologised to the community members. But that's not all, pressure is brewing in Pegoa's head. He walked sluggishly towards his house, praying for blessings as if he is still shocked.

The encounter was suppressed by a jolt. Before anyone could even rationalise, Deve was handcuffed. It's fast and gallant. The crowd lost their words, a tremendous *epiphany*, a moment of revelation. A pin-drop silence, as if the devil has vanquished all mankind. Nothing to say but to watch the suspect lead away, jaws buried in his chest.

Bernard's eyes were feasting to feed his unadulterated curiosity. Of all his precarious suspicions, Deve's involvement is shocking, he couldn't even imagine the one he trusted was the devil in disguise. His subconscious mind swiftly connected the most likely conceivable scenarios. *The burnt Police vehicle? The masked man? The mysterious killer?*

EPILOGUE

Lieutenant Kilua is good at his job. Not forgetting his colleagues, Officer Julie and Officer Bryan. The work is easier for Lieutenant Kilua, much easier. It took him only six hours to get the details out of the two suspects. He is now working on a report.

They used the bag Officer Peter had as evidence to connect the dots. The bag was obtained during the arrest and belongs to the suspect. The items include a mask, a bayonet, a scalpel, rubber material, wires, and detergents.

Deve has no remaining cards to play, but to come clean. He confessed his affiliation with the Isatabu Resistance Movement, stating his continuing involvement as a messenger. He was also responsible for the burning of the police vehicle and also for the attack of Officer Julie.

The reason for such undertakings is obvious; it's all about land inheritance. As *Thibo tribe themselves, both the suspects* felt envious after being sidelined in all land dealings by the tribe. Jemes' family, including Chief Jonah, often expressed to other *Thibo clans* that they have no right over *Ghombua land*. Not to remind you again, it's on Guadalcanal.

For Pegoa, this had been going on for as long as he could remember. After he got married, he was engulfed with the lurking fear his children will be treated the same, or worse off. Deve was used. He was close to the boys, he is one of the BANDITS, which immunised him to any suspicious thoughts of his involvement. Deve holds on to all the aces.

Unlike Pegoa, Sukulu is an opportunist. Elder Moses was right when he mentioned *Judas* is *among us*. Sukulu is just that. He plays the role of the chief only to get the benefits deserved for the status.

The national broadcaster, the mid-day news aired the arrest made by the Australian Defense Force of the most wanted rebel leader of the Isatabu Resistance Movement, Steel face. This news brings smile to the local Solomon Islanders. In the other news, two suspects of Ghombua were arrested for various charges. The midday news prompted Lieutenant Kilua to pump his arm in the air and dial a number.

'Atkinson speaking.'

'Bossman, you hear the news?'

'Yes mate, you'd done it.' Atkinson acknowledged the news. 'Great job.'

'It's teamwork,' Lieutenant Kilua said.

Atkinson paused. 'I can't believe the rebel leader surrendered. That's the news of the year.'

'Steel Face is behind bars. That's the kind of news we want to hear,' Lieutenant said.

'I heard they took Jim Pegoa for questioning. What is he to do with this?'

'Big fish, remember?' Lieutenant said.

Atkinson cannot swallow the news. The operation manager already informed him earlier but hearing it from the Chief of Police is even more intriguing. 'Big fish. But I thought the bandits-?'

'I know, we have to swim with the small fish to get close to the big ones.' That is all the Lieutenant will say.

'Big fish.' Atkinson pondered on the news. Still cannot believe his ears, knowing that his land coordinator was arrested. 'Pegoa is the suspect?'

'Welcome to Guadalcanal, my friend.' Lieutenant Kilua said, 'have a good day,' and he hung up.

Before I forget,
what became of the BANDITS?

Bernard Maneboko - recruited as a cadet for Tetere Police station. At first, he shouldered a hostile feeling toward Officer Peter Pai (Security incognito Dan Bako), but slowly and surely, time heals the ill feelings. He is in charge of the group aiming to apprehend the ex-militants around the island. Capitalising on the advanced ammunitions of the Australian Defence Force, they brought many criminals to justice. Lieutenant Kilua embraced highly on the achievement, knowing that he made the right decision to employ Bernard in the first place.

For the other members:

Alfred Riola (Alo) - He was employed as a carrier for the Australian Defence Force with the help of Bernard. He continued to send money home to support his old mum.

Nimrod Gimo (Nimo) - was promoted from the crew and employed as a full-time logging truck driver.

David Bokito (Deve) - He was engaged to Elizabeth (Pegoa's daughter) but circumstances didn't allow him to proceed.

Irvin Tumusipu (Osama) – employed full-time Security officer at *Tuvu* camp after Dan was reinstated. He works well with Mendana and Suiono.

Thomas Tumusipu (Toxic) - permanently renamed *Paska* which he accepted over time. Assistant to Suiono and continues to bring free-range chickens for him.

Sikua Ruka (Stonie) - recruited as a kitchen assistant at the logging camp, with a strict condition to abstain from drugs, of which after thoroughly consideration, he finally agreed.

Of all the members, some keep their words, some not. Still, they live their life to the fullest, tackling their challenges head-on on a daily basis, like everyone else in the community. Above all, they have all the reasons to pride themselves a few times –the BANDITS.

Finally, music that keeps me going every night when working on this project:

I hope you too will find some of these songs entertaining whilst you read the book.

1. The heathen - by Bob Marley

2. Crisis - by Bob Marley

3. Fugitive - by Lucky Dube

4. Better days - by 2Pac

5. Wherever I may roam - by Metallica

6. Radioactive - by Imagine Dragon

7. Run - by Pink

8. Civil war - by Guns N' Roses

9. I will not bow - by Breaking Benjamin

10. Heavy - by Linkin Park

11. Patience - by Damian Marley

12. Wrecking ball - by Miley Cyrus

13. When we stand together - by Nickelback

14. 21 guns - by Greenday

15. Heathen - by 21 Pilots

16. Heartless - by Hinder

17. Scars - by Papa Roach

18. Live like a warrior - by Matisyahu

THE END, Joshua

First and foremost, I want to say thank you to the First Nations
Writers Festival team for their wise discretion and judgement.
Without you, this book would not have come this far. Special
thanks to Anna Borzi AM, you are the queen of this project, your
invaluable advice and support is truly appreciated.

I want to make special mention to my family members for their
support and encouragement when I worked on this book.
This is for you and your children to come.

Finally, to my friends, schoolmates and work colleagues whom
I have come to know, you are part of this project all along its
progress to now.
Thank you to all of you.

Milton Keynes UK
Ingram Content Group UK Ltd.
UKHW010633141123
432548UK00002B/186